THE INHERITANCE

The Inheritance
Copyright © 2025 by Ilona Andrews
Ebook ISBN: 9781641973397
POD ISBN: 9781641973403

Cover art and interior art by Candice Slater

NYLA Publishing
121 W. 27th St, Suite 1201, NY 10001, New York.
http://www.nyliterary.com

THE INHERITANCE

BREACH WARS
BOOK 1

ILONA ANDREWS

CONTENT WARNINGS

This story is not a tornado that will rip your house apart. This is a well-maintained rollercoaster that passed all safety inspections with flying colors. It might be intense, but you will walk away from this ride. For those who like to know what's coming, here are the warnings before the drop:

Themes of romantic breakup and divorce, parental abandonment / family estrangement, violence including graphic scenes, mental health themes like panic attacks and anxiety, grief, harm to monster animals (the dog lives!), insects, arachnids.

LETTER TO THE READERS

This was not the plan.

That is to say that THE INHERITANCE was just supposed to be a fun short serial on the blog. A novella conceived to help, in our small way, anyone who's going through it. Right now things are pretty tough for many people. Traditionally, in times like these, we escape the daily stress through entertainment. Books, movies, TV shows. They become a lifeline, especially when they are serialized. Every new installment gives us something to look forward to.

At some point Ilona turned around in her chair and said, "Let's do a fun free novella for the blog." And I said, "How long are you thinking?" She said, "The schedule is already full, so short. Twenty-five thousand words?"

I laughed. Immediately. I'm laughing as I'm typing this. Because I knew that it would not be twenty-five thousand words. Later I heard her tell Jeaniene Frost about it, and I could hear her laughing through the phone. It's funny, because in her heart, Ilona honestly believed that it would be a short, simple, uncomplicated story. Whenever she says that about a new work, she is absolutely sincere. And it never ends up that way.

Long or short, I liked the idea, so we set about writing it. Predictably, it kept getting deeper. We had to come up with a universal magic system. Different classes and talents. (We've included a list at the end of the book.) Procedures for entering the breaches. Guild politics.

Writing something like this story immediately raises big questions. What would happen to all of us, individually and collectively in the aftermath of such a catastrophic global event? How would we all live in this new world? Would everything collapse into a post-apocalyptic hellscape, or would we find a way to fight back and keep on keeping on? Would we give up like Roger or persevere like Ada?

Ultimately, I believe the main theme of THE INHERITANCE is one of hope and love. Of people adapting to their new normal, horrific as it is, and not only surviving but becoming stronger.

Or maybe it's just a fun story about going into caves and killing monsters. That is up to you. Thank you for reading our story, and I hope you have fun.

Gordon Andrews

Yes, there is nothing more fun than having your husband and your best friend cackle at you in unison, and then you say, "No, I mean it," and they just laugh harder. Gordon is right. This was so not the plan, but it happened this way, and now THE INHERITANCE is a novel, and there will likely be one sequel. I give up.

Thank you for giving our work a chance. We appreciate it, and we hope you come to like Ada as much as we do.

Ilona Andrews

THE INHERITANCE

W e are at war.
This war isn't about wealth, resources, or territory. It's a war of biological extermination. The very existence of humanity is at stake.

The moment the first gate burst, sending a horde of monsters to rage through our world, our future was changed forever. The invasion brought us unimaginable suffering, but it also awoke something slumbering deep within some of us, a means to repel and destroy our enemy. Powers beyond comprehension. Abilities that are legendary.

The war is ongoing. If you are a Talent, your country needs you. The world needs you. I can't assure you that it will be safe. I can't tell you that it will be easy. But I promise you that every gate we close means the difference between life and death for the people you love most.

Be the hero you always wanted to be.

Take my hand and answer the call.

Elias McFeron
Guildmaster of Cold Chaos

[1]

Health insurance with a thousand-dollar maximum family deductible.

Prescription drug coverage with an eighty percent discount off list prices.

The first time I heard about gates, I imagined them to be these portals glowing with a magical blue light. Too many video games, I guess. They were nothing like it. This one was a hole. A deep, black, vertical hole that punched through reality, swirling with pale mist. The tendrils of white smoke curled and slithered within it, but none escaped into our world.

The gate appeared in front of the Elmwood Park Rec Center eight days ago. To the left was Elmwood Public Library, all red brick and tinted windows. To the right was a funeral home followed by perfectly ordinary, three-story boxes of apartment buildings covered in tan stucco. Behind us, to the east, lay Chicago. And straight ahead was an interdimensional tear. Just another Monday.

If someone told me ten years ago that I would be standing in front of a hole leading into a dimensional breach filled with monsters and preparing to risk my life and go inside, I would've

3

politely nodded, walked away, and later told Roger I'd met an unhinged person. Of course, a decade ago I was thirty, happily married, with a daughter in elementary school, a son just out of diapers, and a low-risk private sector job I loved. A different life that belonged to a different Adaline.

The future looked bright back then. Until the invasion shattered it.

Free emergency medical care when injured in the line of duty.

I took this job for the benefits, and when it got to me, like now, I recited them in my head like a prayer.

Dental, a one hundred fifty-dollar deductible, fifty percent off braces.

Things that came with age and children: appreciation of the dental plan with orthodontics. Braces were hellishly expensive.

Vision plan, fifteen percent discount off glasses and contacts.

The gate gaped like a dark maw.

At least thirty-five yards tall. Maybe taller. The threat scale ran from blue to red, and the prep packet put this gate at the low-orange risk level. On a dying scale of one to ten, it was about seven.

This was my one hundred and sixty-eighth gate. I'd gone into orange gates many times before. I didn't want to go into this one. It made my hair stand on end. And the presence of the funeral home wasn't helping.

"Ominous sonovabitch, isn't he?" Melissa murmured next to me.

"Mhm."

The mining foreman crossed her arms on her chest. She was a tall woman, two years older than me, with auburn hair she religiously dyed every four weeks and the kind of face that said she had everything under control. We met years ago, on one of my earlier gate dives, bonded over kids, and stayed friendly ever since.

After the first gates burst, some people gained strange abilities that couldn't be explained by science. To be fair, science tried its hardest, but if it walked like magic and talked like magic, most people decided it was magic. These abilities were called talents, and to make things extra confusing, people who had them were also called Talents.

Talents fell into two broad categories: combat and noncombat. Combat Talents got a boost to physical prowess and developed abilities like forcefields, summoning energy weapons, or shooting fire from their fingertips. Noncombat Talents got a random skill that was useful only in specific circumstances.

Melissa was a noncombat Talent. She could sense ores. She had to be right on top of them and actively concentrate, but that talent, combined with her previous experience in iron mining, let her rise to the position of the Mining Team Foreman.

Melissa ran her mining crew like a well-oiled machine. She didn't get rattled, but she was staring at this gate like it was about to reach out and bite her. Something about this hole set both of us on edge.

Melissa narrowed her eyes. "Anja, tie your damn shoelaces."

One of the younger miners rolled her eyes and crouched. "Always on my case…"

"Exactly. I *am* always on your case. I'm on everyone's case. If we have to run for our lives out of that gate, I don't need any of you tripping over your feet, because I'll have to double back and get you. You have two toddlers to come home to."

"Yes, Mother."

Melissa heaved a sigh. "Everybody is full of sass today."

Around us the mining crew checked their gear, twelve people in indigo Magnaprene coveralls and matching hard hats. Nobody seemed unusually worried. Toolbelts were adjusted, rock drills and shears tested, the generator and floodlights on four industrial carts inspected. The usual.

The escort, five combat Talents in tactical armor, had done their precheck ages ago and were now waiting. Aaron, a bastion class fighter, sat on a crate, leaning against another crate, his eyes closed. His massive adamant-reinforced shield rested on the ground next to him. Three recon strikers mulled about, armed with SIG Spear rifles. They specialized in ranged combat and rapid disengagement, which was tactical speak for shoot the shit out of everything and then run for the exit.

London, the escort unit leader, surveyed the mining crew. He was a blade warden, which meant he could both dish out lethal damage and summon a protective forcefield that made him invulnerable for two minutes. He carried a brutal-looking tactical axe, and on the few occasions I saw him use it, he cut through interdimensional monsters like he was chopping salad.

Both the mining crew and the escort wore indigo gear marked with the emblem of Cold Chaos, an upright sword wrapped in lightning in white on an indigo background. I wore a white hard hat and grey coveralls with a patch of the Dimensional Defense Command on my sleeve. The mining crew and the escorts were private contractors belonging to the Cold Chaos Guild, while I was a representative of the US Government. My official title was Dimension Breach Resource Assessor. The guilds called us DeBRAs, and they were supposed to keep us alive at all costs.

If things went to shit, Aaron would put himself between the mining crew and the threat, the strikers would shoot down whatever got past him, and London would grab me, wrap us both in his warden forcefield, and drag me out of the gate so I could report the disaster to the DDC. Of everyone here, I was the least expendable, as far as the government was concerned.

It didn't make me feel any better.

The mist swirled inside the hole, sending tendrils of dread toward me. I resisted the urge to hug myself.

Twenty days of recuperation leave. Which was long overdue. Maybe that was part of the problem.

Basic Housing Allowance.

6

Child Tuition Assistance.

CTA was the big one. It helped me cover tuition for Hino's Academy. Things were tight but I hadn't missed a payment yet. The school had stellar academics, but I'd picked it for their underground shelter. If a gate ruptured and a flood of invading monsters washed over the city, Tia and Noah would be safe until the military and the guilds repelled it. Competition for the school was fierce, but since I was DDC, the kids were given special treatment, along with the children of guild members. Advertising that Hino was the school of choice for the children of Talents was good for the academy's prestige.

"Ada, London is checking you out again," Melissa said.

Next to me, Stella, Melissa's baby-faced protégé, snickered quietly. She was twenty, and flirting was still exciting.

A large German Shepherd sitting at Stella's feet panted as if laughing. Bear came from an illustrious line of police dogs with heroic careers. She had the typical GS coloring, big brown eyes, huge ears, and petting her was off-limits. I'd asked before and was told no. Bear was working like the rest of us. Petting would be distracting.

"Brace yourself, he's coming this way," Melissa murmured.

I turned. London was heading straight for us. His real name was Alex Wright, and he was from Liverpool, but everyone called him London anyway. People with combat talents were resistant to wear and tear, and at forty-five, London was still in his prime, tall, broad-shouldered, with blue eyes, wavy brown hair, and an easy smile. His job was to keep the miners and me safe, and since he was my designated babysitter, he and I spent a lot of time in close proximity. Even so, he'd been paying me too much attention lately.

London stopped by us. "Everything okay here?"

"Everything was fine until you showed up," Melissa said.

He grinned at her. "Just doing my due diligence."

They usually had a fun back-and-forth going. It put people

at ease. I worked with guilds all over the Eastern US. In some mining crews, the tension was so thick you could cut it with a knife and make a sandwich. Cold Chaos was light and bright.

Their bickering was amusing, but in reality, London was in charge. Melissa gave orders to the miners, but in the breach London had authority over everyone, me included. Disobeying his command meant endangering the entire team, and it wouldn't be tolerated. If London got a bad feeling, he could halt the entire operation and pull everyone out, and Melissa couldn't say a word about it.

"Are you worried about us, Escort Captain?" Stella tilted her head, and her mane of dark curly hair drooped to one side.

"It's my job to worry, Miles. Have you been doing your sprints?" London asked.

"I have," Stella told him. "Fifteen seconds for the dash."

A hundred meters in fifteen seconds was damn impressive. It was good to be young. God, I was twice her age. How the hell did that even happen? I was twenty only a few years ago, right?

"Not bad," London said.

"I can beat both of them," Stella reported, nodding at me and Melissa.

"Talk to me after you've pushed three human beings through your hips and put on forty pounds from the stress of keeping them alive," Melissa told her.

London turned to me. "Where do you dash, Ada?"

Why are you doing this? You know nothing will come of it. "Gate Park."

All government gate divers ran - not for distance or endurance – but to survive. A 100-meter sprint, a walking lap around the track, rinse and repeat for an hour, then go home, and take ibuprofen for the aching knees. Three times a week. Five would be better, but three was what I usually managed. The DDC had mandatory PT tests every six months to keep us in shape. When a noncombatant faced a threat in the breach, running to the gate was the best and often the only way to stay alive.

"Maybe I'll join you sometime," London said.

Again, why? "You're out of my league. It would be a waste of your time."

"Never," he told me.

"How fast do you dash, Escort Captain?" Stella asked London.

"Let me put it to you this way: I could pick Ada up and give you a three-second head start, and you still wouldn't beat my time."

London smiled at us and moved on.

"Is he lying?" Stella asked Melissa.

"No," the mining foreman told her. "Combat Talents are on another level. We can't keep up."

London was sending out all sorts of interested signals. He was nice to look at, charming, and he'd clearly been around the block enough to know what he was doing. By now, he'd had enough experience not to fumble and enough patience to pay attention when it mattered. If I agreed to go on a date, it would go smoothly and end well.

However, the DDC forbade fraternization with guild members. I was supposed to stay neutral and refrain from forming any personal attachments. Even the work-hours friendships like the one with Melissa were frowned upon. Getting involved with a guild Talent would get me fired, and I had two kids and a mortgage. As fun as London would be in bed – and he would be very fun – he wasn't worth losing my job.

My phone vibrated. Hino Academy. *Please don't be a problem, please don't be a problem...*

"Yes?"

"Ms. Moore?"

Gina Murray, the assistant principal. That wasn't good.

"We have a problem."

Of course, we do.

A woman emerged from the gate and waved. A scout the assault team had left behind. An hour had passed without incident, and it was time to go in.

"Alright people!" London called out. "You know the drill. Last gear check. Move out in two minutes."

"What happened?"

I needed to fix this fast. Phones didn't work inside the gate. There was no connection, and if you tried to take a picture or record audio, you only got static. London had to stick to schedule and account for any delay. If we went inside five minutes late and a disaster struck, even if it was completely unrelated, the Guild would drag him over hot coals for it.

"Tia left campus without permission."

Melissa rolled her eyes.

"Okay." *What was that kid doing...*

"Before she left, several students and a member of the faculty heard her make a self-harm threat."

"What?"

"We are required to contact the police..."

"Please don't do anything. Let me speak to her first. I'll call you right back!"

I ended the call and stabbed Tia's number in my contacts.

Beep.

She wouldn't. Tia wouldn't. Not in a million years.

Beep.

Beep.

I knew my kid. She would not.

"Yes, mom?"

"Are you going to hurt yourself?"

"What?"

The mining crew formed up in front of the gate. London gave me a pointed stare.

"Oh look, Stella's dog is malfunctioning," Melissa said too loudly.

Stella pretended to shake Bear's leash. "Won't turn on. Something broke."

London headed for us.

"The Academy called. You told them you were going to hurt yourself and left campus."

"Well, you know what, maybe I should kill myself because they just assigned us a fifth essay due next week..."

"Tia!" I couldn't keep the pressure from vibrating in my voice. "This is really serious. I need you to be honest with me. Are you thinking of hurting yourself?"

London cleared the distance between us. "What's the hold up?" he asked quietly.

"Give her a minute," Melissa told him. "It's her daughter."

"No. I was in the cafeteria, I failed Latin again, and then there was the fifth essay due..."

London met my gaze. "Three minutes."

Thank you, I mouthed. Three minutes was a gift.

"...Mr. Walton made a snide comment about not applying myself and I said, 'Just kill me, it will solve all my problems...'"

And...?

"...And then I went to get Starbucks! I always sneak out to get Starbucks. Everybody does it. Nobody cares!"

It wasn't a real threat. Someone overreacted. The relief washed over me like an icy flood. Not a real threat.

"Mr. Walton hates me!"

"Tia, I'm about to go into the gate. The school wants to call the cops."

"What? Why?!"

"If this happens, things will get very complicated, and I can't help, because I'll be inside the breach. I need you to return to school and fix this."

"I was already on my way! I'm almost there."

11

I started toward the gate.

"I'm walking into the school building right now."

"Kiss their ass, do whatever you need to, but make sure you fix it. I love you."

"I love you too. Mom..."

The gate loomed.

"Here we go," Melissa muttered.

"I have to go, Tia."

"Mom!"

"Yes?"

"Don't die!"

"I won't," I promised. I hung up, powered the phone off, and slipped it into the zippered pocket of my coveralls.

"Remember," London called out. "We go in together as one, we come out together as one. Nobody gets left behind."

The mist swirled in front of us, held back by an invisible boundary. I took a deep breath and stepped into the dark.

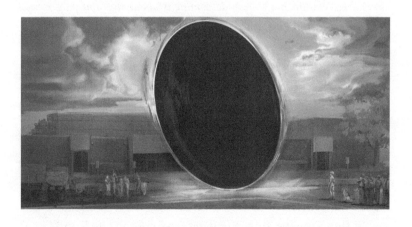

STEPPING THROUGH THE GATE FELT LIKE TRYING TO PUSH YOUR way through dense, rubber-thick Jello.

I blinked, trying to adjust to the low light.

A stone passage stretched in front of me, illuminated by patches of bioluminescent lichens, moss, and fungi. They climbed up the walls, glowing with turquoise, green, and lavender, some curling like fern sprouts, others spreading in a net like bridal veil stinkhorn mushrooms.

The otherness slapped you in the face. It didn't look familiar, it didn't smell right, and it didn't feel like home. The hair on the back of my neck rose. Fear dashed down my arms like hot electric needles. I wanted out of this gate. The urge to turn around and run back to the familiar blue sky was overwhelming.

This burst of panic used to happen every time I entered a breach. I'd tried everything in the beginning: counseling, breathing, counting, cataloging random things I saw... My primary prescribed some Xanax, which I couldn't take because it was strictly off limits for gate divers. Slowed the reaction time down too much.

Medication wouldn't have worked anyway. Nothing had worked until one week we got a cluster breach. Four gates opened simultaneously in close proximity, and I was the only DeBRA in range. I went through four breaches in forty-eight hours, and by the middle of the third my panic switch got permanently broken. This anxiety was an unwelcome blast from the past, and it needed to go away right now.

It was probably residual stress from the school call.

"Alright," Melissa called out. "We have a limestone cave biome. The assault team found a large chamber with promising mineral deposits, so we have a nice short hike ahead of us. Watch your step. Do you remember how Sanders fell into a crevice and got stuck, and we spent ten minutes pulling him out while he was farting up a storm and giggling? Don't be Sanders."

Sanders, a tall bear of a man in his mid-thirties, chuckled into his reddish beard. "I didn't have chili this time, I swear!"

A light laughter rippled through the crew. Melissa was going right down her playbook: item one, put everyone at ease the moment the crew stepped into the breach; item two, reach the mining site; item three, profit.

"We have Adaline Moore with us this morning. She is the strongest DeBRA in the region, which means if there is good pay in this hellhole, she will find it for us," Melissa announced. "Another day, another dollar. Isn't that right, Assessor Moore?"

"That's right." I matched her tone. "Living the dream."

Another ripple of laughter.

"Once more..." one of the miners called out.

"Don't you say it!" Melissa growled. "You know better!"

"...into the breach!"

"Damn it, Hotchkins!"

The actual quote was "unto the breach," but it had mutated long ago. Guild superstition held that if you said the line just as you entered the breach, you would come out alive, but you would kiss the chance of a big score goodbye. It didn't matter. Someone always said the line.

"I swear if you jinxed us, I will fire you myself..." Melissa carried on.

Aaron looked at London. The blade warden nodded, and the massive tank started down the passageway, moving fast. Time was money. The mining crew followed, keeping the four equipment carts in the middle, the strikers guarding the flanks like border collies obsessed with their herd.

I joined the flow of people. Melissa and Stella walked behind me and London on my right. Elena, the assault team's scout who'd come back to escort the miners, fell in step next to London. Lean, with a harsh face and blond hair pulled into a tight ponytail, Elena didn't walk, she glided.

In theory, being on the mining crew was the safest part of the gate dive. Safe was a relative term. Walking across a narrow beam over molten lava was also safe, as long as you didn't fall.

"Doing okay?" London murmured.

"Yes," I lied.

"Is Tia alright?"

"Yes. She's a smart kid. She will handle it. Thank you for the three minutes."

"You're welcome." He glanced at me, his eyes concerned. "Not feeling this one?"

"No."

Gate divers were like ancient sailors. We ventured into the unknown that could kill us at any moment. In the breach, survival depended on luck and intuition, and our rituals were an acknowledgment of that. We knocked on wood, we muttered lucky sayings under our breath, and we trusted our instincts. My instincts were pumping out all of the dread they could muster.

"Anything specific?" London asked.

"It makes my skin crawl."

"Don't worry," he promised quietly. "I'll get you out of here in one piece."

I glanced at him.

"I mean it, Ada. The only way you go down is if I'm down, and I'm really good at surviving. We get in, get out, and you can go home and sort the kid issues out. Tomorrow will be like this never happened."

"Thank you."

He nodded.

Ten years had passed since Roger had abandoned us. I'd been on my own for a decade, taking care of the kids, paying the bills, surviving. Every decision in my life was up to me, and I made them without support or help from anyone else. I'd become used to it, but London just reminded me how it felt to share all of that with someone. Someone who cared if you lived or died.

This was the worst moment to wonder about things. I promised my daughter I would come back. I had to concentrate on that.

The passageway forked. We turned right. Hotchkins, a short,

dark-haired man, spraypainted a backward orange arrow on the wall. He would do this every time we made a turn. It was a proven fact that people running for their lives had trouble orienting themselves.

Ahead a glowing stick shone among the rocks. Beyond it eight furry bodies sprawled on the ground in a puddle of blood. My foot slid on something. A spent shell casing. The cave floor was littered with them. The assault team had made a stand here.

We passed the bodies, skirting them to the sides. The dead things were large, about the size of a Great Dane, with long lupine jaws and massive feet armed with hook-like claws. Their pelts, chewed up by bullets, were shaggy with blue-grey fur. They didn't look like anything our planet could've spawned.

"A variant of Calloway's stalkers," London said. His voice was perfectly calm.

"Yeah. There were a lot of them, and they are spongy. They soak up bullets like they're nothing and keep coming," Elena said. "And they spit acidic bile."

"Good to know," London said.

"We did our best to clean up, but the place is a maze." Elena kept her voice low. "Passages going everywhere, so we may run into some. We didn't see anything more dangerous until we went much deeper, so there is that."

"No worries," Stella offered from behind them. "Bear will let us know if anything is coming."

Elena gave her a cold smile. "*I* will let us know if anything is coming."

"Don't pay her any attention, Bear," Stella murmured. "She didn't mean anything by it."

Bear twitched her right ear. One day I would pet that dog.

Elena kept gliding forward, her face portraying all of the warmth of an iceberg.

A lot of combat Talents developed similar abilities, so many that the government began to classify them. Tank classes, like

London's blade warden or Aaron's bastion, had a lot of defensive skills, so they drew the attention of the enemy and absorbed damage. Damage dealers, like strikers or pulse carvers, attacked the target, causing rapid destruction.

Elena was a pathfinder, a scout class that came with heightened hearing and vision, upgraded speed, and an unerring sense of direction. If she concentrated hard enough, she could hear a person murmuring behind a closed door two floors above her. But as awesome as Elena was, I would trust Bear over her any day. There was a reason every guild brought canines into the breaches. The transdimensional monstrosities wigged them out, and they let us know when something came near. Dogs were the best early warning system we had.

The cave passage kept branching. Left, left, right, another right, each tunnel glowing with swirls of colorful lichens and fungi. Elena was right, the place was a maze. At least we didn't have that far to go. I had seen the preliminary survey of the breach, and the mining site was half-a-mile from the entrance, off to the side.

The way was clear, the tunnels were empty, and Bear stayed quiet. Just like any other gate dive. It should've felt routine, but it didn't. I kept expecting some kind of awful shoe to drop.

Ten years ago, when the first set of gates appeared out of nowhere near the major population centers, they'd taken humanity by surprise. We'd cordoned them off so we could carefully study them and before anyone had a chance to adjust, the gates burst, spilling a horde of monsters into the world.

We knew a lot more about the gates now. Beyond every gate lay the breach, a miniature dimension stuffed to the brim with creatures so dangerous, they were biological weapons rather than living beings. That dimension connected Earth and the hostile world like a gangplank linking two ships. The breaches were how the enemy got from their world to ours.

Every breach had an anchor, a core that stabilized it. Once

the breach appeared, the anchor began to accumulate energy. When it got enough, the gate would burn through the fabric of our reality and rip open, releasing the monsters into our world to rampage and murder everything they came across. The more dangerous the breach was, the longer it took to burst.

There was a brief period, anywhere from a few days to a few months from the moment the gate appeared, when the monsters couldn't escape yet, but we could enter the gate from our side. It gave us a chance to extinguish the anchor and collapse the breach. The moment a gate manifested, the clock started ticking.

At first, destroying the anchors was the sole responsibility of the military, but it quickly got prohibitively expensive. Regular humans were no match for the breach beasts, and casualties were high. And it was discovered that the breaches contained a wealth of materials: strange ores, medicinal plants, and monster bones with incredible properties. Resources that could aid our fight and make us stronger. It wasn't just about destroying the anchors anymore. We had to strip the breach of anything valuable before it collapsed.

Within months after the first Talents manifested their abilities, they banded into guilds, and governments around the world began to outsource gates to them, taking a percentage of the profits. Economic and security crisis solved at the cost of volunteer lives.

By now, the process of gate diving was almost routine. As soon as a gate appeared, it was graded, its threat level measured, a government assessor like me assigned, and the appropriate guild contacted. The guild sent a team in to do a preliminary survey and let the DDC know when they were ready to proceed, at which point I arrived at the site.

The attack began with the assault team, heavy hitters with combat talents, who entered the gate and cut and burned through the miniature pocket dimension until they found the anchor and destroyed it. The journey to the anchor took days, sometimes weeks.

While the assault team worked their way to the anchor, the mining crew came in and stripped the breach bare, extracting anything that could be of use and would help humanity keep fighting. Each breach's resources were unique and precious. My job was to assess the space, guide the mining team, and make sure that the government got their thirty percent cut.

Once the anchor was destroyed, the assault team would rush back to the exit, because without the anchor, the gate would collapse in three days. Nobody knew what happened to the breaches once the gate closed. Hopefully everybody got out before the gate vanished, and when the next one appeared, we would do it all over again.

Ahead Aaron stopped. Finally. It was time to earn my paycheck. The sooner I found something of value, the sooner we all got out of here.

Apprehension curled around me like a cold snake. I could just turn around and run back to the gate, quit, and never go into any breaches again. I could absolutely do that. But then whatever this breach held would stay in it instead of becoming weapons, armor, and medicine.

I took a deep breath and pushed forward, past the miners, to do my job.

[2]

A massive cavern spread in front of us, awash in bioluminescence like some bizarre rave. It resembled an enormous egg set on its side, with the wider end to the right ending in a solid wall and the narrow end to the left splitting off into several dark passages. The cavern's floor sloped to the center where a wide stream ran through the cave from left to right. The water was like glass, perfectly clear.

At the banks, the stream branched into several small pools bordered by rimstone dams, some shallow, others deeper. The pools flowed into each other, stretching toward a flat island on our right. The stream split around it and emptied into a lake, its waters moving slowly and disappearing under a spectacular flowstone wall where layers of calcite formed a frozen stone waterfall.

Melissa turned to London.

The blade warden surveyed the cavern. "Go ahead."

"I need lights, people!" Melissa called out.

The mining crew spread out, planting floodlights along the nearest wall. The only flat space available was directly by the entrance, and the mining crew managed to fit three out of the four carts on it. The portable generator on the central cart sputtered into life, and bright electric light illuminated the cavern. The sloping floor was ridged with calcite, and it looked slick. A good way to break a leg.

"Much better," Melissa declared. "It's almost like we know what we're doing."

London nodded to the tank. Aaron moved to the left and planted himself in the narrower part of the cave, between the dark tunnels and the mining crew. London stayed at the entrance, guarding our exit route. The three strikers fanned out along the perimeter.

It was my turn to shine. The cavern walls were awash with swirls of bright green mixed with rust-colored metallic deposits. Promising.

I took a deep breath and *flexed*.

The official term was talent activation, but to me it felt like flexing a muscle I didn't normally use. The world turned crystal clear. The edges of the rimstone dams and contours of the flowstone waterfall came into sharp focus, as if I'd adjusted my eyes to a higher resolution. The outlines of individual mineral deposits glowed slightly.

I focused on the closest wall, scanning and evaluating, sorting through different hues. Malachite, copper-rich chalcopyrite, decent but not exciting. Cuprite, quartz, calcite, trash, garbage, junk...

A patch of funky plants to the left glowed with dull, pale pink. Healer Slipper. A weird variant, but definitely in the same ballpark as the more common varieties. If processed, it would yield a potent broad-spectrum antibiotic. A decent haul, if nothing else showed up.

Unlike Melissa, who only sensed ores and only when she was on top of them, I evaluated everything in my environment, organic or inorganic, and my talent tagged it with glowing colors. Red meant something useful, something I needed or wanted. Blue was toxic, yellow was dangerous, and occasionally I would get weird shades like white or brown, which told me nothing.

Of all the noncombat Talents, the assessors were the most confusing for the scientific community. Nobody, including me, had any idea how my abilities worked. I could look at something and just know that it was a poisonous liquid, or a chunk of iron, or a plant with coagulation properties, but the exact mechanism by which that knowledge was deposited into my brain remained a mystery. If this was a video game, I would've cast an Identify spell, and a little window would pop up, telling me information about the item, but this was real life. There was no window. Just me.

So far, the cavern had been relatively disappointing. The more dangerous the breach was, the better the loot. Usually, orange gates offered a little more. I pivoted slightly, turning away from the wall.

The inside of the stream lit up like a Christmas tree. Well, that was something.

"Gold in the water," I announced. "Check the pools."

"Go!" Melissa barked.

The miners scrambled over calcite walls. The pools directly in front of them ran a little deeper, and the water came up to their thighs.

Sanders thrust his hand into the pool and pulled up a tangerine-sized gold nugget. "Holy shit!"

The mining crew erupted into a controlled frenzy. Three of the miners went into the pools with small buckets, while the rest positioned themselves on the slope and shore, in a human chain leading up to the mining carts.

I kept scanning. Gold was okay. Just okay.

"We got time, people," Melissa called out. "Don't hurt yourself. Gold is heavy. Don't get greedy, no more than thirty pounds per bucket. Slow is smooth, and smooth is fast."

A bright swath of deep crimson flared on the edge of my vision. I'd learned long ago that the intensity of the glow was situational. If I was starving, my talent would start tagging all the food sources in the vicinity with bright red, ignoring valuable mineral deposits right under my feet. The more I wanted something, the more saturated the glow was, and whatever this was glowed with the red of a priceless ruby.

I turned slowly, following the irregular contours of the radiance, and focused. A thick vein running from the center of the cavern all the way to the far wall...

It couldn't be. I squinted at it to make sure I wasn't imagining it.

No, it was there. And the crimson got deeper at the other end of the cavern. There had to be at least ten cubic yards there, maybe more.

"Melissa?"

"Yes?"

"Dump the gold."

The mining crew stopped. Sanders closed his fists around a handful of nuggets and hugged them to his chest. Gold fever was a real thing. Something about the bright shiny yellow metal made people lose their minds.

I pointed to the beginning of the vein along the wall of the island, by the two pools closest to the shore. "Adamantite. From here to there. Solid, less than a foot down. We'll need more carts."

Melissa splashed into the stream to the adamantite vein buried under calcite deposits and put her bare hands onto the stone. She grunted, squeezed the rock surface with her fingers, shook from the strain, and stumbled back.

"Goddamn! Team One here! Team Two there! I want those drills running five minutes ago!"

The gold went flying. The mining crew grabbed their drills. Safety glasses and noise-dampening headphones went on, and they waded into the river and attacked the dams and the island.

Gold was expensive but adamantite was twelve times more valuable, because it could be refined into adamant. In the same family as osmium, adamant was incredibly durable. Adamant-enhanced armor could withstand machine gun fire. Adamant-coated blades cut through solid metal and monster bones like butter without losing their edge.

We found it rarely and usually in small deposits. A cubic yard of adamantite was a record-breaking haul that would mean a big bonus for every guild member that entered this breach. We had a lot more than a cubic yard here. In all my time crawling in and out of the breaches, I had never found a vein half that large.

The drills chiseled at the rock with a dull roar. The first chunk of adamantite fell free, a dark, almost black basketball-sized rock that looked like frozen tar in the crystal-clear stream. The drills stopped as everyone stared at it. Melissa tried to lift it out of the water, couldn't – it was ridiculously heavy - and laughed.

"We're gunna be rich!" someone yelled.

"Ada, I love you!" Melissa declared. "Marry me!"

"Sorry, I don't want to ruin such a good friendship."

People laughed. Next to me, London cracked a smile.

"Friend zoned," Melissa groaned.

"It's not you, it's me, Mel. I'm the problem."

More laughter.

Melissa shook her head. "Back to work, people! And someone help me with this rock."

The miners resumed their drilling.

The vein continued under the stream, veering across the

cavern floor to the left and behind the far wall. Getting adamantite from under the water would be cumbersome, and our time was short. The wall deposit lay deeper, but it was a better bet. Once they were done with the island, I would tell them to move there.

I went down the slope to the water. London nodded to Elena, and the scout followed me.

The best place to cross was to the left, by Aaron, where the stream was relatively shallow. I headed there and waded in, careful where I put my feet. The rocks were damn slippery, and the water came up past my knees. Magnaprene wasn't the most comfortable fabric, but it was waterproof.

I hiked over the shallow calcite ridges to the wall, pulled a can of fluorescent paint from the pocket of my coveralls, and set about tracing the contours of the deposit in bright Safety Yellow. Elena crossed the stream and lingered on my left, looking toward the tunnels.

I painted the cave wall. A hell of a find. Not that I would get anything out of it other than bragging rights. Government employees didn't get gate loot bonuses, and that wasn't why I'd taken this job.

The steady roar of the drills filled the cavern.

I was thirty-three when I saw my first glow. One of the larger US guilds somehow obtained permission to sell sebrian knives to the public. Sebrian was found only in breaches, and the knife prices started at a thousand dollars for a tiny pocket blade. Our advertising agency had taken the contract and promptly sent it to me with the key phrase of "rugged luxury."

I was sitting in my office staring at the knife and trying to figure out the right approach, when the blade turned pale pink. The glow refused to fade, and when I focused on it, something in my brain clicked. The weight, the density, the structure of the metal somehow popped into my mind and combined into a specific … profile was the best word.

I drove to the ER. I thought I was dying. Twenty-four hours later the DDC came calling with a contract and a patriotic sales pitch. Assessors like me were rare, and the government hoarded us, to the point of making it illegal for guilds to hire their own private assessors. The guilds had poured an obscene amount of money into lobbying against that law but got nowhere.

The invasion wrecked my life. I'd looked at that contract and realized I could do something about it. Every time I went into the breach, I found something to make us safer. Today it was adamantite. A drop in the bucket, but it was my drop.

I finished tracing the deposit and set the can on a rock.

Elena peered at the dark passageways, turned, her face sour, and called, "Stella!"

Stella, who was on the other shore watching the miners, didn't move.

"STELLA!" Elena roared.

The dog handler spun around.

The scout waved her over. "Bring the dog!"

Stella splashed through the stream, Bear on a leash, and trekked over the ridges to us.

"I need you to check the tunnels!" Elena yelled over the drilling noise.

"Which tunnel?"

"Start with the left!"

Bear yanked at her leash, jerking Stella backward, toward the stream. Stella said some command I didn't catch.

Bear yanked on the leash and erupted into barks.

Elena waved her arms. "Control your dog –"

Something burst out of the middle tunnel. It swept past Aaron, a vaguely humanoid shape in pale blue garments, so fast it was a blur. Four other blurs chased it, wrapped in dark grey. They tore past the bastion in a flash.

Aaron's top half - shield, armor, and body - slid to the side and fell to the ground.

For a horrifying moment, I stared straight at the stump of his torso, still standing upright. It was *standing upright*.

The blurs wrapped around us. I froze. They spun about me like a whirlwind, the four grey beings striking and slicing, while the creature in blue parried with impossible speed. I caught a glimpse of arms in dark armor gripping silver blades and inhuman faces with fangs bared. A second, and they tore across the cavern toward the wall and the mining crew.

Untouched. I was somehow uninjured.

I turned to Stella on my right.

Her head was missing. There was her torso in indigo Magnaprene, her neck, but no head.

The headless body crumpled to the ground.

A gasp came from the side. I turned on autopilot, still trying to process Stella's missing head. Elena's guts spilled out of her stomach. The scout clutched at herself. Dark blood poured out of her mouth. She made a horrible gurgling noise and fell.

This couldn't be happening. It was a weird, horrible nightmare. I was dreaming that I found the magic motherlode of adamantite and then monsters came and killed everyone.

The air smelled like blood and bile. To the left four inhuman creatures tore at their prey in the blue robe, running on the walls and leaping in for the kill only to be knocked aside. Two miners floated in the stream, face down, and the water was red, so red...

Oh God. It's real. It's all real.

Panic smashed into me like an icy hammer. I had to get out of here. Now.

The only safe exit was on the other side of the stream. I sprinted across the ridges to the water.

To the left, the fight swung back and forth along the lake's shore.

I slid over the first rimstone dam, tore through the pool, climbed over the other side, and landed into the stream. Water came up to my thighs and I waded through it, squeezing every drop of speed out of my body.

Half of the mining crew was still drilling.

"Run!" I screamed, waving my arms. "Run!"

Sanders turned, plucking the headphones off his left ear. He saw my face, whipped around, saw the creatures, hurled the drill aside, howled, and ran. The line of miners broke as people charged to the exit.

The world shrank. There was only me and the water trying to stop me. I just had to make it across the stream.

At the cave entrance, Melissa was scrambling up the slope, toward London. The blade warden stared straight at me. Our gazes met.

Help me...

A door slammed shut in London's eyes.

No. No!

Melissa shoved Anja Presa out of her way. The slender woman slid on the rocks and fell, rolling down to the stream.

I can't die here. I have to get home to my kids!

I was running so fast. Faster than I'd ever run in my life, and I wasted precious breath on a scream. "Wait! Wait for me!"

London yanked something off his belt. A grenade. He carried aetherium concussive grenades to be used as a last resort.

"Throw it!" Melissa howled and ran past him.

London looked straight at me. His face was cold like ice.

Alex! No!

He dropped the grenade. It rolled toward the stream, bouncing over the limestone. The blue forcefield of his warden talent flared into life, wrapping around London. He turned and fled into the tunnel.

The world exploded.

The blast slammed into Sanders ten yards ahead of me. Water punched me off my feet. I flew like a rag doll and smashed against solid rock. My right leg snapped like a tooth-pick. My spine crunched. Agony splashed across my side and bit into my ribs. My ears rang, my head swam, and the air in my lungs turned to fire.

I tried to breathe and couldn't. There was water on my face. I was in the stream face down. I had to get upright, or I would drown.

I wrenched myself up.

Bright white aetherium smoke filled the cave. I couldn't see anything, I couldn't hear anything, I couldn't breathe. I could only hold still as the pain drowned me.

"Mom! Don't die!"

I won't. I promise.

I forced myself to take a tiny breath. It felt like jagged glass cutting its way through my throat. I coughed through it and willed myself to take another. And another, swimming through the pain, one tiny sip of air at a time.

The smoke drifted up. My vision cleared. I was sitting in one of the pools by the shore, with the water up to my armpits, my back pressed against the rimstone wall. Next to me a severed human head rested on the pool's bottom. The dark curly hair swirled with the current. Stella.

It should've hit me like a semi, but instead I simply noted it, the same way I noted the blood spreading from my right leg and the broken glass that ground in my lungs with every breath.

I pulled the leg of my coveralls up, out of the boot. A jagged bone cut through the skin of my calf. A compound fracture. Okay. I tugged my pant leg over it.

I had to get the hell out of here. Out of this cavern. Out of the breach.

The exit was no more, blocked by a wall of rubble. London's grenade collapsed the ceiling of the tunnel. He and Melissa left me to die.

The clump of alien creatures passed along the opposite wall,

all but floating over the debris that had sealed the exit. I didn't hear any gunfire. Our escorts were dead.

The aliens darted to the right, absorbed in their fight. They weren't targeting the humans. Aaron, Stella, Elena, they were simply in the way, cut down in passing as the four creatures in grey tried to kill the being in blue. And if their fight swung this way, I would be in the way, too.

I had to get out of the line of fire.

The wall in front of me, where the exit used to be, was at least forty yards away and sheer.

I looked over my shoulder. There was a niche in the wall behind me, next to my yellow paint marks, a natural depression in the rock. A place to hide.

I turned around. My right leg screamed. Standing was a no go. I would have to crawl on all fours.

I clenched my teeth and crawled out of the pool.

My right leg burned, sending stabs of hot pain through my knee. I could do it. Stay low, move slowly, don't present a threat. It was only pain. I could endure pain.

Twenty yards to the wall.

Fifteen.

I hit my knee against a sharp rock, and my weight landed on my injured leg. The world went white for a second. I sucked in a small breath and kept moving.

Ten yards. Almost there.

Almost.

My fingers touched the stone. I turned around and tucked myself into the niche, pressing my back against the wall. There was a trail of my blood across the cave floor.

The creature in blue was still moving, but only two grey blurs remained. The third lay on the rocks, a smudge of dark fabric that shifted whenever the fight drew closer, stretching toward it like a living thing. I couldn't see the fourth.

To the right something moved by the rock.

I sat very still.

A furry head with big ears poked out from behind an outcropping.

Bear.

I licked my lips, trying to get my mouth to work. "Bear." I could only manage a whisper. "Come."

The German Shepherd crawled toward me, pressed against my thigh, and let out a soft whine.

"They left you, too."

I hugged the dog to me. We sat by the wall and watched the fight tear across the cave. The blurs were so fast. How could anyone move that quickly? It should've been biologically impossible.

One of the remaining grey blurs collapsed.

The last grey attacker shot toward us. It took me half a second to realize it wasn't a coincidence. It was aiming for me.

There was no time to run, no time to do anything. I threw my arm in front of Bear on pure instinct. The grey blur loomed above us... and stopped.

I finally saw it clearly, a tall creature with four arms, wrapped in a tattered grey cloak. Its hands had too many fingers, long and clawed, and each hand clenched a sword. It stared at me with terrifying eyes, huge and round, and its mouth, on the face of white pearlescent skin, was a wide, dark slash filled with nightmarish teeth. A blue blade protruded from its chest.

This is also real.

The grey cloak stretched toward my face, like some strange amoeba, its strands long and viscous.

The blue blade twisted.

The creature spat purple blood and went limp.

The sword slid backward, disappearing into the creature's body as whoever wielded it pulled it out. The cloaked being fell to the side and slid a few feet down the slope.

A tall figure stood behind it, clad in a shimmering, ice-blue robe. The silhouette looked chillingly human, too tall, with limbs that were too long, but unmistakably familiar. The head was a solid chunk of metal, twisted into a sleek horned shape. The same metal, blue with gold filigree, sheathed their body under the robe. No visible skin. Even the fingers of their right hand, gripping the blue sword, were coated in metal. Their left arm was missing, cut off just below the biceps, and bright red blood spurted from the cut.

None of my briefings had ever mentioned a being that appeared this human. Animals, monsters, inhuman sentients with strange anatomy, vaguely humanoid beings, yes. But never this.

The figure touched their helmet. It split apart and retracted into itself. An older woman looked at me. Her skin was a muted pastel pink in the center of the face, darkening to a vivid turquoise near the hairline. A straight nose with a blunt tip, a narrow-lipped mouth with the same pink lips, and upturned eyes with blue-green irises, slightly too large for an Earth native, but not enough to alarm anyone.

Aside from the skin color, she looked so human, it was terrifying. There were crow's feet at the corners of her eyes and laugh lines by her mouth. Either the DDC did not know, or they knew and kept it a secret at the highest level.

The woman stared at me. Her eyes were sad and mournful.

I stared back.

She swayed and fell.

What the fuck do I do now?

The sound of hoarse breathing echoed through the cavern.

She saved me. If she hadn't stabbed the grey attacker, I would be dead.

Another hoarse breath. Another.

Fuck it.

I shifted on all fours and crawled the few feet to the woman.

Her arm was sheared off as if by a razor blade, the cut so precise, it was like an anatomy slide. I could see the bones among the bloody muscle. Blood shot out with every breath.

"We'll need a tourniquet. Hold on."

I dug in the pocket of my coveralls, extracted the paracord I always carried, and pulled it loose. Paracord was a shitty way to make a tourniquet, but she was bleeding out and I had nothing else. I folded the paracord lengthwise until I had about a three-foot stretch of cord, wrapped it around what was left of her arm, and pulled it into a knot. The blood was still spurting.

I patted myself. I needed... Here. I pulled a slim flashlight out of my pocket. I always brought one as a backup to the light in my hard hat. I pressed the flashlight into the knot and tied another knot over it.

"This will hurt, and you'll lose what's left of the arm. I'm sorry. We have to stop the bleeding."

I twisted the flashlight, tightening the knot. Once, twice, three times.

The woman reached out with her right arm and touched my hand. Her fingers were cool, their touch feather-light.

"I'm sorry," I told her.

The blood stopped spurting. Now I just had to secure this...

The woman touched her own forehead. Her fingers dipped into the skin, sinking into a seemingly solid skull.

It had to be a hallucination. I was losing it from blood loss and pain.

The woman pulled something out of her head. It was round and glowing, like a brilliant jewel lit from within. It was so beautiful. The colors swirled and danced, a stunning, mesmerizing gemfire.

I had to look away, move, run, do something, but I had no will to move. The gemstone was too beautiful to resist. It was coming toward me, held in the woman's long fingers. Closer. Closer.

The gem touched my forehead.

The Universe unfurled with light and color. A soft voice whispered inside my head.

"Treasure your inheritance, my kind daughter."

Everything went dark.

[3]

I opened my eyes. A jagged stone ceiling spread above me, glowing softly with swirls of alien growth.

I hadn't imagined the nightmare. It happened.

I stared at the ceiling for a long breath and checked my watch. The digital skin was dark, with a spiderweb of cracks across it. Must've happened when I smashed into that rimstone after the blast.

Lying here would accomplish nothing. I had to get out of this hellhole.

I sat up slowly. The generator was still going, and three of the five floodlights had survived, illuminating the cavern with bright puddles of electric light. The inside of my head burned, my back throbbed, and my right leg felt like someone had rolled an asphalt compactor over it. But I was still breathing.

"Is anyone alive?"

Silence. Just me and the corpses.

"Anyone?"

Something nudged my side. I whipped around. Bear sat next to me, her smart brown eyes focused on my face with unwavering canine intensity.

I wasn't by myself. The dog was with me.

"Hi Bear."

Bear tilted her head. Her left side was dark and wet. Blood. It started near her shoulder and bled down over her leg onto the paw. Shit.

"Hold on, girl."

I pushed to my feet. My right leg trembled but held my weight. Oh good. I took two steps before I remembered the bone sticking through my skin.

I pulled my right pant leg up. An angry red welt marked my calf, smudged with dried blood. That was it. The wound was gone.

I'm losing my mind.

My leg was broken. I had looked at it and then hid it with my coveralls. The pant leg was stained with dark red, the result of a massive bleed. I'd left a blood trail across half of this cavern. I looked up. There it was, a ragged chain of dark smears.

I felt the edge of rising panic and shoved those thoughts right down before they dragged me under. It didn't matter right now. I had to see what was going on with Bear's shoulder.

I made my way to the nearest pond. An indigo hard hat lay on the rocks. I had a sick feeling that Stella might have been wearing it.

Nope, not going to think about that either.

"Come here, Bear."

The shepherd padded over.

"Stay."

Bear looked at me. All the commands Stella gave her were in German, and I could only remember a couple. The word for stay wasn't one of them.

"Stay."

Bear sat.

Good enough.

I needed to clean the blood off her, but who knew what the hell was in this water.

I *flexed*.

The water looked perfectly clear to my enhanced vision.

My talent pegged it as clean, but there were limits to what I could sense. If Bear had an open wound, and I dumped a bunch of alien bacteria into it... But then I crawled all over in that water with an open wound – which was mysteriously not open anymore, and yeah, not thinking about that – and I almost drowned in it. I was pretty sure I'd swallowed a bunch of it. Which was neither here nor there, except if there was some vicious pathogen in it, we were both fucked.

There was water in the canteens. All miners carried some. We would have to save that for drinking. There was no way to tell how long it would take us to get out of this cave.

Suddenly my mouth was dry.

I dipped the hat into the stream, scooped some water, and gently poured it over Bear's flank, half-expecting the dog to bolt. Bear sat like a rock.

"Stay. What a good girl. The best girl. So good."

Three hats later, the water ran mostly clear. A gash carved Bear's skin over her shoulder. It was shallow and not too long. Most of the blood must have come from somewhere else. Someone else.

I exhaled. One of those carts should have a med kit on it.

"Let's get some antiseptic on that."

I needed to get across the stream and the slight wobble in my leg said that if I fell, I would regret it. The best place to cross was still the same – the shallow part where Aaron lay in two pieces.

I picked up Bear's leash and made my way to the crossing. If she yanked me off my feet, there would be hell to pay. I waded into the stream, ready to drop the leash at the slightest tug. Bear whined and followed me. I slowly shuffled across the stream bottom.

"Slow is smooth and smooth is fast."

The words came out like a curse. Melissa's face was branded into my memory. I could replay it in my head like a recording. Six years. I couldn't even remember how many breaches together. She knew my children's names. She looked straight at me and yelled at London to throw the grenade.

"I thought she was my friend, Bear."

Bear didn't answer.

"I saw Melissa push Anja out of her way. And that over there is Anja's body. She was twenty-six years old." ·

Sanders, Hotchkins, Ella Gazarian, they were in front of me when I was sprinting for that exit. My memory served up Sanders being swept away by the blast.

"They were her guildmates. They trusted her, and she fucking left them, and worse, trampled over them trying to escape. Sanders is probably the reason I survived. He took the brunt of that aetherium grenade."

We cleared the stream and carefully went up the shallow slope to where the carts waited. Water sloshed in my boot. The other one was wet, too.

I tied the leash to the cart, found the first aid kit, and flipped the heavy latches open. A nice big bottle of antiseptic rinse. We were in business.

"Stay, Bear."

The shepherd sat again.

I opened the antiseptic and poured it over the wound. Bear shook but stayed.

"You are so good. Such a good dog."

I capped the bottle and grabbed a tube of antibacterial gel.

"Melissa's priority was the mining crew. But London's priority was keeping everyone safe, and if that failed, keeping me alive. He was in charge."

I remembered the cold calculation in London's eyes, too. The way his face iced over when he hurled the grenade. The set of his mouth. I squeezed the gel onto Bear's wound.

"He was looking straight at me, and his eyes said, *'Fuck you. I'm not dying here today.'* His shield lasts two minutes. Two minutes, Bear! That man is fucking invulnerable with the shield up. I was halfway across that stream when he bailed. If he just activated his shield and waited ten seconds, I would've been on the other side of the cave-in. The rest of the mining crew would've been on the other side with me."

Bear tilted her head, looking at me.

"The hostiles weren't even paying attention to us. They were fighting each other, and they cut us down because we were in their way. We could've run all the way to the gate. Even if the creatures had followed us, they couldn't exit into our world. They are trapped in the breach until the anchor gets enough energy to rip the gate open."

Bear tilted her head to the other side.

"You know what he said to me? He said, 'I'll get you out of here in one piece. The only way you go down is if I'm down, and I'm really good at surviving.' Well, we know he didn't lie. That asshole is excellent at surviving."

I screwed the cap back onto the gel tube.

"The Cold Chaos assault teams are good at clearing the prospective mining sites before moving on. I've never seen their escorts deal with anything more serious than a skirmish. The most London had to do was to cut down an occasional left-over creature popping out of its hiding place. This – everything that happened – was the reason why Cold Chaos sent him into the breach. When the worst-case scenario occurred, he was supposed to step in and that fucker... All those people..."

A sob choked me.

I shut up.

Being an escort captain came with a lot of responsibility, and you didn't just become one. It wasn't enough to be powerful or trusted. The position required experience. London had put in · years with the primary assault teams. He was seasoned. He looked at those hostiles slicing people like they were weeds in passing, and in a split second he knew that he had never encountered anything like them and nothing he had in his arsenal could stop them. He saw death, and he made a deliberate choice to save himself.

He could've waited. He could've stood in that gap with his invulnerable warden shield up and let the rest of us escape, but it was a risk, and he chose his life over ours. The only reason Melissa made it out was because she happened to be close enough and he would need a witness to back up his story. When your job is to put yourself between noncombatants and danger, coming out of the breach alone wasn't a good look.

Even if they fired him, he would live. That's all that mattered to him. And if he had been one of the ordinary miners, I wouldn't have a problem with that, but he wasn't a miner. He was a high-ranking combat Talent. We trusted him. I trusted him, and he threw an aetherium grenade in our faces and ran.

"When death stares people in the face, they revert to their true self, Bear."

London's true self was a cold, calculating coward.

I checked myself for scrapes and bruises. I didn't find any. I had some red welts here and there but no broken skin. I'd crawled on my hands and knees across a rough cave floor dragging my broken leg behind me. My hands and knees should've been raw, but I didn't find any abrasions. I rubbed some gel over the red mark on my leg just in case.

Don't think about it. That was best.

The generator was next. The industrial model was rated for seven to nine hours run time. The fuel indicator was almost empty. I'd been in this cave for at least seven hours.

If London made it out of the gate, he would immediately

report what happened to the guild. London and Melissa didn't stay long enough to see how the fight turned out, so for all they knew, there were still active hostiles in this cave. Since body-cams only recorded static in the breaches, Cold Chaos would have to rely on London's testimony, and I was sure that Melissa would confirm whatever he said. She wouldn't just suddenly grow a heart and admit that she climbed out of the cave over her guildmates' bodies. As she so often told me, she had mouths to feed.

This was going to go one of three ways.

One, London made it out and reported that I was dead. This was the most likely outcome, because otherwise he would have to own up to leaving me behind.

Two, London made it and reported he left me behind. Not likely. If the DDC found out that he bolted out of the cave abandoning me, Cold Chaos would face heavy sanctions. There would be a fine at best and revocation of gate access at worst. Cold Chaos would come down on London like a ton of bricks.

Three, London and Melissa died en route. Like Elena said, this breach was a maze, and we hiked half a mile to get to this cavern. It was possible that something equally terrible burst out of a side passage and killed those two. I doubted that. London was a fucking cockroach. He would survive.

Even if they died, by now carts filled with resources should've been coming out of the breach. The procedure was to grab the good stuff and get it out ASAP. At least seven hours had passed without any activity. Even if London and Melissa didn't make it, the guild knew that the mining crew was either in trouble or dead.

No matter which of these three outcomes happened, protocol required the assault team to be notified. Radios didn't work in the breach, just like the rest of the electronics, but each assault team carried a "cheesecake." A beeper stone.

Beeper stones occurred in the steppe and mountain biomes

41

and had a core of denser material running through them. When shocked with electricity, they glowed and vibrated. If you broke a piece off and then shocked the core of the main stone, the broken off piece would also light up and vibrate. Distance didn't seem to matter. As long as both fragments were in the same breach, shocking the core would activate the other chunk. The first gate diver who discovered this effect compared it to the Cheesecake Factory's restaurant pager and the name stuck.

By now Cold Chaos' guild coordinator would have gone into the breach with a piece of a core stone and shocked it with a taser. The moment the charge hit that rock, the cheesecake the assault team carried would light up and start humming. It was the breach equivalent of an SOS signal. The assault team would realize that a fatal event occurred, and they were being recalled. They would turn around and head back for the gate.

They were only an hour ahead of us. By now they should have been here to neutralize the threat and retrieve the bodies. Nobody came for the corpses or for the incredibly valuable adamantite. That meant only one thing: the assault team was dead.

Bear whined softly. I reached out and petted her back.

Right now, Cold Chaos was likely putting a new assault team together. The level of threat in this breach was beyond anything I had seen. They would need their top Talents for this, and those people were usually occupied. High ranking guild members made more than celebrity actors, and the guilds worked them to the bone for that money. Getting them all in one place could take days.

The gate opened eight days ago. Judging by the power readings, Cold Chaos had anywhere between four to eight weeks to clear it. They thought everyone was dead, so they wouldn't be in a hurry.

There was another unpleasant possibility. If London did own up to leaving me behind, Cold Chaos could choose to deliberately delay. If I was alive, they would face intense scrutiny. Things would be a lot simpler for them if I was dead. Given enough time in the breach, I would be.

There would be no rescue. I was on my own. If I died here, the kids would be alone. Roger would let them go into foster care. I was sure of it. They were living reminders of his failure as a father, and he had very little tolerance for being held accountable these days.

I'd made a promise to my daughter. I would keep it.

Digging through the cave-in was out of the question. The integrity of the cave ceiling in that passage was shot, which meant moving any of the rocks risked another collapse. No, I would have to go around, through one of those passageways.

I glanced at the end of the cavern. The tunnels stretched into darkness. I would have to go into that darkness, make my way through the breach filled with monsters, ones that probably killed an entire assault team, find the gate, get out, and make sure Cold Chaos didn't have a chance to stop me. Too easy.

I would need supplies. And a weapon. In a few minutes, the generator would die and take the lights with it.

I had to act fast.

JOHN COSTA, THIRTY-TWO YEARS OLD, HONORABLY DISCHARGED after eight years in the Marine Corps. He and his husband had just celebrated their fourth wedding anniversary, and before the dive, he had shown off the necklace he received as a gift – a clover charm in gold with a small breach emerald in the center. For luck.

John sprawled on the rocks, face up. The left side of his skull and face were sliced off, and the cut was so sharp, it was like half of his head simply disappeared. His one remaining eye stared up at me, dull and lifeless.

43

I squatted by the body. My leg whined in protest, so I sat on the ground and picked up John's SIG Spear.

"This probably won't work," I told Bear.

Bear enthusiastically panted.

Originally the SIG Spear was developed as a civilian version of the US Army XM7, a multi-caliber rifle that answered the military's need for small arms with greater firepower. It offered higher muzzle velocity and better long-range shot placement. This version of the SIG Spear was developed specifically for the gates. I knew all of this because I had been briefed on it and taught how to fire it.

There was just one problem.

I turned the rifle on its side and found a small black selector. It could be turned only two ways: toward a stylized bullet etched into the gun or toward the identical bullet with a line through it. Fire, no fire. As my retired Marine firing range instructor put it, private-proof. So easy even a soldier could do it.

The selector was in the safety position. John died too fast to fire off a shot.

I flipped the selector toward the bullet, raised the rifle to my shoulder, and pressed the trigger. Nothing. As expected.

A small red light flared on the rifle and faded.

The use of guns inside the gate was strictly controlled. Only smart guns were permitted, and only combat-rated Talents could carry one. Nobody wanted the civilians grabbing weapons dropped by their injured escorts and firing them in a wave of panic. Nobody wanted to hand a working firearm to the enemy either. That technology needed to stay in human hands as long as possible.

Each smart weapon was keyed to the heartbeat biometrics of its owner. In a pinch, it could be unlocked by entering a code given only to the assault and escort team members. A new code was issued for every gate dive.

They didn't give me the code. I was a noncombat Talent. I would never need this code, because I had a big strong blade warden with an invulnerable forcefield to protect me.

"When we get out of here, I'm going to punch that smarmy weasel in the face."

I flipped the gun over to the code lock. The small screen had space for six digits.

123456
654321
000000
111111...

Nothing. I could sit here for hours and not get anywhere.

"If there are more of those four-armed creatures on the other side of the breaches, guns won't be much of an advantage for us, Bear. They still need a human to aim and fire. Parrying an attack at that speed requires a top-tier combat Talent, and we don't have too many of those."

I went through John's pockets and came up with two energy bars and a Ka-bar knife. I took the knife, his canteen and the bars and moved on to the next corpse.

Anja's corpse was next. She wasn't cut, but there were chunks of rock embedded in her chest. Killed by London's grenade.

She wore the same shoe size as me, 8 in women's. I took her boots. They were dry.

"I've turned into a ghoul, Bear. I'm now robbing the dead."

Panic crested inside me, and I shoved it back down again. Don't think, just do.

Fifteen minutes later I'd worked my way around the cavern back to where I'd passed out. There were fourteen human bodies in the cave. Nine of the twelve miners, four of the escorts, and Elena.

George Payne was the oldest miner on the crew. He was fifty-four, and his years had been hard-won. He'd brought a backpack. Inside I found Motrin, a Chapstick, some tissues, a small towel, a packet of jerky, a Leatherman multitool, a pair of dry socks in a Ziploc bag, and way too many Tiger Balm patches. I dumped the patches and kept everything else.

The rest of my haul consisted of eight energy bars, seven 32 oz canteens, two KitKats, one portable first aid kit, and a pack of THC gummies. I stuffed the candy and energy bars into the pocket of the backpack, shoved the first aid kit in, and pushed as many of the canteens as I could inside. Only four canteens fit. That and the one on my waist made five.

"A Ka-bar." I showed the knife to Bear. "That's the weapon we have to work with. This is all of our firepower. Right here in my hand."

Bear didn't seem impressed.

If the escort team had melee damage dealers instead of strikers, I would've had my pick of edged weapons. Not that it would've done me much good.

I hefted the Ka-bar. "We're going to make it out of here if I have to cut my way through every last monster in this fucking breach."

Big talk. Whatever killed the assault team was probably still out there. Jace, the assault's team tank, was protected by over a hundred pounds of adamant, which he wore like sweatpants because he was literally strong enough to bench press a car. Blue Savant shot lightning from his fingertips. Ximena, a pulse carver, had a reaction time of fifty milliseconds and could dice a horde of monsters into pieces with her twin swords.

I had a Ka-bar and needed ibuprofen for my knees after a 100-meter dash.

What was the alternative? Sitting here and dying?

I had gone through all of the human dead. The grey attackers were next. There were four of them, lying in different spots around the cavern. I walked over to the nearest body. The grey shroud wrapping around the four-armed corpse shivered.

I stopped.

The shroud stretched toward me in long strands, like algae swaying with the currents. Behind me, Bear whined.

I *flexed*. The grey shroud burst into a blazing violent orange. It was plant based and also animal based, an odd hybrid somewhere in-between. A mixotroph like the single-celled Euglena, which used photosynthesis like a plant but moved and ingested food like an animal. And if it touched me, I would be dead. I had no idea how I knew it, but I was absolutely sure. It would kill me.

I backed away. The shroud shivered, as if vibrating in frustration, and settled back onto the corpse.

Orange was yellow and red, and while yellow meant danger, red indicated something useful or valuable. Whatever that tinge of red meant, it wasn't worth exploring. All four attacker corpses were shrouded. Going near them was out of the question.

I swallowed and turned to the woman in blue.

I'd successfully avoided thinking about her and the gem up to this point. But there was no choice now.

What did she do to me? She did something. I didn't feel that different. Did she really put a gem inside my head? Was that why my leg healed?

But if you had a magic gem that could fix broken bones in a matter of hours, it was highly likely said gem could also regrow limbs. Why give it to me? Why not keep it and regenerate the arm?

Treasure your inheritance, my kind daughter.

All the questions. Zero answers.

The dead woman lay on her back. Her face had lost its vibrant color. The pink and turquoise dulled, muted, as if she were a wilted flower. Her blood-soaked robe stuck to her body, and the puddle of blood by her arm had congealed to a dark viscous gel.

Logic said I had to search her, but something about it felt fundamentally wrong, like committing sacrilege.

I circled the body and *flexed*. The corpse turned a faint violet, so light it was almost white. A sliver of deepest black lay by the woman's side. The sword. My talent had no idea what to make of it, so it registered it as a slice of darkness. That only happened once before. Two years ago, the DDC made me sign a bunch of forms and then showed me an object that looked like an oversized metal brooch studded with small gems. It came from the forehead of a huge breach beast, and they wanted it assessed. The object had turned solid black in my vision. I'd failed to determine what it did or what it was made of.

I blinked my power off and knelt on the rocks by the sword. I remembered it being slender and blue, but now it seemed shorter and dull, washed-out grey in color. There was no wrapping on the hilt. The whole thing was one continuous chunk. It looked metal, but nothing I'd ever seen before.

A sword was much better than a knife.

"I'm sorry you died," I told the corpse. "I need your sword to survive."

And now I was talking to dead people.

I touched the sword. The metal felt cold, then instantly warm. The blade turned blue. The handle flowed in my fingers as if liquid and wrapped around my wrist.

Panic punched me. I jerked my hand away on pure instinct, flailing around like there was a poisonous bug on my arm. The band of metal around my wrist snapped open, and the blade clattered to the floor.

I froze, staring at it.

The sword lay on the stone, inert, once again a dull, muted grey.

A moment passed. Another.

The sword didn't move.

Okay. One more time.

I reached for the sword. The moment my fingers touched it, the metal flowed again, anchoring itself around my wrist and fitting perfectly into my fingers. The urge to fling it away gripped me.

I clenched my teeth and waited.

The sword waited with me.

Was I controlling it? Was this some alien artificial intelligence? Was it alive somehow?

Nothing was happening.

I took a deep breath.

The sword flowed through my fingers to my forearm and wrapped around it like a pale-blue metal bracer.

I quashed the scream before it left my mouth. My fingers were free. I moved my arm around. The bracer stayed as if glued.

I moved as if to stab. The sword streamed into my palm, lengthened into a half-formed blade, and stopped. Was it waiting for a target? I lowered my arm. The blade slithered back into a bracer.

"Magic sword," I told Bear.

The shepherd eyed the bracer and kept her distance.

I had a weapon now and I was almost ready to go. I glanced around to make sure I didn't miss anything. I'd made the full circle around the cavern. The pool where Stella died was right in front of me. Her head was still on the bottom, dark hair swaying with the weak current.

I needed to fish Stella's head out of the water and put it with her body. When the guild eventually came for the corpses, they might miss it, and Stella's parents would need a whole daughter to bury.

The hair swayed.

I had to do this. It was very simple: wade into the water, pick up the head, put it with her body.

Oh my God. She was twenty years old. She was alive this

morning. She was breathing, walking, talking, and now she was dead and her head was in the water, and Tia was only four years younger. Would somebody be taking my daughter's head out of a pool like this one so I could look at her face one last time? When they got Stella out, they would put her in a box, and then they would bury her, and her mother would never see her again.

How do you survive this? How do you go on after this?

Her parents couldn't be much older than me. They would have to live the rest of their lives without her. There was nothing anyone could do. This was done. She was dead.

Tears wet my eyes. I splashed through the water, picked up her head, and climbed out, slipping on the rocks. Her body lay on its back. What do I do? Do I put it on her neck? Do I leave it next to her?

I was holding a kid's head in my hands and trying to figure out how best to leave it with her corpse.

Someone wailed like a hurt animal, and I realized it was me. Tears came, so many I couldn't even see.

I put the head gently by her side, dropped to the ground next to her, and cried. I cried and screamed for Stella, for her parents, for Sanders and Anja, for their children and loved ones. I cried for Costa who was missing half of his face and for Aaron who lay in pieces.

I sobbed for all of them, all the bodies in this cave. And I cried for myself, trapped here, left to die, and for my children who might never see me again.

Bear padded over to me and lay by my side. I hugged her and cried harder. It was just the two of us, the cave, and the raw pain of my grief.

Gradually, the sobs subsided. I ran out of tears. For a while I sat there, silent, staring at Stella's body. Slowly, very slowly, self-preservation woke up and took over. Nobody was coming for me. Nobody would help me. It was up to me.

Nothing new. I'd been on my own since I turned eighteen

and my mother informed me I had two weeks to move out. Then Roger came along, but he was gone now, and I'd been on my own again for a decade since.

I could do this.

I wiped my face with my sleeve, swapped my socks for the dry pair, put on Anja's boots, and got up.

Bear stared at me.

"Time to get a move on."

I swung the heavy backpack onto my back and picked up Bear's leash.

I was halfway to the tunnels when the generator sputtered and died, plunging the cavern into darkness.

[4]

2,119 miles away from Elmwood

R ight leg hurt, left arm hurt, everything fucking hurt. There was alien slime dripping from his armor, and it stank like yesterday's vomit.

The gate loomed in front of him. Elias McFeron stepped through it.

Blue sky. Finally.

He took a deep breath and tasted home. That first gulp of Earth's air. There was nothing like it.

Behind him the rest of the assault team staggered out. He'd force-marched them for the last three days, all the way from the anchor chamber. It was a hard pace even for the top Talents, and it took longer than expected because the markers they had placed to guide their way through the swamp had sunk.

The first responders dashed toward him with the stretcher. Elias let them get in position, lifted Damion Bonilla off his shoulders, and carefully transferred him to it. The pulse carver's blood-smeared face was a mask of pain.

"Thank you, Guildmaster. I'm sorry."

Elias nodded. "Nothing to be sorry about. Rest. You've earned it."

The first responders carried Bonilla off. His legs were bloody mush below the knees, but he would walk again. The healers would fix him. They fixed anything except dead if you got to them in time.

This was the last time. Elias had promised himself that every time he went into the breach, but this time he meant it. He would strip off the armor, take a long shower in his hotel, board the guild jet with the rest of his team, and go home. He would eat well, sleep in his own bed, and then in the morning he would put on a suit, go into his office, and do paperwork like a normal fucking human being. That's where he belonged. Running the guild, which had plenty of blade wardens without him.

The medics swarmed the assault team. A young kid with a healer's white caduceus on his jacket ran up to him. Elias waved him off and squinted at the familiar orderly chaos in front of the gate, looking for the mining crew. He'd sent a scout ahead with the orders to wrap it up. The miners were on the left, stowing their gear. He counted them out of habit. Fifteen and eight escorts. Good. Everyone was out.

A familiar tall, lean figure in a black Tom Ford suit tugged at his attention. Leo Martinez, who seemed to be born to wear elegant suits and be the public face of a guild, the only man standing still in the flurry of activity. His XO, who should've been back at HQ, 2,000 miles away. Something had happened.

Leo started toward him.

Elias made himself walk forward. Whatever it was, he didn't want to deal with it but avoiding it would make things worse.

A sharp sound cut through the human clamor, like the noise of a thousand paper sheets being ripped at once magnified through concert level speakers. The gate collapsed.

Leo reached him. "Cutting it a little close, sir."

"Happens." Elias headed for the familiar black SUV. The back hatch rose as he approached, and he began stripping his armor and tossing it into the plastic-lined vehicle. "What is it?"

Leo kept his voice low. "We had a fatal event."

He'd figured that. "Where?"

"Elmwood Gate. The assault team is presumed dead. We lost nine of twelve miners, including a K9 and handler, four of the escorts, a scout, and a DeBRA."

Elias stopped for a moment. Twenty-eight people. Good people. He'd approved the line up himself. It was a solid team that should've been more than adequate for the low orange gate. He'd personally trained them, he'd gone into breaches with them, and now they were dead. Half of them under the age of thirty. He'd sent kids to their deaths again.

This wasn't a fatal event, this was a catastrophe. What the hell went wrong over there?

Leo's face was carefully neutral. "The DeBRA is—"

"Adaline Moore." The best DeBRA in the Eastern US died in their gate dive.

"Yes, sir. I've got the mining foreman, the surviving miners, and London under lockdown."

"London made it out?"

The crisp line of Leo's jaw got sharper. "Yes, sir."

"Hmm."

"I've reported to the DDC," Leo continued. "Cora Ward owes me a favor, so she will sit on it for as long as she can, but sooner or later this will get out and when it does, both the Hermetic Alliance and the Guardian Guild will scream bloody murder. The Guardians, in particular, have been vocal about our share of the gates."

Adaline Moore had been in high demand. DeBRAs of her caliber were rare and monopolized by the DDC. Elias liked to know who he was working with, so he kept tabs on the assessors. Adaline was divorced, with an absentee ex-husband, two children, and a cat, and her life revolved around work and family. The very definition of a noncombatant. Her children were now orphans.

Leo was right, the fallout from this would hit them like a hammer, but the political mess and the PR nightmare weren't important right now. He would deal with that later. "What does London say happened?"

"Humanoid combatants. Highest red level."

"What kind of humanoids?" They had come across humanoid combatants in the breaches, but the word humanoid was used loosely, as in anything that was bipedal and somewhat human in shape.

A slight edge slipped into Leo's voice. "He doesn't know. He's never seen anything like them before."

Perfect.

"His entire crew and the DeBRA are dead, and he doesn't know. Did he see the DeBRA die?"

"He says he did. The mining foreman backs up his story."

The foreman made it out, too. "What about the other two miners?"

"They aren't saying much. One didn't see anything, and the other is keeping his mouth shut."

Elias deposited the last bit of gear into the SUV and slapped it shut. The vehicle rocked. His control got away from him a hair.

Leo got behind the wheel, Elias climbed into the passenger seat, and they drove out, past the police barricade and the onlookers onto I-205, heading north, toward the airport, where the guild jet waited.

"From what London described, we will need the primary team," Leo said. "Kovalenko is on loan to Texas' Lone Star Guild and Krista is on vacation in the Caribbean. Jackson is in Japan."

And they would have to wait for Jackson because they would need their best healer. When it came to Talents, quality far outpaced quantity. Jackson was a top-tier healer, capable of near miracles. In the breach, where split seconds mattered, he was irreplaceable. Sending in five mid-tier healers wouldn't have the same impact. No, they needed Jackson. Both for his heals and his forensic capabilities. They needed to know how their people died.

"Jackson has the longest travel but should make it within forty-eight hours. The real problem is the tank," Leo said. "Both Karen and Amir are inside gates right now, and both have gone in less than twenty-four hours ago. We can substitute Geneva, but she lacks experience…"

"No need," Elias said. "I'll take them in myself. Tell Krista I authorized triple rates. We can swing by Dallas and pick up Kovalenko. We have twenty-eight people in that breach. We must recover the bodies so their families will have something to bury."

If there was anything to recover. With the kind of delay they were facing, they could get there and find only bones stripped bare. Dead people became meat, and meat didn't last long in a breach. He would shower and sleep on the plane. The office would have to wait.

"Are we pulling them to HQ or straight to Elmwood?" Leo asked.

"Straight to Elmwood. Nobody goes into that gate until I get there."

"Understood."

Elias looked at the city soaking in the dreary rain of the Pacific Northwest outside the window and glanced back at his XO. "Was London injured?"

A hint of bright electric lightning flared in Leo's eyes, turning them an unnatural silver white. He pronounced words with crisp exactness. "Not a scratch, sir."

"Hmm."

He had to get to Elmwood. The sooner, the better.

THE CAVE PASSAGE GAPED IN FRONT OF ME, A NARROW TUNNEL painted with bioluminescent swirls of strange vegetation. It split about twenty yards ahead, with one end of it curving to the right and the other cutting straight into the gloom.

I had a light on my hard hat but decided against using it. It didn't illuminate much, while making me easy to target, and I had no idea how long the battery would last. It was better to save it for emergencies. The pale green and pink radiance of the foreign fungi and lichens offered some light, but it made the darkness seem even deeper.

It was like I'd turned five years old again, lying in my bed in the middle of the night, too afraid to move, until the need to pee won out and forced me to make a mad dash to the bathroom. Except that back then, if I got really scared, I could flick the lights on. As long as you had electric light, it gave you an illusion of safety and control. Without it, I felt naked. It was just me, Bear, and the tunnels filled with underground dusk.

There would be no dashing here. We would go carefully, quietly, and slowly.

A cold draft flowed from the tunnel, bringing with it an odd acrid stench.

57

Bear whined softly by my side.

Whining seemed entirely appropriate. I didn't want to go into that gloom either.

"We don't have a choice," I told the dog.

Something rustled in the darkness, a strange whispering sound.

Bear hid behind me.

"Some attack dog you are."

That's probably why she survived. If she were braver, she'd be dead.

"The exit is to our left. This is the closest tunnel to it. The other two branch off to the right, which will take us further from the gate."

Before the assault team left to find the anchor, they had surveyed the mining site and the immediate area around it. Their maps showed three tunnels in the north end of the cavern leading into a tangle of passageways and chambers. Of the three, this tunnel, the furthest to the left, was most likely to connect to the main route.

Likely but not guaranteed. The maps only showed about half a mile of the tunnels. For all I knew, we would hike for hours only to run into a dead end. If that happened, I would turn around and retrace my steps. Walking was better than waiting and I had to get on with it while I had my strength and food to keep me going.

I started forward, picking my way through the glowing growth. It looked almost like a coral reef, except there was no water.

We took the left branch and kept moving. The tunnel was about thirty feet high and probably the same width. An almost round hole in the rock, as if some massive worm had burrowed through the mountain. Hopefully not.

Back by the entrance, we'd passed by some stalker bodies, and Elena mentioned that the assault team didn't wipe them all out. Taking on a single stalker would be difficult. There had been eight corpses, and the stalkers typically traveled in groups. If a pack of them attacked us, the best strategy would be to run and hope the tunnel narrowed ahead so they could only come at me one at a time. If I saw a crevasse, I would have to make a note of it in case I needed to double back...

For some reason, I could actually see both sides of the tunnel with a lot of clarity. My eyes should have adjusted to the darkness, that was to be expected, but I could pick out small details now, like the cracks in the stone. The walls weren't glowing, and the shining growth in this area was kind of sparse. Hmm.

The passage veered slightly left, then angled right. Normally, cave passages like this varied in size and shape. This one was too uniform. Whatever dug it out had to be huge.

We rounded another gentle turn, and I stopped. Ahead ridges of growth sheathed the floor and walls of the tunnel, like someone had raked solid stone into shallow curving rows. Between them bright red plants thrust out, shaped a little like branching cacti or Sinularia corals, almost like alien hands with long twisted fingers decorated with narrow frills. The tallest of them was about two feet high, but most were around eight inches or so. There were hundreds of them in the tunnel. The red patch stretched into the distance. Forty yards? Fifty?

Something about the red plants gave me pause. I crouched by a patch. The frilly protrusions weren't leaves. They were thorns, flat and razor sharp.

I *flexed*, accessing my talent. The red patch snapped into crystal clarity, flaring with a bright green. Yellow was dangerous, blue was toxic. Green usually meant a lethal mix of the two.

I focused, trying to dig deeper.

The Grasping Hand. The thorns carried lethal poison. If one of those cut me or Bear, we would die in seconds, and the Hand would devour our bodies. In the distance, I could see a lump that was once a living creature, soon to become one of those ridges, drained of all fluids.

How did I know that? This hadn't been in any of the briefings. I had never seen this before. I hadn't read about it, no one had talked about it, and I should not have detailed knowledge of this carnivorous invertebrate. I shouldn't even know it's an invertebrate. The best my talent could do was identify it as animal and possibly dangerous.

The knowledge was just in my head. I *flexed* again, concentrating on the bright red stems until they glowed with green again.

A dark plateau unrolled in front of me, acres and acres of red stems, some ten-feet-high, blanketing purple rock with giant dinosaur-like reptiles thrusting through the growth, the stinging thorns sliding harmlessly from their bony carapace...

This was not my memory.

Fear washed over me. My heart pounded in my chest. I went hot, then cold. What the hell was happening to me?

Bear nudged me with her cold nose. I petted her, running my hand over her fur, trying to slow my breathing. Was this my inheritance? Memories from I didn't know who, obtained I had no idea where.

I stared at the patch. I could have a nervous breakdown right here and now, or I could keep going.

It didn't matter where the damned memory came from. It warned me about the danger. It might not have been mine, but I knew it was true. Blundering into that growth was certain death.

The Grasping Hand grew in clusters, probably determined by the availability of nutrients. Each of those clumps or ridges used to be a body. This growth was relatively young, the stems short and somewhat sparse.

If I was careful, I could pick my way through it. The problem was Bear. There was no way to communicate to the dog that she had to stay away from the thorns. One tiny scratch and it would be all over. I had to keep Bear safe. No matter what it took. I owed it to Stella, and if Bear died... Bear couldn't die. We would leave this place together.

I could carry her. She was a big dog, she had to weigh... I *flexed* again. Seventy-six pounds.

And that was a lot more precise than normal. My talent helped me ballpark weight and distance, but not with that much accuracy. I focused. Seventy-six pounds and four ounces or thirty-four kilograms and five hundred and eighty-six grams. Fuck me.

I didn't just get vision. My talent had gotten a mysterious upgrade. Who the hell knew what kind of consequences or side effects this sudden precision bump might have.

Since I had it, I might as well use it. I focused on the field of red. Forty-eight yards or one hundred and forty-four feet. Or forty-three point eighty-nine meters.

Great. All I had to do was pick up a seventy-six-pound dog and carry her across half the length of a football field. While carefully avoiding deadly thorns.

I could always double back and try one of the other tunnels. But none of the other passages led toward the exit. We'd been walking for almost two hours. It would be a long trip back, and there was no guarantee we wouldn't run across this same problem in another tunnel.

Also, very few things could get through the Grasping Hand without some kind of body armor. It was a deterrent, a little bit of safety behind us. Nothing would come at us through that patch.

If I put Bear on my shoulders, I could make it. But not while I carried the backpack. The canteens were bulky and heavy, and the backpack pulled on me. If Bear squirmed, she would throw me off balance and both of us would land right into the thorns. It was the pack or the dog.

All of the water and food we had was in that pack. I could try to throw it ahead of me, but there was no telling where it would land or how far. Dragging it behind me was out of the question. It could get stuck and pull me back, and the thorns would either shred it or deposit poison on it. I had no effective way to neutralize it.

If I got through, I could find a safe spot on the other side, tie Bear to something, and come back for the pack. Yes, that had to be it.

I dropped the pack, pulled a second canteen out, and hung it on my coveralls. I had to take only what I absolutely needed. The antibacterial gel, a couple of bandages, knife, both candy bars, three of the energy bars, and Motrin went into my pockets. That was all that could fit.

God, I didn't want to leave the pack behind, but Bear mattered more. It would be fine. I would come back for it.

I took off my hard hat, pulled one of the spare canteens out of the backpack, poured water into the hat, and offered it to Bear. She lapped at it. I drank what was left in the canteen and waited until the shepherd stopped drinking. I took the hat, tapped it on the ground to get the last of the liquid out, and put it back on my head. It was the only helmet I had.

There was a command guild dogs were taught to make them easy to carry. I'd heard the handlers use it before. What the hell was it? Lie, rest… Limp. Limp, it was limp.

I tore the packet of jerky open, pulled a piece out, and offered it to Bear. She sniffed it and gently took it out of my hand.

"Good girl. See? We're friends."

I took another piece of jerky and crouched by the shepherd. "Limp, Bear."

She stared at me.

"Limp."

Another puzzled look.

I was sure that was the right command. I scooted close to her and put my arm around her. *Please don't bite me.* "Limp."

The shepherd leaned against me, slumping over. I put my hands around her hind and front legs, heaved her up onto my shoulders. If she were a human, it would be fireman's carry, but since she was a dog, it was more like a fur collar. I stood up.

Bear made a surprised noise halfway between a whine and a growl. I offered her another piece of jerky. A warm wet tongue licked my fingers, and she swiped the jerky from me.

"Good girl. Stay. Limp."

I put my hands on her legs, took a deep breath, and walked into the field of red death.

Ten feet. Fifteen…

I zigzagged through the field, threading the needle between the thorn ridges.

The law required Cold Chaos to immediately notify the government of my death, but the DDC had a lot of discretion as to when the public announcement of this disaster went out. And Cold Chaos would use every crumb of their influence to convince the DDC to sit on that news as long as possible. Their chances of mitigating this disaster would be much better if they recovered the bodies, presented a clear explanation, delivered a record haul of precious adamantite, and closed the gate, all of which required time.

The DDC would oblige, because Cold Chaos was a major guild and it had built up a lot of goodwill. As much as I hated them right now, if you asked me this morning which guilds I preferred to work with, Cold Chaos would've been in my top three. Having a top guild crumble wouldn't be in the interest of national security, so the DDC would likely delay the press release, at least for a few days, to give Cold Chaos a chance to get their shit together. But my kids would be notified, probably within twenty-four hours.

This gate was local to Chicago. I didn't fly here, I drove for twenty minutes. Elmwood was less than five miles from my house in Portage Park. Even if the mining session ran overtime, by now I should be heading home. My children would be calling my phone, and when I didn't answer, they would know that something went very wrong. The DDC wasn't oblivious. In the morning, an agent would show up at our house and tell Tia and Noah that I was missing in the breach. They wouldn't tell them I was dead until they recovered my body or the gate was closed.

There would be nobody to cushion the blow. Roger wouldn't lift a finger to help. Roger's father and stepmother basically disowned him in favor of his younger brother and never showed any interest in their grandchildren.

My mother was unreachable. After my father died a decade ago of a heart attack, she moved back to her native UK, and I didn't even have her phone number. She viewed having children as a duty she had to fulfill. She had me, she provided food and shelter until I reached adulthood, and that was the end of her obligation to me and society in general.

I was an only child, and I didn't have any friends, at least none who would step in. I did have a will and a law firm appointed as an executor, but the kids would need warmth, kindness, and guidance.

I had left a death folder both with physical copies of the documents and with scanned PDFs on my laptop. There were things in there I didn't want my kids to find unless I was truly gone, but there was also a plan of action. I had gone over it with them several times. They knew what would happen.

The moment the DDC released the news of my death, the other major guilds would scream bloody murder and keep screaming across every media channel that would give them airtime. They wouldn't be doing it for my sake. They would do it to take out their competition.

Everything about the guilds was political. They were constantly fighting over who got which gates and how many of them. Closing dangerous gates raised the guild's prestige, which in turn led to more high-profile gate assignments and boosted the guild's Talent recruitment. It also brought in a staggering amount of money. Each gate was both a potential death trap and a treasure trove of resources. The higher the danger, the better the haul.

An average guild miner made twice my annual wage. Melissa pulled in over three-hundred thousand per year before bonuses, which could easily double her salary. London likely cleared two to three million per year. And all of those earnings hinged on the guild's ability to secure the gates and the assessors' talent. Without someone like me, the miners would just blunder around, testing random rocks. I made everyone a lot of money.

The DDC was sensitive to public opinion. The department was seen as the main defense against the invasion, much like the CDC was the main defense against an epidemic. Maintaining the public's trust was crucial. If the rival guilds managed to whip up enough outrage, the DDC would eventually bow to that pressure and Cold Chaos would lose their top billing. It would take them a long time to recover.

If I was missing or presumed dead, the other guilds and the media would pounce on my children like sharks. I'd seen it time and time again. They would drag them from one show to the next, exploiting their fear and grief and making them into a target for scammers.

Look at these grieving orphans! We must hold Cold Chaos accountable for their suffering. Your father abandoned you. Your mother was torn apart in the breach by monsters. Tell us how that made you feel. Cry for us. Cry louder.

Tia and Noah both knew to refuse all interviews, but they were only kids. They would be so scared and vulnerable…

I had to make it home.

Sixty feet. Almost halfway there. *Slow is smooth and smooth is fast.* I would make Melissa eat those words when I got out.

Bear must've been a shoulder cat in another life because she sat steady like a rock. Come to think of it, carrying her should've been a lot harder. Maybe it was the adrenaline...

Bear stiffened under my hand. A low growl rumbled from her mouth. She craned her neck, looking at something in the tunnel behind me. I didn't have room to turn around and check what was happening.

Ninety feet.

Another growl.

Running would get us killed. I wove my way through the ridges. Whatever was coming up behind us would have to deal with the Grasping Hand as well. It would be fine.

Growl.

One hundred and twenty feet.

Fine. Just fine.

A dry skittering noise came from behind me. It sounded insectoid, as if a giant cockroach was scrambling through the tunnel at top speed.

Bear snarled, trying to lunge off my shoulders. I wobbled, careened, caught myself at the last moment and kept going, feverishly trying to keep from slicing my legs to ribbons.

Bear erupted into barks, jerking me to and fro.

"Stay! Limp! Stay!"

The chittering chased us.

Almost there. Almost through. Just a little longer. Just a little bit...

Bear threw herself to the left. I spun in place, my boot catching on the nearest clump of thorns, shied the other way, and jumped over the last ridge. My boots hit the clear ground. Alive. I was alive somehow. The thorns didn't penetrate through the boot.

I dropped Bear to the ground and spun around.

The awful chittering sound filled the tunnel behind us. I *flexed* and saw the dark outline of four-foot-long chitinous legs.

"Run!" I turned and sprinted down the tunnel. The dog dashed ahead, pulling me forward with the leash.

It wouldn't get through the Grasping Hand. Surely, it wouldn't.

I glanced back, *flexing*. A massive insectoid thing tore out of the tunnel. It sampled the red field and plowed right into it. Shit!

I flew across the cave floor, drawing even with Bear. No turnoffs, no branching hallways, just a death trap with the thing behind us charging full speed ahead.

The tunnel veered right, curving. We took the curve at breakneck speed. I slid, caught myself, and dashed forward. Ahead the mouth of a tunnel opened to something lighter, glowing with eerie purple. We raced to it and sprinted into the open.

I *flexed*. Time stretched. It was the strangest thing. The world slowed down as if throttled to half speed. My enhanced vision thrust the feedback at me and I saw everything instantly.

A huge cave lay in front of us, its jagged walls rising high up. You could fit a ten-story office tower into this chamber. Natural stone bridges crossed high above, a waterfall spilled from a fissure in the wall far in the distance, and straight ahead, in front of us, a small lake lay placid, its color a deep blue. Short shrubs grew along the shore, about a foot high, with leaves the color of purple *oxalis*, dotted with glowing mauve flowers.

Two stalker corpses lay in the flowers, torn apart, and in the lake itself, a large shape waited, hidden in the water. It flared with bright yellow. Danger. Chances of survival: nil.

The world restarted with my next breath. I didn't have the luxury to freak out about it. We had to run. Now.

I pulled Bear to the left, where a chunk of the wall protruded in a miniature plateau. We couldn't crawl onto it, but there were boulders around it. It was the only cover we had. Anything else would bring us too close to the lake.

We dashed through the flowers. My heart was beating a thousand beats per minute.

A screech erupted from the tunnel.

We reached the ledge, and I ducked behind a large boulder and pulled Bear close. She squatted by me, and I hugged her, my hand on her muzzle, and whispered, "Quiet."

The shepherd stared at me with big brown eyes.

A monster burst out of the passageway. Its front end resembled a silverfish that had somehow grown to the size of a rhino, with razor-sharp, terrifying mandibles. Its tail was scorpion like, curving over its head, and armed with another set of flat pinchers, studded with sharp protrusions.

The monster paused. Its tail blades sliced the air like two huge shears.

I held my breath.

The creature skittered forward, straight for the stalker corpses on the shore.

The thing in the lake waited, still and silent.

The bug monster reached the closest stalker corpse. The mandibles sliced like two sets of shears, cutting the body into chunks, dissecting it. The first shreds of flesh made it into the creature's mouth.

The thing in the lake struck. A blur erupted out of the water, lunging onto the shore. Somehow the bug monster dodged and scampered back, out of reach.

The lake owner paused, one massive paw on the torn-up corpse. It was huge, ten feet tall, thirty-five feet long, and it stood on four sturdy legs armed with eighteen-inch claws. Its body was a mix of dinosaur and amphibian, dark violet, with scales that shimmered with indigo and pink as it moved. A massive fin-like crest crowned its head and flared along its spine all the way to the tip of a long, thick tail. Its head with four small deep-set eyes and a wide, triangular mouth filled with razor-sharp teeth was straight dragon. There was nothing else to compare it to. It was a lake dragon, and it had sighted an intruder in its domain.

The bug monster scurried backward, then sideways, its tail raised high, ready to strike.

The dragon's flesh rippled. Pale pink spots appeared on its sides, near its crest, glowing softly. Was it a warning or was it trying to mesmerize the bug?

The monster silverfish veered left, then right, but did not retreat. Bugs weren't known for their strategic thinking. There was meat on the shore, and the bug wanted it.

The silverfish lunged forward, the bladed tail striking like a hammer. The dragon shifted out of the way and the chitin shears hit rock instead of flesh. The dragon lunged, swatting at the bug with a taloned paw. The silverfish dodged and charged in from the side.

I grabbed Bear's leash, leaving her six inches of lead, and moved carefully away, past the boulders, along the ledge, toward the back of the cavern. Bear made no noise. She didn't bark, she didn't growl, she just snuck away with me.

Behind us, the bug monster screeched. A deep eerie hiss answered, almost a roar.

I picked my way along the wall, through jagged boulders. On our left, the cavern's sides were smooth and almost sheer. On our right, the river that flowed from the waterfall rushed to the lake.

I *flexed* again. The water was twenty-two feet wide and seven feet deep. Too deep to easily cross, and the other shore sloped up, littered with large rocks. A chunk of cave ceiling or one of those stone bridges above must've collapsed and broken into big chunks. Too hard to climb.

I kept scanning. There had to be a way out of this deathtrap.

My vision snagged on something ahead, where the wall curved left. A dark gap split the rock face, twelve feet high and fourteen feet wide. I focused on it.

No dice. The gap was fifty-three yards away, and my talent told me that there was nothing valuable in the rock wall around it, but I couldn't tell how deep it was. My ability was always tied to my vision. I could sense things buried within rock, but I still had to look at the rock while doing it. If I closed my eyes, I got nothing, and that fissure was just a dark hole. Once I entered the gap, I could scan it but until then, it was a mystery.

There could be other passages on the other side of the cavern, but I didn't want to risk it. There could be nothing there.

The boulders ended. The ground here was almost clear and sheathed in the mauve flowers. We'd have to leave cover to get to the gap.

I glanced over my shoulder. The bug monster had circled the lake. It was on our side now, still facing the dragon, but two of its left legs were missing and a long gouge carved across its chitin carapace. It wasn't darting quite as quickly. The huge lake monster kept advancing, its crest rigid, the spots on its sides almost blinding. A wound split its right shoulder, bright with magenta blood.

We had to risk it.

I tugged Bear's leash, and we padded into the open, heading for the gap. My enhanced vision snagged on the flowers. Deep blue. Poisonous when eaten. Everything in this fucking breach was trying to kill us.

Something thudded. I risked a glance. The bug had crashed into the wall, falling on its side, and the dragon bore down on it, mouth gaping. At the last moment, the silverfish flipped and dashed away, heading straight for us.

I ran, pulling Bear with me. We flew across the cave, scrambling over rocks. The air in my lungs turned to fire.

The bug was right behind us. I felt it there. I didn't need to flex, I knew exactly where it was.

The gap loomed in front of us.

Bear and I scrambled into the darkness. For a moment I was running blind, and then my night vision kicked in. Ahead, the passage narrowed down to four feet wide.

Yes! The narrower the better.

An awful scraping noise came from behind us, the sound of bug legs digging into the rocks.

Beyond the narrow point lay darkness. It was too deep and too dark.

We dashed through the narrowed gap, and I slid to a halt, yanking Bear back. We stood on a seven-foot ledge. Beyond it the ground disappeared. There was no way down. There was just a gulf of empty dark nothing.

We were trapped.

The wall behind us shook.

I spun around.

The bug rammed the stone, trying to get its tail through, but the gap was too narrow. It screeched and struck the rock again. The mandibles shot toward me through the gap, slicing.

I jerked my right arm up on pure instinct. The cuff around my wrist flowed into my fingers and snapped into a long sharp spike, and I drove it into the bug's head. The blade sliced through the right mandible and bit into the armored carapace. The mandible hung limp. I yanked the blade free and stabbed again, and again, and again, thrusting and jabbing in a panic-fueled frenzy. To my right, Bear launched forward, exploding into snarls, bit the mandible I had partially severed, and ripped it free.

The bug screeched. Pus-colored ichor wet its head. It tried to back up, but its head was wedged into the gap.

I kept jabbing. Bear bit and snapped, foam flying from her mouth.

Stab, stab, stab...

The bug collapsed. I drove the sword into it seven more

times before my brain finally processed what I was seeing. The giant silverfish was dead. It wasn't even twitching.

I heaved, trying to catch my breath. We killed it. Somehow we killed it.

Bear snarled next to me, biting a chunk of the bug she had torn off. All her fur stood on end.

"Good girl," I breathed. "Finally snapped, huh?"

Bear growled and bit down. Chitin crunched.

The bug shuddered.

I jerked my sword up.

The silverfish slid backward, into the gloom of the dark passageway, and behind it, I saw the outline of a massive paw and pale glowing spots.

I dropped into a crouch and hugged Bear to me in case she decided to follow.

The silverfish vanished, swallowed by the darkness. The pale pink spots winked out.

North Tunnels

Hiding spot

Entrance

Map of the Mining Site

[5]

The plane shuddered as it hit an air pothole. Elias put his hand on the glass of the ginger ale sitting on his desk to keep it from flying off.

Across from him, Leo sat very still, his eyes unblinking. His XO didn't like planes. It wasn't the flying; it was the lack of control. And if Elias mentioned it, Leo would just feel more self-conscious and withdraw deeper. He learned long ago that comfort and logic didn't work for times like these, but distraction did wonders. The sooner he sorted through his thoughts, the faster he could put Leo's sharp mind to analyzing the Elmwood disaster instead of focusing on being stuck in a metal tube hurtling through the atmosphere thousands of feet above the ground.

Elias peered at the mining site map on his tablet. Compasses didn't work in the breaches, so traditional directions didn't exist. Instead, the moment you entered, you faced north and the gate behind you was always due south. It was obviously simplified but it worked, and all breach maps followed this principle.

The cave biomes were Elias' least favorite, and this one was a fucking maze. A tangle of tunnels, passages, and chambers, resulting from eons of erosion, as water shaved and carved the stone. A chunk of another world, wedged between Earth and elsewhere.

Gate dives had stages. Of all of them, the assault phase was the main and most important. Humanity entered the gates to destroy the anchor and collapse the breach. Everything else was secondary to this goal, no matter how much some people wanted to twist it. Yes, mining paid the bills, but the focus of the mission was to keep the invasion at bay.

Like many others, Elias felt the anchor the moment he stepped through the gate. It tugged on him, a knot of energy, a distant nexus of power that demanded attention. The stronger you were, the more it pulled on you. To Elias, it was inescapable, like an evil sun. It called to him, and he hunted it down until he cut through its defenders, forced his way into the anchor chamber, and shattered it.

The trick wasn't just carving a bloody path to the anchor. The real challenge was to destroy the breach and come out alive. Successful gate dives required preparation. The breach protocol was written in the blood of the gate divers.

On the surface, Malcolm, the leader of the assault team, had followed the Cold Chaos protocol. Like Elias, Malcolm could feel the anchor and he also had the benefit of Lila Mason, a pathfinder, with enhanced anchor sensitivity. They quickly identified the most likely assault route. It punched almost straight north from the gate. They mapped about three miles of it, clearing the hostiles, went back to the gate, and began looking for the prospective mining sites.

Determining a good mining area was more art than science. Things would have been so much simpler if they could hire their own assessors, Elias reflected. As it was, they were forced to play the guessing game.

It was about control. If the government didn't trust the guilds to share the spoils, the DDC could simply station observers to log everything that came out of the gate. Instead, they chose to hoard the assessors. They wanted to dictate what came out of the breaches and how much. If the DDC wanted more sebrian, the DeBRAs would find sebrian deposits and ignore aetherium that would sell for ten times as much.

It was also the way to bring problematic guilds in line. Three years ago, the DDC had an issue with Halcyon, and the DeBRAs stopped finding valuable resources in Halcyon's gates. Six months later, Halcyon was on the brink of bankruptcy, and they threw in the towel.

The DeBRAs were spies. They mingled with the guilds, they saw how they operated, and they were actively discouraged from forming any personal attachments to the guild members. That's why most guilds limited the assessors' access. They were given a survey to review, came in during the mining stage, and then left as soon as the last of the mining was completed.

Except that Ada Moore never left Elmwood.

The mining site Malcolm chose lay off to the east, roughly a mile from the gate, at the end of a branching tunnel. It ticked all of the boxes outlined in the guild protocol for cave biome mining: a large stable cavern, close to the gate, with a good mix of promising mineral deposits and an abundance of vegetation in case those minerals turned out to be trash.

It also had to be defensible, and that's where they ran into a problem.

Elias looked at Leo. His XO leaned forward slightly.

"You are Malcolm," Elias said.

Leo nodded.

Elias tapped the map of the mining site on the screen. It showed a massive cave with a stream running north to south. The entrance, through which the mining team had accessed the site, lay in the lower left, in the west wall. The east and south walls had no accessible egress. The north wall, at the top, showed three tunnels spiraling into a labyrinth of passageways and small chambers, half of them carrying running water.

"You find this site," Elias said. "You sweep it. It's clean. Your next move?"

"I set up aetherium charges in these three tunnels and detonate."

Exactly. "Why?"

Leo swept his fingers across the three passages and the maze beyond. "It's a mess. Everything is connected. The only way to secure the mining site is to prevent access completely. One way in, one way out."

"Agreed. Malcolm would have known that."

"Yes."

The two of them peered at the map. This was basic shit, and yet Malcolm left the tunnels as they were.

"Why?" Elias murmured.

"I don't know."

"What's your best guess?"

Leo considered the map. "Perhaps he was unsure whether he picked the right path to the anchor and thought he might have to double back and take one of the tunnels instead."

"Yes, but with the firepower in that team and the mining crew's equipment, he could easily reopen one of the entrances. Why gamble with the miners' lives?"

Leo shook his head. "I don't know."

Malcolm had been with Cold Chaos for five years. An Interceptor class Talent, he was a maneuverable, fast damage dealer who positioned himself behind the tank, which allowed him to rapidly respond to the changing battlefield. He fought with a spear, could summon plasma javelins, which he hurled at incoming threats, and could teleport about twenty yards once every hour or so.

The man had an uncanny situational awareness. He was slightly precognizant, anticipating the enemy's actions as well as his team's. He could predict how and where an opponent would attack and how his people were likely to respond to it. He sensed when someone would need assistance, and he was always where he was needed the most.

His only flaw as a team leader was that occasionally he made impulsive decisions. Nine times out of ten, he reacted as expected but once in a while he would roll the dice. To his credit, he was good enough to compensate when his gamble didn't pay off, but he'd come close to disaster a couple of times.

Malcolm was experienced and smart, and he knew the procedure. And yet he left the tunnels as they were.

Elias moved on. "Next question: why only one mining site? The protocol suggests at least three. Why this one?"

Leo frowned. "You think he found something in that cave? Something he had to have?"

"That's the only thing that would make sense."

Leo's eyes flashed white. The moment he was left to his own devices, he would take a deep dive into Malcolm's life. Leo took mysteries as a personal challenge.

As the assault team leader, Malcolm had absolute authority over the gate dive. Neither the mining foreman nor the DeBRA would question his decisions. If he said something had to be done, only London could push back, and according to the records of the meeting, the escort captain had mentioned the potential vulnerability of the mining site just once and then dropped it.

In Malcolm's place, Elias would have spent another three days on a survey and then doubled back and collapsed those tunnels. Then and only then would it have been safe to bring in the miners. Instead, Malcolm charged in, pushing the mining crew to the site as soon as the guild regulations allowed.

Elias leaned back. "Let's say Malcolm glitched out for some reason. He gets impulsive once in a while, but London doesn't."

Leo nodded. "London is careful and risk averse."

Risk averse. Interesting way to put it. Elias would have to remember that.

The XO frowned. "When the team came out with the survey, London would've had to sign off on it. He is the escort captain."

"Exactly. The record says he mentioned the tunnels once and never spoke about them again. Did you ask him about it?"

"No. It didn't occur to me." A hint of frustration showed on Leo's face. He was his own worst critic. "I should have. It seems obvious in hindsight."

The intercom came to life. *"We're beginning our descent into Dallas."*

"Don't worry about it," Elias said. "London isn't going anywhere. In a few hours we will ask him about that. And a lot more."

Leo nodded and buckled his seat belt.

THERE WAS NO WAY DOWN.

I had scanned the darkness three times. It was a bottomless pit. No route below, no ledges we could drop down to, no escape. The only path out was the same way we came. Through the passage and back into the lake dragon's cavern.

I gave it about five minutes after the last of the noises faded, and then Bear and I snuck forward to the mouth of the tunnel. We made it just in time to see the lake dragon pull the bug's corpse under the water. It would be busy for a while. As long as we avoided the shore, we should be safe.

I searched the perimeter of the cave, staying as far from the lake as I could. There were no other tunnels, but there was a path up, along a ledge that climbed fifty feet above the cavern floor. We took it and picked our way onto a natural stone bridge. It brought us across the cavern to a dark fissure in the opposite wall, barely three feet wide. We squeezed through it, and it spat us out into a wide tunnel.

Ahead the passageway gave way to a large natural arch, and beyond it I could see more ledges and passages, a warren of tunnels, some dark, some marked by bioluminescence. Unlike the banks of the river, studded with jagged rocks, the floor of the tunnel was relatively flat, with ridges of hard stone breaking through here and there like the ribs of a buried giant skeleton. Fossilized roots braided through solid rock between the stone ribs. The air smelled sour and acrid.

Next to me, Bear took a few steps to the side and sniffed something. I focused on it. Stalker poop.

"No," I whispered and tugged the leash.

She came back and looked at me with slight disapproval. Sniffing strange poop was what dogs did, and I was clearly preventing her from fulfilling her duty.

I could see the other signs now: the faint trail leading to the fissure, more feces, stains from urine on the rocks. These tunnels were stalker hunting grounds. They came through here and took the bridge down to the water below, and because the bank of the river was hard to get to, some of them made their way to the lake to drink. The lake dragon nabbed them like a crocodile ambushing wildebeests.

This wasn't just a cave stuffed with random monsters. This

was an ecosystem. The lake dragon was an apex predator; the giant bug was probably a rank below, and the stalkers were mid-tier. There must be prey species somewhere in these tunnels. There was certainly enough vegetation to support small herbivores.

I could see the pale stains on the rocks, where stone had been bleached by generations of stalkers urinating on it. None of this environment looked new. This was an established bionetwork that developed over years, possibly centuries. All of this must've belonged somewhere, to a different world.

This was the longest I had ever been in a breach and the furthest I had gone into one. Assault teams spent days, sometimes weeks in the breaches, but my normal MO was to get in, find the resources, stay just long enough for the miners to finish, and get out. I had no idea if all breaches were like this, but if they were, what would happen to this place when the anchor was destroyed? Did this environment disintegrate, or did it simply return to its place of origin?

The gates had been opening for ten years, and we knew so little about them. Usually the assault teams made it out in time, but occasionally the gates collapsed while people were still trapped inside. Sixty-two percent of those instances were considered to be fatalities. Nobody escaped. In the rest of the cases, people were jettisoned back to the point of the gate's origin. A large percentage of those survivors showed brain damage with retrograde amnesia. Some had to relearn basic skills like writing and holding a spoon.

Sooner or later, Cold Chaos would put another assault team into this breach. I had to get out before they shattered the anchor.

Bear growled softly.

I *flexed*. Four shapes were closing in on us, sneaking through the gloom. My talent grasped them, and knowledge came flooding in.

The *re-nah*. Fast, deadly, able to regurgitate acidic bile that would burn exposed skin on contact. Pack hunters, cautious alone, brazen in large numbers. The strongest of the group would attack first, drawing attention, while the rest would flank the prey. Their hearts, on the right side, were possible to reach with a long narrow blade, but the best target was at the base of their throat, just under their chin. A small organ that functioned like a secondary motor cortex. It made them fast and helped them coordinate their movements when they swarmed, and when damaged or destroyed, it induced partial paralysis.

A memory unfurled. *A clearing in a deep alien jungle, re-nah streaming from the caves in the mountain side, forming a massive horde. Eyes glowing, fangs bared, two males fighting, each trying to rip out the other's throat...*

I reached down and released Bear's leash.

Around us the cave was perfectly silent, except for the faint sound of water dripping somewhere out of sight. The bracer on my wrist flowed into my hand, its metal familiar by now, slightly textured and comfortable, like a favorite kitchen knife I had used for years. I focused on the blade. Long, flat, an inch and a half wide. As much damage as possible in a single thrust. The organ would be hard to hit on a moving target. Still better than a heart, though.

Drip. Drip. Drip.

There were no thoughts anymore. I just stood still and waited.

Drip. Drip.

Almost there. They were crouching along the walls, measuring the distance, shifting forward, paw over paw. One large male, two smaller ones, and a female hugging the left wall.

Drip.

The large male charged. He tore out of the gloom like a cannonball, jaws gaping. There was no time to think. I just reacted. My sword slid into the soft tissue of his neck. The male crashed, its momentum carrying him forward despite his locked limbs. Somehow I dodged, and then Bear was on him. The stalker was twice her weight and almost twice her size, but his legs no longer worked. She ripped into his throat, tearing at the wound I'd made.

The remaining males lunged, one from the left, the other from the right. The right one came high, snarling and loud, while the one on the left silently aimed for my legs.

I sliced, turning as I cut. The sword slashed the right stalker across the muzzle, carving a bright gash in his pelt. The beast recoiled, but I kept going, cutting as I twisted. My blade caught the left stalker's leg. There was almost no resistance as the sword glided through flesh and bone. The left stalker yelped and scuttled back on three legs, its front leg severed clean.

Bear ripped into the three-legged stalker. The other beast pivoted and charged toward her. I sprinted, slicing like my life depended on it. The right stalker's head slid off its shoulders.

Bear and the three-legged beast were a clump of fur and teeth, rolling on the ground. I *flexed*, willing the moment to stretch out like a rubber band. It did. The frantic whirlwind of bodies slowed, and I narrowed my sword into a spike, and drove down into the base of the stalker's neck. It went limp.

Time snapped back. A terrible weight smashed into my back. My knees buckled. Scalding teeth sank into my right shoulder.

Pain tore through me, turning into an ice-cold rage.

I turned the sword into a dagger, bent my elbow, and stabbed the blade straight into the female stalker's face. She dropped off me, backing away to the fissure. I chased her, blood running down my arm. She made it all the way through the gap before I caught her. She spun to face me and bared her teeth, her nose wet with blood. I bore down on her and kicked as hard as I could. My foot connected with her head. She stumbled back and slid off the stone bridge. For a moment she hung on, digging her claws into the bare rock, but her talons slipped, and she plunged into the river below.

Bear. Shit.

I spun around and sprinted back into the tunnel. The three stalker bodies lay unmoving. Bear sat in the middle. Her shoulder was bloody, and there was a long streak of red across her right side. She panted, her eyes bright, her mouth opened in a happy canine smile, like she just ran around through the surf on some beach and was now waiting for a treat.

She saw me, grabbed the smallest stalker by the paw, and tried to drag it toward me. *Hi, I'm Bear and these are my dead stalker friends. Look how fancy.*

I dug into my pocket, fished out some jerky, and offered it to her. She took it from my fingers, dropped it to the ground, went back to the stalker, bit it some more, came back, and ate the jerky.

"Good girl, Bear. Best girl."

We were both bleeding, but we were still alive. Four stalkers! We took down four…

I should be dead. And Bear should've been dead with me. It took the assault team a bucket of bullets to stop eight stalkers, and Bear and I killed four. A creature the size of a Great Dane had jumped on my back, and I stayed upright. It should've knocked me off my feet.

It wasn't just the weird hallucinations and the unusual precision of my talent. I was changing. Physically changing.

The thought pierced me like a jolt of high-voltage current. The hair on the back of my neck rose.

The year after the divorce had twisted me. I used to like flying. In my head, flying was married to vacation, because the flights of my childhood took me to the beach and amusement parks. Suddenly I was terrified to board a plane. The fear was so debilitating, I couldn't even talk while boarding. I became obsessed with traffic, avoiding driving whenever I could. I developed a fixation on my health that bloomed into hypochondria.

I ended up in therapy, where we got to the root of the problem. I had realized that Roger was truly, completely gone and if something happened to me, the kids would be alone. I was desperately trying to exert control over my environment, and when I failed, my body locked up and refused to respond. It took years to get over it, and the hypochondria was the hardest to defeat. Every time I thought I'd finally broken free, it would come back with a vengeance over some minor thing like a new mole or some weird pain in my arm.

In a way, becoming an assessor was the best thing for me. Facing death on a regular basis didn't leave room for anxiety. I was too busy surviving.

In this moment, it was like all those years of therapy, exercise, and rewiring my brain's responses never happened. Was I dying? Was that glowing thing in my head eating at me like cancer? No doctor would be able to get it out of me. There was no treatment for whatever the fuck it was. The woman had called me her daughter. Would this gem reshape me into someone like her? What if I wasn't human anymore? What if I got back to the gate and it wouldn't let me exit back to Earth?

The grip of anxiety crushed me. I couldn't talk, I couldn't move, I just stood there, desperately cataloging everything happening in my body. My breathing, my aches and pains, the strange electric prickling feeling in my fingers. I could hear my own heartbeat. It was fast and so loud...

A cold nose nudged my hand.

I still couldn't move.

Bear pushed her muzzle into my fingers, bumping me. I felt her fur slide against my hand.

Bump. Bump.

I exhaled slowly. The air escaped out of me, as if it had been trapped in my lungs. I swallowed, crouched, and hugged Bear. Gradually the sound of my heart receded.

Yes, I was changing. No, I had no control over it, and I didn't know what I would become at the end of this process. But I was getting stronger. There were three stalker corpses on this cave floor. I made that happen.

I petted Bear, straightened, walked over to the nearest furry body, and *flexed*. One hundred and forty-three pounds. I grabbed the stalker by the front paws and lifted it off the ground. My shoulder whined in protest. I clenched my teeth against the pain.

I was holding one hundred and forty-three pounds of dead weight. It wasn't resting on my back, no, I was *holding* it in front of me.

I wonder...

I spun around and threw the corpse. The stalker flew and landed on the cave floor. My shoulder screeched, and I grabbed at it. Okay, not the brightest moment.

The stalker corpse lay ten feet away. I threw one hundred and forty-three pounds across ten feet. Two weeks ago, I'd used a forty-five-pound plate for some overhead squats at the DDC gym, because someone was hogging the Smith machine, and I had a hard time holding it steady for ten reps.

"We're not in Kansas anymore, Bear."

Bear looked at me, padded over to the corpse I threw, and bit it.

"No worries. It's dead. You are the best girl, Bear, you know that?"

Somewhere in the tangle of the tunnels a creature howled. We couldn't stay here. We had to keep moving.

I pulled the antibacterial gel out, slathered some on my bleeding shoulder, popped four Motrins, and turned to Bear.

"Okay, girl, let's treat your battle wounds."

SOMETHING WAS WRONG WITH BEAR.

We had cut our way through the stalker tunnels. Our trail was littered with corpses, and we had just killed our fifteenth beast. It hadn't gotten easier, not at all. I was so worn down, I could barely move. My body hurt, the ache spreading through the muscles like a disease, sapping my new strength and making me slow.

Bear stumbled again. I thought it was fatigue at first, but we had rested for a few minutes before this last fight, and it hadn't helped at all. I had kept her from serious injury. She'd been clawed and bitten once, but the bite had been shallow, so it likely wasn't the blood loss.

Bear whined and fell.

Oh god.

I dropped to my knees by her. "What is it?"

The shepherd looked up at me, her eyes puzzled but trusting.

I *flexed*, focusing on her body, concentrating all of my power on her. What was it? Blood loss, infection…

The faint outline of Bear's body glowed with pale blue-green, but I got nothing more. I had to push deeper. I focused my power into a thin scalpel and used it to slice through the surface glow.

It resisted.

I sliced harder.

Harder!

The glow broke, splintering vertically into multi-colored layers, and before I had a chance to stop, I punched through the top one. It was almost like falling through the floor to a lower level.

On this lower level, Bear's body lit up with deep blue, the glow tracing her nerves, her blood vessels, and her organs. I had never before been able to do that, but that didn't matter now.

Toxin. She was filled with it. I saw it, tiny flecks glowing brighter as they coursed through her like some deadly glitter. I had to find the origin of it. Was it from a stalker bite? No, the concentration of poison wasn't dense there. Then what was it? Where was it the highest?

Her lungs. That fucking glitter saturated her lungs, slipping into her bloodstream with every breath. I had to go deeper. I pushed with my power. Before, it was like trying to slice through glass. Now it felt like punching through solid rock, and I hammered at it.

The top layer of the blue glow cracked, revealing a slightly different shade of blue underneath. I hit it again and again, locked onto the glitter with every drop of willpower I had.

The tiny specks expanded into spheres. What the hell was that?

I pounded on the glow, trying to enlarge it. The spheres came into greater focus. They weren't uniformly round; they had four lobes clumped together and studded with spikes.

What are you? Where did you come from?

A flash of white cut my vision. It lasted only a moment, but I knew I hit a wall. I wasn't going any deeper. I would have to work at this level.

I blinked, trying to reacquire my vision.

My thighs were glowing with blue.

I jerked my hands up. Pale glitter swirling through my arms and fingers. This dust, this thing was inside me too, and I couldn't identify it.

We were both infected, and it was killing us.

Panic drenched me in icy sweat. I wanted to rip a hole in my legs and just force the glitter out.

Bear whined softly like a puppy.

I was losing her. She trusted me, she followed me, and she fought with me, and now she was dying.

"You can't die, Bear. Hold on. Please hold on for me."

Bear licked my hand.

The urge to scream my head off gripped me. Wailing wouldn't help. If only I could identify the poison.

Why couldn't I identify it? Was it because it was inside us and it had become part of us? Or was I just not strong enough to differentiate it from our blood? It had started in the lungs, so we must have inhaled it.

I took a deep breath and exhaled on my hands.

There it was! A trace of the lethal glitter. I focused on it. The four-lobed spiked clumps, swirling, swirling... Something inside me connected, and I saw a faint image in my mind. The mauve flowers. We had been poisoned by their pollen.

I *flexed* harder, stabbing at the pollen with my talent. The tiny flecks opened up into a layered picture in my mind, and the top layer showed how toxic it was...

Oh god.

We were almost out of time. We needed an antidote. *Now.*

I strained, trying to access whatever power lay inside me, the same one that showed me the Grasping Hand and gave me the stalkers' name. It didn't answer.

Please. Please help me.

Nothing.

We would die right here, in this tunnel. I knew it, I could picture it, me wrapped around Bear, hugging her as we both grew cold...

No. There had to be an answer. We hadn't come all this way to lay down and die. We did not kill and fight all these damn stalkers –

The stalkers. The stalkers went to the lake to drink. The flowers were all over the shore, but the stalkers had died because the lake dragon had torn them apart. The flowers didn't poison them.

I jumped to my feet and ran to the nearest corpse. My talent reached out and grasped the body. There was pollen on the fur and on the muzzle and a faint smudge in the lungs, but none anywhere else. Not a trace in the blood. They were immune.

The poison had to be eliminated in the bloodstream. If it was purged in the liver or any other organ, there would've been traces of it in the blood vessels but there were none.

This wouldn't help us any. Just because the stalkers had the immunity...

I *flexed* again. Within the stalker, the heart glowed with bright red. My talent flagged something as red based on how much I wanted it. I valued adamantite more than gold, so in my mind gold flared with pink but adamantite was a dark saturated red. The stalker heart was so red, it was dripping with crimson glow.

I flipped the stalker on its back, shaped my sword into a knife, and stabbed the corpse, slicing it from the neck to the groin. Bloody wet innards spilled out. I dug in the mush, pushing slippery tissue aside until I found the hard sack of the heart. I carved it out and pulled the bloody organ free.

Flex.

The heart turned crimson. I smashed my talent against the top layer of the glow, trying to splinter it into layers, and it obeyed. I punched through the top red layer and saw the second, neon blue.

Toxic. It would poison us, too.

The red was stronger than the blue. That meant there was a slim chance we could make it. It was the difference of might-be-dead from the stalker heart or definitely-dead from the pollen. We didn't have hours, we had minutes. The heart had to be the answer.

This was not how the immunity worked. This wasn't how biology worked.

I blinked my enhanced vision off, shut my eyes for a long second, opened them, and *flexed* again.

The heart was still bright red. My talent was telling me it was our way out. I had nothing to lose.

I put it on a flat rock and minced the tough muscle into near mush. I scooped a handful of the bloody mess and staggered over to Bear.

She was still breathing. There was still a chance.

I pried her jaws open and shoved a clump of the stalker mince into her throat. She gulped and gagged. I held her mouth closed.

"Swallow, please swallow..."

Bear gulped again. Yes. It went down.

"What a good girl. The best girl. One more time. Let's get a little more in there."

I forced two more handfuls into her and *flexed*. The concentration of pollen in her stomach dimmed. Somehow it was acting as an antidote. I didn't understand how. It didn't matter. We were all out of choices.

Bear let out a soft, weak howl, almost a gasp. It must have hurt.

"I'm so sorry. I wouldn't hurt you if there was any other way."

If I ate the heart now, there was no telling what it would do to me. I could pass out right here, and we would both become stalker dinner.

About twenty minutes ago we had walked by a narrow stone bridge that spanned a deep cavern. There had been a depression at the other end, a smaller cave within the wall of a larger cave. At the time I thought it would be a good place to rest, because the stalkers could only come at us one by one, but I wanted to get out of the tunnels, and it seemed better to just keep moving. We had to find a place to hide, and that was the closest safe spot I could think.

I should be able to find the bridge again. I just had to follow the trail of bodies and make it there before the poison got me.

I picked Bear up. She felt so heavy, impossibly heavy.

I spun around and trudged back the way we came.

[6]

The guild SUV came to a quiet stop in front of a two-story house. Elias didn't know much about architecture, but he'd spent enough time in Chicago to recognize the style. It was a remodeled Chicago bungalow. Brenda's parents lived in one, and Brenda and he had looked into buying one before…

A cold hand reached into his chest. He held still for a moment, waiting for the feeling to pass. He had no idea if his former in-laws were still alive. For the first year after the funerals, he'd tried to call once a month, until his father-in-law finally asked him to stop. He said it was too painful.

Elias studied the house, trying to anchor himself to the present. The original bungalows were on the smaller side, with a footprint around eight hundred square feet, a full basement, and an attic space on top. They were iconic to Chicago. People often expanded them with second story additions, and some of the popped-top bungalows looked disjointed as if a tornado had picked up half of a completely different home and deposited it atop the original brick or stucco frame.

This one didn't. Whoever remodeled it set the addition back, away from the street, leaving the original façade intact. The house was brick, with the original front room, a trademark row of large windows, and a small porch under the gabled roof with stairs leading to the street level. The second story matched the first – same gently sloping roof, same dormered windows and matching shingles. A garden bed ran along the front wall, offering lavender and white flowers. More flowers bloomed in the box by the windows. To the left, some sort of small decorative tree spread branches with dark red leaves. Adaline Moore loved her house.

Had. Had loved.

"I still don't think this is wise," Leo said from the driver seat.

Twenty-eight people died in the breach. Fourteen members of the assault crew, nine miners, four escorts, and Adaline Moore. Twelve of the deceased left behind minor children. Of all of them, only Adaline Moore's kids had no immediate family to take care of them.

The media devoured any news related to the guilds and gates, and the death of a prominent DeBRA would set off fireworks. At some point the DDC would issue a press release announcing it. Once that news broke, the rival guilds would go into a feeding frenzy of outrage, and Adaline's children would become the center of a news cycle. They would be overwhelmed, used, wrung dry for the sake of a cheap emotional punch, and then abandoned to their grief. If they were lucky, the country would forget they existed. If they were unlucky, someone would take note of two vulnerable orphans with a million-dollar life insurance payout. He had seen this tragedy play out before.

"I won't allow Adaline's children to be fed to the media circus," Elias said. "They are safer at the Guild HQ. I don't need some asshole showing up at their door, sticking a microphone into their faces, and asking how they feel about their mother dying."

"Adaline Moore would have made provisions," Leo said.

"I'm sure she did. Until we know what they are, we will take care of the kids."

"This will be seen as Cold Chaos controlling access to the children because we have something to hide. We are trying to minimize the media's attention. They love conspiracies, and other guilds will spin it in the worst way possible. I worry this will have a Streisand effect. Instead of keeping the story small, we will only make it bigger."

"That's fine. If they want to paint us as villains, let them. We will survive. We are the third largest guild in the country."

Leo sighed quietly.

"I called Felicia," Elias told him.

Felicia Terrell was a powerhouse attorney, and she specialized in guild-related litigation. He spoke to her as soon as he got off the plane. She called him a marshmallow and promised to show up first thing in the morning. The children would be well protected from everyone, including Cold Chaos.

"Still…"

"Leo. This is the least we can do."

Leo sighed again.

Elias opened the door and stepped out. The narrow walkway leading to the steps needed to be pressure-washed. He walked up the steps and knocked on the door.

The Ring camera came to life. Elias looked into it. "Hello, I'm…"

The door swung open, revealing a boy. He was about twelve, thin, with glasses and short light brown hair. "Elias McFeron," the boy said. "From the commercials."

"Yes," Elias said.

Behind the boy, a teenage girl stepped out into the open. She looked like a younger version of Adaline: same large eyes, same auburn hair, same wary look. He never met Adaline Moore, but he had seen a couple of interviews and photographs. Adaline didn't just look at people. She watched them, actively observing, and her daughter was doing that exact thing to him now. He felt himself being evaluated.

"Something happened to mom," the girl said.

"Yes. May we come in?"

The boy glanced at his sister.

"Yes," she said.

Elias walked into the house. Behind him Leo entered and shut the door.

The inside of the home was clean and neat. Dark wood floors, cream walls, a lot of the wainscotting that seemed to match the outside of the house. A staircase to the left, a living room to the right, light green couches with notebooks and art supplies strewn on the coffee table, a white kitchen past it… It felt like a home, warm and lived in. He had that once.

The two kids were looking at him, their faces tense.

"I'm the guildmaster of Cold Chaos," Elias said. "Your mother was working on the mining site in the gate we are responsible for. The miners were attacked."

"Is she dead?" the girl asked.

"Officially, she is missing. However, your mother is a noncombat Talent. She doesn't have any means to defend herself. Only four of our mining team escaped, so the outcome isn't looking good. We won't know what happened for sure until we go back in and eliminate those threats."

"So Mom could still be alive?" the boy asked.

"Yes. There is a slight chance that she might have survived. Nothing is certain until we find the bodies."

"When?" the girl asked.

"As soon as we can pull an assault team together. We will need top-tier people for this breach."

"How long will it take?" the boy asked.

"Several days. Probably at least three. Maybe longer. We have to go in with the kind of team that will win." Elias paused. "I'm inviting you to stay at our HQ until this is over."

"You don't want us talking to the press people," the girl said.

"It doesn't really matter if you talk to the press or not," Leo said. "We will get skewered anyway."

"I'm not going to pressure you to do anything," Elias said. "But if you wanted to stay at our HQ, away from everyone, so you can deal with things, you have that option. I've called a lawyer on your behalf. Whether you come with us or not, she will come to speak with you in the morning. She doesn't work for the guild. She works for you."

"And if we don't want your lawyer?" the girl asked.

"Then you tell her no and she'll leave."

"Why are you doing this?" the boy asked.

"Because your mother trusted us to keep her safe, and we failed her," Elias said.

The boy looked at his sister.

"He is not a threat." She said it with absolute certainty.

"What about him?" the boy looked at Leo.

"Not a threat either. Although he really doesn't think any of this is a good idea."

Leo blinked.

Adaline's daughter looked at Elias, and there was pressure in her gaze. "My name is Tia. This is Noah. We're coming with you, but we have to bring Mellow."

"Who is Mellow?"

Noah reached over to the couch, moved a blanket aside, and picked up a large cream-colored cat. The cat looked at Elias and hissed.

"Don't be a drama queen," Tia told it.

"Mellow is welcome to come," Elias said.

"Good." Tia nodded to her brother. "Go pack."

He put the cat down and ran up the stairs.

"You're a Talent," Elias guessed.

"Yes," she said.

"An assessor?" Leo asked.

"Sort of. Like Mom but with people."

What kind of power was that? "Does your mother know?"

Tia shook her head. "You have to promise me that you'll bring her back."

"I can't do that," Elias said. "I'm not going to lie to you. Your mother is probably gone."

"My mom is alive," Tia said. "She promised she would come back to us. She always keeps her promises."

He didn't know what to say to that.

Tia pivoted to the bookcase and pulled a large black folder with a zipper on it.

"I'm going to get a cat carrier and my things," she said and handed the folder to him.

"What is this?" he asked.

A tiny shiver of fear flashed in Tia's eyes. He watched her squash it.

"Mom's death folder. There is one on her laptop, too. I'll need to grab that. We won't need it, but she would want us to bring it."

Tia disappeared into the house.

"Are they in shock?" Leo murmured.

"No," Elias said. "They are just ready."

Adaline Moore had trained her children what to do in case of her death. They were so efficient at it, they must've practiced.

This was the war at home, he realized. Ten years of it. He was looking at children who grew up with the gates. Tia would've been five, maybe six, when the first gates burst. The boy would've been a toddler. They were prepared to lose their mother. They lived with that possibility every day, and now they were putting on brave faces and trying to stick to the plan.

He had to get into that damn breach.

THE STONE BRIDGE STRETCHED IN FRONT OF ME. IT WAS ONLY twenty-seven yards long, but it felt like a mile. I shuffled across it, one foot in front of the other, my body weak and exhausted, and poor Bear heavy like an anvil in my arms. She was still breathing. I felt her every ragged breath. She was shivering and sometimes she would yelp, but she was still alive.

Almost there.

One step at a time. Almost made it.

Just a little further.

The little cave gaped in front of us. It was a nearly circular depression in the rock, about thirty feet across, its walls smooth, its floor empty.

I tried to set Bear down, but my legs gave out, and we both collapsed. I pulled myself upright and unhooked Bear's leash from around my neck. Three stalker hearts tumbled to the ground. I had cut them out along the way, strung them onto the leash like fish, and then I put that grisly necklace around my neck. It was the only way I could carry it.

I chopped one heart into small pieces. My hands felt so heavy and clumsy. I scooped a handful of stalker stew meat and shoved it in my mouth.

It burned like battery acid.

I swallowed. Fire sliding down my throat. I chopped the

meat smaller. The last thing I needed was to die choking on stalker's heart.

The pieces of raw flesh landed in my stomach like rocks. My hands trembled. I retched and forced it back down.

I'd managed to down one and a half hearts before the shivers came. Cold clutched at me. My teeth chattered, my knees shook, and I could not get warm. I slumped against the cave wall, shuddering. Bear trembled, turned, and crawled to me.

Tears wet my eyes.

Bear slumped against me and rested her head on my thigh. I petted her. We shivered together. Time stretched, each moment sticky and viscous.

The shivers attacked in waves now. They washed over me, broke into stabbing pains, faded, and came again.

I had to stay awake. Something told me that to sleep was to die.

I shook Bear. She looked at me with her warm eyes.

I forced my quivering lips to move. "You have to stay awake."

The shepherd looked at me.

"Stay with me. I'll tell you a story. You were born into this new age. Your parents were probably born into it as well. You don't know, but it didn't use to be like this. It used to be... nice."

I stroked her fur with trembling fingers.

"I remember when the first gates opened. The government called them anomalies back then. One of them was right downtown. The military cordoned it off. Shut down half of the business district.

"At first, everyone was alarmed. There was news coverage, and theories, and the markets crashed. But the gate just sat there, not doing anything. Roger and I drove by to look at it. It was huge. This high-rise-sized, massive hole in the middle of the city, swirling with orange sparks, strange roots and branches twisting along its boundary, just out of reach. I remember feeling this overwhelming anxiety. Like looking at the tornado coming your way and not being able to do anything about it.

"I asked Roger if we should move. He said, 'Let's talk about it.' Roger was my husband and my best friend. Neither of us got along with our parents. I have no siblings, and he didn't talk to his brother, so it was the two of us against the world. We discussed it on the way home. Our jobs were here. We'd just bought the house two years before. Tia was doing well in school. Roger's company was twenty minutes from the site, and I was north of it, so if something happened, we'd have time to get out. We decided to stay.

"For two months the gate just sat there. People stopped talking about it, except to complain about the traffic. Then one day – it was a Monday. I don't know why crap like this always happens on Mondays – one day, I had this long Zoom meeting with the San Diego office, trying to sort out the new advertising campaign. I kept hearing raised voices and then San Diego went offline.

"I came out of my office. Imagine the conference room crammed with terrified people, and they are all staring at the screen, glassy-eyed and completely quiet. There was a newscast on tv, and the journalist sounded so high-pitched, she was squeaking like a terrified mouse. The anomaly had burst and vomited a torrent of monsters into the city. Downtown was a warzone. Bodies torn apart, cars upside down, and creatures that had popped straight out of a nightmare streaming across the screen..."

I remembered the burst of hot electric panic that shot through me. I knew in that moment that whatever plans we made and the future we thought was coming had just died, smashed to pieces with the hammer of an existential threat.

"I stumbled away from the room and called Roger. He answered right away. He said, 'Pick up the kids and go home. Straight home, Ada, no stops. I'll get there as soon as I can.'"

My eyes had grown hot. I swiped the tears off with the back of my forearm. My fingers were stained with stalker blood, and I didn't want it in my eyes.

"These are angry tears. The fucked-up thing is, I remember his voice, Bear. I remember how he sounded. Strong and sure. And I miss that. I miss that voice, I miss the old him, and he is a fucking shithead, and I will never let him back into our lives, but there it is."

I swallowed and checked Bear. She looked at me. Still alive.

"I left the office. The streets were choked with cars. I'm on the corner of Grace and Broadway, right by that pancake place, and a cop is in the middle of the intersection, and this herd of people just tears out of nowhere and stampedes down Grace. The crowd runs past, and the cop is on the street on his back, not moving. I saw that man being trampled to death. Then a body falls on the street from above. I look up, and there are six-legged things crawling on the building to my right and yanking people out of the windows, and up ahead, just past the IHOP, there is a high-rise apartment building. And it shakes, Bear, and then people start raining from it, jumping in desperation and just smashing onto the street. And I know it's about to fall, so I jerk my wheel right, and tear down Grace Street in the direction the stampede had come from, because I have no place to go, and something tells me not to follow the crowd. It was hell on Earth, Bear. I don't know to this day how I got out.

"I pick up Tia, get to Noah's daycare, grab him, and drive home on autopilot. At some point we pass Target, and it's on fire. We get to our house and huddle in the bedroom on the bed. The kids are scared, so I turn Netflix on and for some reason it is still streaming despite the world ending. We watch and wait."

I sat in that bedroom and thought what life would be like if Roger died, and every time I imagined losing him, it felt like someone had cut my soul with a knife. Until today, those were the worst two hours of my life.

"Finally, I hear the code lock, and then Roger walks into the bedroom, wild eyed, disheveled, but alive."

The relief had been indescribable.

"I hug him, but he doesn't hug me back. He just stands there, stiff. I thought he was in shock. I make some frozen pizzas, we eat, and we stay with the kids watching Netflix. Roger is distant. It's like he's gone into some inside place where nobody is welcome. At some point he leaves the bedroom. I wait until the kids fall asleep, check my phone for news, and then look for him.

"He is sitting on our front porch. He has a pack of cigarettes, and he is chain smoking, one after another. He quit when I was pregnant with Tia. Ten years later, that fucking pack still bothers me. I didn't make him quit. He chose to do it. Either he had a secret pack – and who keeps a hidden pack of cigarettes for six years? – or he's been smoking on the side and hiding it from me. Why?

"Anyway, I tell him what I saw on my phone."

That conversation was branded into my memory. I could recite it word by word and in an instant I was right there, back on that porch, with the night encroaching onto the city and the blaze of orange in the distance, where Target was still burning hours later.

"They are saying that the anomalies are gates that lead to some other world or dimension. There are twelve gates in the US. Our outbreak is fifteen percent contained. They think they'll have it under control in forty-eight hours."

"Nothing is under control." His voice was almost a snarl.

I reached out to take his hand.

He shifted away.

"I'm so sorry," I said. "I don't know what happened, I don't know what you saw, but I'm so sorry."

"I took 90 home," he said. "The traffic stopped. Everything stopped. And then the things came. They went after the ones who got out of

their cars first. Then they figured out that we were in the cars. I saw them rip a man apart right in front of me. They threw him on my car. His guts fell out of his body onto the glass. His intestines were sliding on the windshield, and he was still alive. I just sat there and watched him die."

Roger stabbed the cigarette out on the step, crushing it.

"I sat there like that for three hours, waiting for them to find me. I didn't know if you and the kids were dead or alive. I didn't know if you made it home or if you were stuck like me. And the whole time I had this voice in the back of my head telling me that I needed to get the fuck out and take care of my wife and kids. I needed to nut up, get out of the car, and go find you."

Oh my God. "You made it home. That's all we wanted."

He didn't look like he heard a word I said.

"And then I thought, what if you were already dead? What if I never found you? And you know what I felt?"

I couldn't tell if he wanted an answer. "No."

He looked at me, and his eyes seemed feverish. *"I felt relief."*

"What?"

"I felt relief. A burden lifted."

The hair on the back of my neck rose. "You don't mean that."

"I do. Adaline, why would I lie about this now?"

I stared at him, stunned. What do I do with this? How do I fix it?

"The world is ending. This right here..." He held his hands out and circled the street. *"This is done. It's over. It's over for all of us."*

"I think you're still in shock."

"Maybe. But I see things very clearly now. We are living on borrowed time. There will be more of these holes. They're not just going to give up. We can't beat them. I don't know how much time we have left. Six months, a year, a week. Nobody knows."

I'd gone strangely numb. A part of me knew he was talking and making words, but none of the sounds made any sense.

"I'm going to live whatever time I have left on my own terms. Doing what I want."

He fell silent and looked at me. This was the part where I had to say something.

My voice came out wooden. I was so calm, and I had no idea why. "And what is it you want, Roger?"

"Not this."

"Ah."

"Not anymore."

"Is there room for me and the kids in this new life on your terms?"

"No."

The word lashed me.

"We've been together ten years. If you don't want to be married, that's fine, but you don't get to just quit being a father. The kids have known you their entire lives. They won't understand, Roger. They need you. I need you."

"It's not about you or them. This is about me. I need something else."

"Tia loves you. Noah adores you. That little boy can't wait for you to come home. Every day he does a little dance when he sees your car in the driveway. You know what Tia told me while we were waiting for you? She said, 'Don't worry Mom, Dad will kill all the monsters.'"

Roger shook his head. "I can't. I can't kill any monsters. I didn't save anyone. I just froze. And I'm not going to spend the rest of my life feeling like a coward."

"So, you're just going to abandon us? To whatever happens?"

A hint of something cold and vicious twisted his face. "I have a right to be happy. For however long I have left. I'm going to grab my happiness and hold on to it while I still can. This is done. We are done."

"What am I supposed to tell the kids?"

"Whatever you want."

He got up and went inside.

"And now you know how my marriage ended, Bear. I've had

105

a decade to think about it. I understand it better now. I was able to drive away from the slaughter. I escaped. He couldn't. He just sat in that car stuck and waiting to die, and it must've occurred to him that he was doing that exact same thing in his life. He must've realized something about himself that neither he nor I knew until that moment."

I stroked Bear's fur.

"He's down in Puerto Rico. He owns a boat and takes tourists out to the reefs to snorkel with manta rays. He is exactly where he wants to be. And until today, I was where I wanted to be. I manifested as a Talent three years after that first gate break. Yes, I got this job for benefits and pay, because I have bills and kids, but there are other ways to earn money. I do it because every time I find adamantite or aetherium, it makes us a little stronger. It gives us a better fighting chance to repel this invasion, and I will keep finding this shit until all the breaches are broken and all the gates are closed, so my children can have a safe, boring future."

I realized that I was snarling and took a deep breath.

"I don't blame Roger for the divorce. I blame him for being a shit father. I've tried, Bear. I've sent emails, I texted, I offered phone calls. He didn't respond. The only communication from him was through the child support payments. That's how I knew he was still alive."

Another shudder twisted me.

"He works as little as possible, so he makes just enough to survive and maintain the boat. At first he was sending two hundred dollars a month, then a hundred, then he stopped. I kept offering to send the kids to visit him or inviting him to visit us, and he cut that off. He said he didn't want to see them. I finally had enough and had my lawyer email him an affidavit to relinquish his parental rights. I thought it would shock him into having a relationship with our kids. It came back as a scan in twenty-four hours, attached to a blank email, signed, notarized and witnessed by two people. He wanted to get rid of Tia and Noah that much."

I gritted my teeth.

"I didn't tell the kids, but I have the Death Folder with insurance, and the will, and all that crap. It's backed up on my laptop. The children know about it, and that affidavit is in there, with his fucking signature on it. Once my death is announced, they will learn that their father doesn't want them. My children will think they don't have anyone left in this world. People break promises all the time. Roger promised to love me. Melissa promised to be my friend. London promised to protect me.

"Promises must be kept, Bear. Especially to children. I promised Tia I wouldn't die in this hellhole and I meant it. We are going to survive. We will get out of here if I have to crawl on my hands and knees all the way to that damn gate."

DRISHYA CHANDRAN BLINKED HER BIG BROWN EYES. ON PAPER, she was twenty-one. To Elias, she looked about fifteen at most.

It's not that the kids are getting younger; it's that I'm getting older.

"I'm sorry," Drishya said. "I honestly didn't see anything."

They had settled Tia and Noah into one of the HQ apartments. The guild headquarters took up an entire office tower in Schaumburg. Twelve floors of offices, meeting rooms, apartments, R&D labs, sitting in the middle of a twenty-five-acre greenbelt space. The building had a clinic with an emergency room, two restaurants, a gate diver–rated gym, a movie theater, an arcade, a park, and a roof garden. It was a village onto itself, and he'd assigned Haze to look over the children. All of their needs would be met, and Haze would unobtrusively chaperon them if they chose to wander. Elias had called ahead, and when the kids arrived, their apartment featured a brand-new cat tree and a robotic litter box. Mellow hated both, hissed at him again, and hid under the bed instead. He wasn't very fond of cats, and the feeling was clearly mutual.

After the kids were settled, Leo and he turned around and went to Elmwood, where he'd commandeered the Elmwood Public Library as their makeshift office. Guild policy dictated that in case of a fatal event wiping out the assault crew, the gate had to be secured at all times, and he intended to sit on it until they accumulated enough divers to go in.

Through the glass window of the conference room Elias could see the gate looming like a dark hungry mouth, bathed in the glow of the floodlights. No matter how many lives they threw into it, it would never be enough. It was past one in the morning, and he was out of coffee.

"Walk me through it one more time," he said.

"The drill head jammed," Drishya said. "I showed it to Melissa. She said to go get the new one from the cart in the tunnel. I went to get it. The next thing I know Wagner is running out of the tunnel, and Melissa is behind him, and her face doesn't look right. I'm like okay, I guess we are doing that now, so I turned around and ran to the gate. I heard an explosion behind us, so I didn't look back. I didn't even know London made it until I was out."

"Were you the first to the gate?"

"Yes. I was scared."

"Who came out after you?"

"Wagner."

Middle-aged Wagner with arthritic knees somehow overtook both Melissa and London, who sprinted faster than most Olympic athletes. If Melissa and London wanted to get their story straight without being overheard, the only time to do so would be just inside the breach, after Drishya and Wagner exited.

"Why was the cart with the spare parts in the tunnel and not at the site?" Elias asked.

"It didn't fit. The site sloped to the stream and there wasn't a lot of flat ground, so we could only get three of the four carts in." Drishya counted off on her fingers. "Cart One had the generator, lights, and first aid, so it had to come in. Carts Two and Three were for the ore. Adamantite is heavy, so we didn't want to carry it too far. Cart Four with the spare parts had to live outside."

"So there was adamantite at the site?" He'd read Leo's notes of Melissa's interview, but it seemed almost unbelievable that so much adamantite could exist in one place.

"Oh yes. That's how my drill broke. Chipped off a chunk this big." Drishya held her hands out as if lifting an invisible basketball.

"Was the adamantite in plain view?"

The miner shook her head. "No. Buried, and half of it underwater. It took the DeBRA about ten minutes to find it. She had to mark it with paint for us."

Was this why they were attacked? Was something protecting the ore?

Drishya sighed. "It's awful, isn't it? Everyone is dead."

"It is, and they are," Elias confirmed.

"I knew we would get a big bonus when we found the gold, and then the DeBRA came up with adamantite. I was so excited. I thought I could finally put a deposit on the house. My mom isn't doing so well. I've got to get us out of the apartment, and I'm the only one working."

Gold? What gold? "I'm sorry your mother is in bad health, and that you had to go through this trauma. You may want to see Dr. Choi. He has a room set up downstairs."

"I'm okay. I didn't see any of it," Drishya said. "I've only been working for six months. I didn't even know people that well..."

He'd seen this before. Some people grieved when faced with death, others got angry, and some tried to disconnect themselves from what happened.

"I understand," he said. "Still, it might be a good idea. You've lost colleagues in a sudden traumatic way. Things like that can fester."

"I'll think about it," she said.

"So how much gold was there?"

"A lot. It was everywhere in the water, like rocks. We weren't even drilling; we were pulling it out by hand. Nuggets the size of walnuts. I ended up dumping like fifty pounds of it to make room for adamantite, and we'd been only gathering it for a few minutes."

"I see. I appreciate your help, Ms. Chandran. The guild is grateful for your assistance. Please get some rest."

She got up and paused. "You are a lot less scary than I thought you would be."

"That's good to hear."

"Just so you know, Wagner told me not to talk to you."

Elias raised his eyebrows. "Oh?"

"He said that miners don't go into the breaches with guild-masters. They go with escort captains. He said it was something to keep in mind."

"Thank you for your honesty."

She nodded and walked out.

Elias pulled up the interview notes on his tablet. Neither Melissa nor London said anything about the gold. Malcolm wouldn't have seen the buried adamantite, but gold was an entirely different beast. It was just lying there in the stream.

Was it just gold? Was that it? He'd been wracking his brain, trying to find the reason for the lapse in procedure, having this back and forth with Leo, wondering what he was missing, and all this time, the answer was depressingly simple. *Well, no shit, Sherlock, here it is.* Greed.

He had put so many regulations and checks in place, and somehow greed always won. He was so fucking tired.

Leo appeared in the open doorway like a wraith manifesting, met his gaze, and stepped back.

"Come inside and shut the door," Elias growled.

Leo came in and closed the door behind him.

"Sit."

Leo sat.

"Why do baby miners think I'm scary?"

"Because you are, sir. Most people find a man who can cut a car in half with a single strike and then throw the pieces at you frightening."

"Hmm."

"Also, we offer the highest pay and the best benefits among the top-tier guilds, and you are their boss who holds their livelihood in his gauntleted fingers..."

Elias raised his hand. "Did you know there was gold at the mining site?"

Leo's eyes flashed with white. "I did not."

"Apparently it was in the water. Nuggets the size of walnuts. Finally, I know something before you do."

"Congratulations, sir."

Elias let that go, pulled up the map of the site on his tablet, and pointed at the three tunnels, each carrying a current of water that merged into a single stream. "Gold washes downstream."

"Malcolm left the tunnels open because he wanted to maximize the profit from the site." Leo's face snapped into a hard flat mask. "He must've expected that once they cleared the site, they would gather more gold upstream."

"Remind me, how much did Malcolm make last year?"

"Seven million."

"I want to know why gold got him so excited that he risked twenty lives by leaving the tunnels unsecured."

"Twenty?" Leo frowned. "The mining crew, the escort, the scout, the DeBRA..."

111

"And the dog."

"Oh."

"Malcolm took a significant risk. That's not just greed. That's desperation. How are his finances?"

"Squeaky clean as of the last audit, which was two months ago. Credit score of eight hundred and ten, low debt to assets, less than ten thousand owed on credit cards. I'm following up on a couple of things. We should know more in a few hours. Do you want me to get Wagner in to talk to you?"

"He won't tell me anything. Wagner is forty-nine years old. He was a coal miner before the gates appeared, and we are his third guild. He's used to getting screwed over by his bosses."

"So, he developed an adversarial relationship with us despite fair treatment," Leo said. "Seems counterintuitive."

"It doesn't matter what kind of treatment he gets. He's cooked. He doesn't trust us, he will never trust us, and he will always resent us no matter how many benefits he gets."

"That's not even logical."

"It isn't. It's an emotional response. Trust me, we won't get anything out of him. I'd like you to reinterview Melissa instead. As you said, I'm scary, so she may do better with you. Don't be confrontational. Be sympathetic and understanding. Make it us against the government: we need to tell the DDC something and we need her help to make them go away. Imply that her cooperation will be remembered and appreciated."

Leo nodded. "Should I bring up the families?"

Elias shook his head. "Normally the foreman would be the last to get out, just before the escorts. She was at the head of the pack. Either she was incredibly lucky, or she abandoned her crew and ran for her life. Either way, there is guilt there. If you lean too hard on it, she might shut down. Go with *you were just doing your job, and we don't blame you for surviving* instead. Get her a coffee, get some cookies, interview her in a comfortable setting, and see if she thaws and starts talking. If she goes off on

112

a tangent, let her. Don't rush. You are her friend; you are there to listen."

Leo nodded. "Will do."

Elias leaned back. He was so over it. As soon as he hammered the assault team together, he would enter the gate. He couldn't wait to get out of this conference room. There was no politics in the breach. Things were much simpler: the enemy was in front, the support was behind, and the anchor was an evil star that would lead him to victory.

Leo was still sitting in the chair. Some other problem must've reared its ugly head.

"Lay it on me," Elias said.

"We can't find Jackson."

"What do you mean, you can't find him?"

"He was supposed to fly out of Tokyo twenty minutes ago. He didn't make it to the plane, and he isn't answering his phone. I'm on it."

Jackson was arguably the best healer in the US. He didn't drink, he didn't get high, and his biggest vice was collecting expensive bonsai. The man did not go AWOL. It was simply not who he was.

"Do whatever you have to do, but find him, Leo."

The XO nodded. "I will."

SOMETHING WET MY HAND. MY EYES SNAPPED OPEN. SOMETIME between the waves of shivers and searing pain, my will had given out and I'd fallen asleep.

Bear lay next to me, licking the dry stalker blood off my hand. Her eyes were bright, and when she saw me stir, she sat up and panted.

My back ached, but the suffocating fatigue was gone. I felt strong again.

I *flexed*. No glitter. In her or in me. We had beaten the flowers.

For a few moments I just sat there, happy to be alive.

Bear danced from paw to paw, looking at my face as if expecting something.

"Are you thirsty?" I took off my helmet and poured some water into it from the canteen. She lapped it up.

The gashes on her shoulder and back had closed. I parted her fur to check. There was a narrow, pink scar, but even that was fading.

What was it Elena said about the stalkers? *They soak up bullets like they're nothing and keep coming.*

I still had one stalker heart left. I had three to start, then ate one and a half, and Bear had finished the other half while I slept. I focused on the heart, pushing as deep as my talent would let me go. The heart unfurled before me, not just glowing, but splitting into layers of different properties, each with its own color, as it had done when I panicked trying to diagnose Bear. It felt like the most natural thing now, as if my talent always worked this way.

I studied the layers. Previously they had been saturated with color but now they were almost pastel. The heart was now of limited use to me, and nothing it offered met an urgent need.

The red was still first, but the hue was lighter, and it looked different. It took me a second to figure out why it was there – my stomach felt empty despite all that raw flesh eating, and my talent tagged the heart as edible meat.

I pushed through the red to the second slice of color, a light blue. When my talent interacted with the environment, I used to see a simple glow. Occasionally I got swirls of color varying in saturation and vibrancy, which my brain somehow interpreted into data, but what I saw now was nothing like it.

My father used to collect topographic maps, detailed reliefs of mountain terrain in different parts of the world, with contour lines and color-coded heights: lighter color for the greater elevation, medium for the mid-lying areas, darker for the valleys. This was exactly like that, except I knew that the valleys were a healthy baseline, and the peaks indicated how much toxins affected a particular body system. Nervous and integumentary systems were barely influenced, the digestive and respiratory were moderately impacted, but the poison wreaked havoc on endocrine, exocrine, muscular, and circulatory systems.

And I somehow knew that the integumentary system was comprised of skin, hair, nails, sweat, and oil glands. Yesterday I had no idea what that word stood for.

In any case, the color of this slice seemed barely there, so while the toxicity would be deadly to most people, to me it would be a mild inconvenience now. I focused on the next layer, the one glowing under the blue. There was that unsettling feeling of falling through the glass floor again. Another relief, in plain white this time. It took me a moment to figure it out.

Regeneration.

I hadn't seen it before, maybe because I was too focused on countering the poison. The stalkers were damn near indestructible. We've been targeting the glands in their neck, but given time, they would regenerate those. You had to deal enough damage to cause actual clinical death, otherwise no matter how badly they were wounded, they would bounce back. Good to know.

I would bounce back as well. And our new regenerative powers seemed to be permanent, which explained why my talent colored this diagnostic slice in white. The regeneration didn't benefit us. We already had it.

Still, regeneration alone didn't explain why we survived. That was *not* the way biology functioned. Consuming mongoose meat didn't magically mutate your acetylcholine receptors, giving you resistance to snake venom. Eating the stalker hearts should've just poisoned us further, but instead both I and Bear healed our wounds and purged the pollen.

On the other hand, regular biology couldn't account for the emergence of the Talents, compound fractures healing in 7 hours, or a glowing gem passing through solid bone. We were in Arthur C. Clarke territory. Any sufficiently advanced technology was indistinguishable from magic, and this was magic.

I sorted through my environment until I found some pollen traces and split that into layers as well. The toxicity was off the charts, although it was barely blue for me now. I tried to look at the two of them together, the heart and the pollen, by imposing one on to the other, but the picture was too complex. After a few seconds, both sets of layers collapsed, and I saw white again. This time I was blind for at least a minute. I had to be careful not to push myself too far.

The best I could figure out was that mixing the pollen and the stalker blood somehow negated their mutual harm while boosting the regenerative properties of stalker heart meat. We could likely stroll through the flowers now, not that I would risk it unless we absolutely had to, and eating the stalker meat should be safe. At least in theory.

The memory of the horrible battery acid taste sliding down my throat made me shudder.

It was a miracle that we survived. A roll of cosmic dice.

I checked my shoulder. The bite had knitted closed. The gashes on my legs from the claws had healed too. I had escaped death. Again. I couldn't tell if it was the magical gem or my newly acquired regeneration. Possibly both.

Bear licked the hat clean and looked at me.

"More?"

I poured a bit more water out. She lapped it up.

My mouth was dry, too. I tipped the canteen and finished what was left. We would need to find a water source soon. Also, I was hungry. So very hungry. I'd taken my watch off because it broke, so I had no idea how much time had passed. I should've checked the bodies for a watch, but I didn't think of it at the time.

It felt like I hadn't eaten in days. The stalker heart weighed about two pounds, and I had eaten a whole one just like it and then downed another half. I should've been full, but instead I was starving. Water, food, exit. I needed to find all three.

There was something on the opposite wall. Some sort of shapes...

I picked up the hard hat and flicked the light on.

Cave drawings, depicted in rust red and blue. A procession of some kind of beings, resembling raccoons or foxes, maybe? They were leading weird looking donkeys.

Danger.

A vision unfolded in my mind. *A caravan of fluffy creatures departing, some being wrapped in rags begging on the street, and a feeling of alarm. Not deadly danger exactly but ruin. Financial ruin.*

The vision faded.

Cute fluffy foxes who leave you destitute. "What do you think this is all about, Bear?"

The shepherd wagged her tail.

"Yes, I don't know either."

The woman who called me her daughter, the four-armed killers, and now the foxes, all distinct and morphologically different. Three separate species. Representatives of three civilizations? Or was it one complex society?

What the hell was on the other side of the breaches?

Everything the US knew about the other side came primarily from the Houston gate. It was one of the ten original US gates, designated as Prime Four, and for some reason, NASA had been called in to study it.

When the gates burst, the military strike teams had gone inside to close them. In the interviews with survivors, a lot of them reported seeing a second portal. Most of the people didn't get a good look at it, because as soon as they reached the chamber, they were gripped with an overwhelming urge to attack the anchor. The moment someone destroyed it, the second portal collapsed.

In Prime Four's case, they had held off on anchor smashing long enough to peer into the second gate. The reports described a world under a green-tinted sky, and a never-ending column of horrific monsters stretching from the portal across a grassy plain. The creatures kept pushing their way through the portal and attacking people in the anchor chamber, and eventually the military team destroyed the anchor to keep from being overrun.

Since then, the US government made three attempts – that I knew of – to allow for a controlled gate burst. They sent in teams to clear the breach and then sat on the anchor until it accumulated enough energy for the gate to rupture and the second portal to form. Then they tried to put a nuke through it.

We didn't know what happened. In all three cases, the gate collapsed and nobody came out. It didn't seem to have any effect on the frequency or strength of the gates. In fact, after the third attempt, another gate opened just five miles away and it was a dark orange.

We knew nothing except that this was clearly an invasion, and our extermination seemed to be the goal of it.

And I had more pressing things to worry about right this second. We had one canteen of water left, so we needed to get a move on. If we found a water source, I would need to wash up. My coveralls were drenched in stalker blood. My hair was bloody too, and it stuck to my face and neck. I hooked the empty canteen to the loop at my waist, put the hard hat back on my head, and nodded to my dog.

"Once more into the breach. Living the dream."

Bear wagged her tail, and we started across the stone bridge.

[7]

E lias studied London from across the conference table. The man was lean, in good shape, with an expensive haircut and the kind of face most people would describe as attractive. He seemed ten years younger than his forty-five, and the way he sat, although not overtly confrontational, signaled that he was neither nervous nor afraid.

It was that easy confidence, coupled with innate ability, that first prompted Elias to promote London to leader of Assault Team 4 four years ago. He appeared capable and stable, and in practice and training matches he outperformed most of the other top-tier Talents. London inspired confidence. People trusted him to take them into the breach and bring them out safely. A perfect candidate to lead an assault team.

He saw London differently now. What he'd previously mistaken for confidence was instead an ever-present air of polite entitlement. Even now, when most guild members would be sweating bullets in his position, London held himself as if this was a meeting of equals. He wasn't impatient – that would've been impolite and London was never impolite. Rather he managed to make it clear that he considered this entire process a formality, a series of tedious procedural steps, at the end of which he would be released with all his troubles swept under the rug and forgotten.

On paper, he and London were not dissimilar. Both blade wardens, both in their mid to late forties, both with nearly a decade of gate diving. At one point, years ago, the gap between their abilities had been much shorter.

Elias had grown in power every year. Ten years after his awakening, he was stronger, faster, and more experienced than when he had started. He learned to imbue his blade, so his weapons cut through solid steel and stone. His shield lasted a full five seconds longer now than it had when he'd walked into his first gate, and each second was hard won through grueling training and life and death battles.

London hadn't progressed at nearly the same pace. It might have been the limitations of their inborn abilities, but Elias had come to suspect that it was a limitation of will. London was happy in his current position within the guild. He was well compensated for taking a relatively low-risk role, he had no immediate supervisor breathing down his neck, and he rarely spent a night in the breach. Elias could see the appeal. But he also knew that he, himself, would never be satisfied with just that.

He'd thought about it while rereading London's file. Alexander Wright came from an upper middle-class family, had gone to a boarding school, followed that with Cambridge, and ended up with a job in finance. Affluent, comfortable, respectable, just as expected. Unfortunately for Wright, the market collapse following the first gates' bursting bankrupted the firm he'd worked for and wiped out his personal wealth. He was forced to pivot. This struggle was short-lived, since he'd conveniently awakened to his talent. Six months later he was in the US, making a name for himself as London, moving from smaller guilds to more prominent ones, until a Cold Chaos recruiter scouted him six years ago.

That seemed to be a trend with London. He led a charmed existence. It wasn't that he didn't experience adversity, it was that when a crisis occurred, another opportunity always presented itself. He was expected to do well and always land on his feet and had no doubt he would.

Elias had been in a state of crisis from the moment the gates opened. It never stopped. No exit ramp ever appeared, and if it had, he wasn't sure he would've taken it.

His grandfather was a carpenter who got drafted during WWII and served with honor. His father enlisted in the Navy to escape Vietnam, because he knew he would eventually be drafted. He ended up going career, retiring twenty years later, and picking up a civilian contractor job at the Department of Defense. Elias himself had gone to the Virginia Military Institute, and his big rebellion consisted of accepting a commission in the Army instead of the Navy, partially to spite his dad. He was the first college graduate and the first officer in four generations of McFerons. To him, striving for advancement was a given. You always wanted to be better, to do more, to get that next rank, to excel, and to make a difference.

No matter where life took them, London would always slightly look down on him. The condescension of classism was so casual, London himself likely barely registered it. Normally Elias didn't give a fuck what London – or anyone else – thought of him, but right now he needed to remind the escort captain of their respective roles. This wasn't a business meeting. London wasn't doing him a favor. He was called out on the carpet and had to account for his actions. The man was entirely too comfortable, and when people felt that comfortable, lying was effortless. He needed to deliver a powerful, precise punch and knock London off balance, or he would never get to the bottom of this mess.

Elias leveled a heavy stare at London. "Is this another Lansing? If it is, you need to tell me now."

London went pale.

That's right. Remember how you landed in your current spot. Remember why you're no longer the assault leader.

London leaned back in his chair, his expression indignant. "How much longer? How many times do I have to prove myself? Will you ever let it go? What do I have to do?"

Too easy. "Not losing an entire escort team and most of the miners would be a good start."

The words hung between them.

The door swung open. Leo entered the room and sat on Elias' left. They had coordinated this prior to the interview.

"That's unfair," London said. "Nobody could have stopped that. You couldn't have stopped that."

"I would've tried."

"And you would be dead."

Elias pointed to the survey of the mining site printed on a large posterboard. Staying at the library had its perks. "Walk me through it."

London glanced at Leo. "I already spoke to the Vice-Guildmaster."

"And now you're speaking to me." Elias paused to let the weight of his words sink in.

The escort captain shifted his body to the side, leaning to his left in the chair, and crossed his arms. If they were standing in the breach instead of sitting in the office, London's shield would be up.

Elias leaned forward, taking up more of London's view, communicating that the table between them wasn't much of a barrier. His speech was unhurried.

"You know what's so easy about telling the truth? It's always the same. You don't have to think, you don't have to keep track of it. It never changes. Start with the moment you entered the gate. You were four minutes behind schedule. Why?"

London sighed. "Ms. Moore had an emergency phone call regarding her daughter. I judged it to be in the best interest of the guild to allow her to resolve that situation before we went in. That way she could be more fully focused on the assessing."

"What happened next?" Elias pressed.

"We entered the breach and proceeded to the mining site." London pointed to the survey. "We walked for approximately twelve minutes. The transit was uneventful. Seven minutes in we encountered a group of deceased hostiles, which we identified as a variant of Calloway's stalkers…"

The story was largely the same as the notes Elias had read: they got to the site, started mining, then five hostiles emerged from the tunnels and slaughtered everyone. According to London, he saved whom he could by collapsing the entrance. This time though, he mentioned the gold in addition to the adamantite.

"You omitted the discovery of the gold in your original interview. Why?"

"It was not relevant. I was focused on conveying the nature of the threat."

"Fifteen people died or are presumed dead," Elias said. "Everything is relevant."

"I know," the exasperation was clear in London's voice. "I can count."

He wasn't completely lying, Elias reflected. His physical responses when recounting the attack matched those of someone who lived through a near death experience. Whatever happened scared the hell out of London, and that was precisely the problem.

Leo sat slightly straighter. Elias kept his gaze on London. *No, not yet.*

"In your opinion, was the mining site secure?"

London unlocked his teeth. "No."

"What steps would you have taken to make the mining site secure?"

"I would have collapsed the north access tunnels."

Elias glanced at Leo. *Now.*

"Did you review the survey with Assault Team Leader Malcolm?" Leo asked.

"I did. You have a record of that meeting."

"Did Malcolm specify how he selected the mining site?" Elias asked.

"Again, you have the record of the meeting. He selected the site based on the visible mineral deposits of malachite and copper-bearing ores in the walls, the size and relative stability of the cavern, and the proximity to the gate."

"Were you aware of the risks the tunnels posed?" Leo asked.

"Yes."

"Did you raise those concerns with Malcolm?" Elias asked.

"I did."

"What rationale did Malcolm give you for leaving the tunnels intact?" Leo asked.

"He thought he might require an alternate route to the anchor."

"Why not just collapse the tunnels and dig through if needed?" Elias asked.

"I don't know."

"Why didn't you collapse the tunnels after getting to the site?" Leo asked.

London stared at him for a second. "Because it isn't my call." He bit the words off.

"The security of the mining site is your call. You are responsible for the safety of the escorts and the miners," Elias countered. "Do you understand the scope of your duties, Escort Captain Wright?"

London glared at him. Angry red blotches colored his face.

"Malcolm wanted to keep the tunnels open. I brought up the possible risk. Malcolm reiterated his desire to keep the tunnels open. The survey showed no predators larger than the stalkers, and my team was well equipped to handle the stalkers. I requested a secondary sweep of a half mile from the entrance to the tunnels. The scout confirmed the sweep was done. You are *not* going to hang this on me. Malcolm fucked up. Malcolm is dead."

It was all pouring out. They broke him.

"We can split hairs all day, but in the end, all of us in this room know that the ultimate responsibility lies with the assault leader. As the escort captain, I must maintain a good working relationship with the assault leader. That is the system that *you* put in place. *You* put Malcolm in that position, and *you* put me in my position."

Shifting the blame again. If it wasn't his fault, it was Malcolm, and if it wasn't Malcolm, the system, the guild, and Elias were to blame.

"Malcolm and I respected each other. I was not going to go behind his back, because I had to work with him in the future. I brought three people out with me, three people who otherwise would have been dead. I am *not* going to take the blame for what happened. This outrage and scrutiny are disingenuous. A fatal event happened; people died. People die in breaches every day. This was no different. Either get used to it or get out of the game."

London's brain finally caught up with his mouth. He shut up.

Nobody said anything.

"You can judge all you want," London said. "But you weren't there. You didn't see them. The speed... They were so fast, they blurred. My reaction time is half that of an average human and I couldn't follow it. Elias, seriously, whatever assault team would have been in that fucking cave, none of them would have made it. You want me to say I ran? Yeah, I did. Like I told you, I saved who I could and got out."

Elias leaned forward. "Look me in the eye and tell me that everyone else in that cave was dead when you threw the grenade."

"They were dead. All of them. The miners, the K9, the scout - everyone was dead. I saw the DeBRA cut to pieces. You have my word."

They hounded London for the next ten minutes, but they didn't get anything else. Elias knew they wouldn't. In the end, they told him to stay put at the site and let him go.

Elias leaned back in his chair. London was lying. It was in the eyes. That direct unblinking stare when he said, *"You have my word."*

"It wasn't the gold," Leo muttered.

"It wasn't."

London's demeanor confirmed what Elias already deduced from the record of the survey meeting. He didn't know about the gold, and he didn't see it as relevant.

No, this problem ran deeper.

Leo steepled his fingers, his tone methodical, almost clinical.

"Assault Team 3 is the best performing team in the yellow and orange tiers. Malcolm and London worked together frequently. London saw Malcolm as his professional equal. In his mind, they were laterally positioned. If he pushed against Malcolm, there would've been tension and conflict. London abhors tension. He didn't want to rock the boat. Was it a misguided professional courtesy?"

"And professional arrogance," Elias said. "You heard him. Nothing larger than a stalker was found. Breaches are unpredictable. Nothing can be taken for granted. He's grown complacent."

Leo's eyes flashed with white. "He's lying. I can't prove it, but I feel it."

"It's the lack of guilt," Elias told him.

People who lost their teams in the breaches came out fucked up. Some were manic, others catatonic. He had to put divers on suicide watch before. That's why they had a psychiatrist, a psychologist, and several therapists on staff.

"London is too aggressive, too confrontational," Elias said. "He's absolved himself of all responsibility. He's right about one thing – I put him in that position. The buck stops with me."

"It's been three years since Lansing," Leo said. "He hasn't fucked up until now."

"That we know of. One of two things happened in that breach. Either London is telling the truth, and he is a hero who saved three miners, or he's a coward who abandoned his team to their death."

"Which do you think it is?" Leo asked.

"I think he saw something that terrified him, and he bugged out. The only way to prove what happened is to examine the mining site and the bodies, assuming there is anything left of them. I need cause to remove him from his position."

"And with Melissa backing him up, we don't have any." Leo frowned. "If we demote him, it will look like we made him into a scapegoat."

"That's not our biggest problem. If we demote him without proof, he will jump ship to Guardian or any other guild willing to take him. He looks good on paper. He will aim for escort captain again, because he likes that job, and the next time shit hits the fan, more people will die." Elias exhaled. "We need to get into that breach ASAP."

"Agreed," Leo said.

"Did you find Jackson?" Elias asked.

"Not yet. We're doing everything we can."

"I know."

Sitting on his hands was driving him out of his skin, but going into that breach without Jackson was suicide. It was both about the speed and the potency of healing. Two years ago, he was stabbed in the heart and lost his left hand, and because Jackson was there, he pulled the spike out of his chest and kept swinging, while his hand regrew itself in minutes. Something took out Malcolm's team and terrified London so much that he fled for the exit. They couldn't risk any more lives.

"You need to rest, sir," Leo said quietly.

Elias looked up. Outside the window the morning was in full swing. He'd slept four hours in the last forty-eight.

"We have bunks set up downstairs," Leo said. "If anything happens, if I hear anything, I'll wake you up."

Elias didn't feel like sleeping, but his body needed it, and he knew he would pass out the moment his head hit a pillow.

"Wake me up as soon as you find Jackson."

"I will, sir."

FLEX.

The stream didn't glow. I stared at it some more, but I was getting only clear water. It flowed from a gap in the rock, forming a narrow but deep current that ran across a massive cavern.

Chomp, chomp...

"Will you please quit doing that?"

Bear raised her bloody muzzle from the stalker's body and gave me a puzzled look.

"I mean it."

She licked her lips.

We'd been moving through the tunnels for hours. We ran across two silverfish bug things and took them out. They turned out to be slower than I thought. Or perhaps Bear and I had gotten faster. I lost count of how many stalkers we'd killed. This latest trio of two females and a male died a couple hundred feet into the passageway and I carried the largest body to the stream.

Bear had developed a disturbing liking for stalker meat. Every time we had a fight, and I got distracted, she chomped on bodies like they were premium dog food. She tried to eat the bugs too, but they must've tasted foul because she took a bite and never went back for seconds. I had stuck to my supplies so far, but both the energy bars and the KitKats were a distant memory. We had run out of water hours ago.

I looked at the stream again. Bear padded next to me, looked at the water, and whined. She'd tried to drink already but I stopped her.

In a perfect world, I would have boiled the water, but I didn't have any way to make a fire. And even if I could, my plastic hard hat was the only vessel we had. It would melt. Well, I could probably boil water in a canteen... It was moot anyway. I didn't have a lighter or any fuel. What I had was two empty canteens and a very thirsty dog, who was currently dancing on the bank in anticipation.

Fuck it.

I nodded at the stream. "Go get it."

The shepherd bounded to the bank and began lapping up the water, splashing it all over the place.

I smiled. "Is any of that actually getting into your mouth?"

Bear paused to give me a look and went back to drinking.

I scooted upstream and dipped my hands into the breach water. The stalker blood faded a little. I scrubbed my fingers. There was dark grime under my fingernails, and I shuddered to think what kind of bacteria was breeding there.

I cleaned my hands as best I could, cupped them, and brought some water to my mouth. It tasted clean and cold.

I filled both canteens, filled my hat, and poured it over my coveralls, trying to wash the dried blood from the Magnaprene. It took forever. Finally, I straightened. Bear lay next to the water, twitching her left ear.

"We drank, we showered, it's time for a feast."

I walked over to the stalker's corpse, crouched, shifted my sword into a knife, and paused. Bear had been eating them along the way every chance she got, and so far she didn't have any shivers.

Mmm, raw alien meat.

I didn't have any choice. If we had found some plants or fruits that were safe, I would have eaten that, but the caves offered mostly fungi. They were conveniently glowing and hellishly poisonous.

"Stalker. It's what's for dinner."

Bear panted.

I stabbed the stalker and gutted it. I was never a hunter. The only skinning I had ever done was limited to removing the skin from chicken thighs I bought at a grocery store. Getting the pelt off took a while. Finally, I cut a ham free and tossed it to Bear. The shepherd chomped on it.

I carved a paper-thin slice from the other leg and sniffed it. It smelled kind of gamey. Disgusting. It smelled disgusting. Back home, I bought a special composite cutting board just for raw chicken, because I could put it through the dishwasher. All of my wooden cutting boards were scrubbed after each use, and all of my meat was cooked to the correct temperature. I owned three cooking thermometers.

This meat was raw. Not rare. Just raw.

"Tacos would be so nice right now. Or shepherd's pie. I make really good shepherd's pie, with creamy mashed potatoes and a crust of melted cheese on top."

Bear chewed on the stalker ham.

"You know what my favorite dessert is? Sometimes, when life's too hard, I go to Dairy Queen and get a Turtle Pecan Cluster Blizzard. It has pecans and little bits of chocolate. I don't really like pecans, and I'm not much of a chocoholic, but there is something about that Blizzard. It's like happiness in a cup. I could so use one right now."

My stomach was begging for calories. If I counted from the moment Bear and I left the mining site, I'd been hiking for days and between the hikes I'd been fighting for my life. My body kept healing my wounds, and all that regeneration had to have a caloric cost.

I was starving. Everything ached. If I *flexed* right now, the meat would be bright red. I had to eat, or I would become someone else's dinner. I couldn't afford weakness.

I surrendered to my fate and bit into the thin slice.

No flash of pain. No broken glass. It tasted vile and it stank, but it was meat. I was squatting by the river in a breach and eating raw meat. I'd gone completely feral.

I would make it out of this cave, and then I would never think of this again. I would erase this from my memories.

I chewed the meat and tried to think of something else. Luckily for me, I had plenty to ponder.

When we crossed the stone bridge out of that small cave, I sensed something. It was far in the distance, hidden behind countless cave walls and solid stone, a knot of... something. I couldn't quite describe it. It felt almost like a hot magnet. It pulled on me, but not in a pleasant way. It was more like a psychic ache, like a splinter that got stuck in my awareness.

The stalkers and other creatures had kept me busy, so I mostly noted it and kept moving. But right now, with no distractions, it nagged at me. It could've been anything, but the most plausible explanation was usually the right one.

I'd become aware of the anchor.

Most of the gate divers didn't feel the anchor until they were right on top of it. The distant awareness usually came with extraordinary power particular to top-tier Talents. Not all the powerful guild members could feel the anchor from far away, but everyone who did was in the upper layer of the talent pool.

I leaned over the stream and tried to look at my reflection. I couldn't really see myself. The light was too diffused. My arms and legs didn't look that different, but then I was wearing coveralls.

I would have to find a reflective surface somewhere. I didn't want to dwell on it. As long as I still looked enough like myself to be recognized, I would be fine. I'd been checking my blood through the lens of my talent, and I was reasonably sure that I would pass the DDC blood tests. My regeneration ability lay far deeper, on a cellular level.

The bigger problem was the anchor. It was closer now than when we started. We were walking toward it. I didn't want to go toward the anchor. I wanted to go toward the gate and the exit. But right now, I didn't have much choice. Even if I wanted to backtrack, I couldn't. We had threaded the labyrinth of the tunnels like a needle, and I didn't remember the way back.

The assault team had taken a route to the anchor that led away from the mining site. In theory, if I found the anchor chamber, I could try to find that route and use it to reach the gate. However, the closer you got to the anchor, the more difficult the fights became.

I had two choices: to wander aimlessly in these caves or to head for the anchor. Even if I failed to find the route the first assault team had taken, eventually Cold Chaos would send in the second-strike team. Joining up with them would be too dangerous. There was a solid chance that Cold Chaos wanted me dead to avoid the massive PR storm and sanctions that would result from admitting that London abandoned me. So running into the embrace of the Cold Chaos assault team wouldn't be smart. But I could retrace their steps or follow them to the gate, staying out of sight. I'd gotten very good at moving quietly.

The anchor was the only logical choice. I would have to chance it. At least I had a direction now.

Fifteen minutes later, Bear departed to poop in the corner by some rocks and came back.

"Good to go?"

The dog wagged her tail.

Maybe we could take a breather...

The cave wall by Bear's poop moved.

"Come!" I barked.

Bear ran over to me.

The wall trembled and broke apart, cascading to the floor.

I jumped over the stream. Bear leaped with me. We cleared fifteen feet and landed on the other bank.

Chunks of the wall streamed to the stalker carcass. I *flexed*. Bugs, about a foot across, with a chitin carapace that perfectly mimicked the stone.

I backed away.

The bug whirlpool broke open, revealing a bare skeleton. Not a shred of flesh remained. If we had fallen asleep here...

"I fucking hate this place. Come on Bear. Before the cave piranha bugs eat us too."

I headed into the gloom, my loyal dog trotting at my side.

I CROUCHED ON A NARROW STONE LEDGE PROTRUDING ABOVE A vast cavern. Bear lay next to me gnawing on a stalker femur.

Long veins of luminescent crystal split the ceiling here and there and slid up the walls, glowing like overpowered lamps, diluting the darkness to a gentle twilight. My talent told me it was jubar stone, a breach mineral that shone like a floodlight. The biggest jubar stone I had seen until now was about the size of my fist.

Two hundred and sixty-two feet below us, at the bottom of the cavern, enormous lianas climbed the stone wall, bearing giant flowers. Each blossom, shaped like a twisted cornucopia, sported a funnel at least ten feet across and fifteen feet deep, fringed by thick, persimmon-colored petals that glowed weakly with coral and yellow. It was as if a garden-variety trumpet vine had been thrown into the chasm and mutated out of control into a monstrous version of itself.

Strange beings moved along the cavern floor, clad in diaphanous pale robes. Their torsos seemed almost humanoid, but there was something oddly insectoid about their movements. They strode between the flowers, carrying long staves and pushing carts.

As I watched, one of them stopped at the opposite wall far below and tugged on the long green tendrils dripping from a large blossom. A spider the size of a small car slid from the flower. It was white and translucent, as if made of frosted glass.

The being checked it over, prodding it with a staff topped with a large chunk of green glass or maybe a huge jewel. My talent couldn't identify it from this distance. The spider waited like a docile pet.

The being dipped a slender appendage into their cart, pulled out a glowing fuzzy sphere that looked like a giant dandelion, and tossed it to the spider. The monster arachnid caught it and slipped back into its flower.

The spider herder moved on to the next blossom.

It was surreal. I'd been watching them for about two hours and my mind still refused to come to terms with it. There were hundreds of flowers down there, and most of them held spiders. The herders had been clearly doing this for a long time – their movements were measured and routine, and they had made paths in the faintly glowing lichens sheathing the bottom of the cavern.

I was watching an alien civilization tend to its livestock.

"Do you know what this is, Bear? This is animal husbandry."

Bear didn't seem impressed.

If I had to herd spiders, this would certainly be a good place. From this angle, the cavern looked almost like a canyon, relatively narrow with steep, mostly sheer walls. They had a water source – the narrow ribbon of a shallow stream twisted along the cavern's floor. I couldn't see any other entrances, although there had to be some, probably far to the left, behind the cavern's bend. If stalkers or other predators somehow invaded, they would be easy to bottleneck. It was an ideal, sheltered location except for one thing.

Another spider herder emerged from behind the bend on the left. My ledge ended only a few feet away on that side so I couldn't quite see where they came from. This one was pushing a larger cart.

"Here we go," I murmured to Bear.

She flicked her ear.

The spider herder paused. Above them, about forty feet off the ground, a large blossom glowed with gold instead of red. The herder raised their staff and leaped at the wall, clearing ten feet in a single jump. They climbed up the vine, shockingly fast, reached the flower, and thrust the staff into the blossom.

I glanced to the right. Across the cavern, a fissure split the wall near the ceiling, a crack in the solid stone about eight feet tall and five feet across at its widest.

Nothing moved. The fissure remained dark.

The spider herder swirled the staff as if scraping the pancake batter out of a bowl.

The fissure stayed still.

The spider herder pulled their staff out. Three dense clumps of spider silk hung suspended from the top, glowing softly with cream-colored light. They were about the size of a beach ball.

A segmented body squeezed out of the fissure and dove, three pairs of translucent wings snapping open in flight. A wasp-like insect the size of a kayak zipped through the air, glinting with blue and yellow like a blue sapphire wrapped in gold filigree.

Bear jumped up and growled.

The spider herder saw the wasp and scrambled down, but not quickly enough. The giant insect divebombed across the cavern, hooked one of the spider eggs with its segmented legs, tearing it from the bundle, and shot up, buzzing along the wall into a U-turn. A moment and it squeezed back into the fissure, taking its prize with it.

The spider herder stared after it for a long moment, climbed down, and deposited the two remaining egg sacks into their cart.

I had seen a similar scenario play out hours ago, when I first found the cavern. I had backtracked since then, exploring as many of the tunnels around it as I could. All of them either dead-ended or led to a narrow, bottomless chasm that ran parallel to this cave. I returned to the ledge a while ago and have been sitting here since, observing and deciding how to proceed.

I closed my eyes and concentrated. The anchor was still straight ahead and to the left of me, radiating discomfort. I opened my eyes. I was looking right at the bend of the cavern.

If we wanted to get to the anchor, we would have to pass through this underground canyon. There was no way around it. Backtracking wasn't an option. We were truly lost at this point.

Unfortunately, I had a feeling that the spider herders wouldn't welcome our intrusion into their territory.

Another wasp squeezed out of the gap and dove down, aiming for the cart. The spider herder let out a loud clicking sound. A green spider the size of a donkey raced around the bend of the cavern and leaped into the air, knocking the wasp into the wall. The insect and the arachnid tumbled down through the vines and rolled onto the floor. The wasp jabbed at the spider with a stinger the size of a sword, but the spider clung to it and sank its fangs into the wasp's neck. The insect's head fell to the ground.

The spider herder made another clicking noise. The green spider abandoned the wasp and scuttled over to the cart. The herder pulled out a glowing yellow globe and tossed it to the spider. The arachnid caught it and ran back around the bend.

"Look, Bear, your cousin from another dimension got a treat."

Bear tilted her head.

The spider herder leveled their stave at the wasp's body. A moment passed. Another. A bolt of green lightning tore out of the gem and struck the carcass. The insect sizzled and broke into dust.

The activation time was a bit long. The wasps would have no

trouble evading, considering the delay it took to fire, but once the beam hit, the results were devastating.

If Bear and I strolled down there, assuming we somehow got down off the ledge, trying to make our way past the herders would be impossible. Between the green spiders and that green lightning, we wouldn't get through, not without some serious injuries.

I glanced at the fissure. There was a wasp nest behind it. Spiders were excellent wall climbers. Theoretically, the spider herders could mount a full assault against it, but there were three problems with that.

First, the fissure wasn't wide enough. The wasps were long and narrow, and they folded their wings to get through. The white spiders would never fit. The green ones could try to squeeze in there, but they would have to enter one at a time, and the wasps would swarm them.

Second, the wasps could take flight if they detected the assault and simply wait it out. The spiders couldn't sit by that wasp nest indefinitely, and waiting by it exposed them to the aerial assault.

And third, the entirety of the wall around the nest was sheathed in mauve flowers. Toward the top, where my ledge met the fissure, the wall wasn't strictly sheer. It broke down into a series of outcroppings, and the mauve flowers clung to the rocks like some deadly African violets. There was no way to approach the nest without going through them.

When one of the white spiders popped out of the highest flower, I had a chance to scan it. They were not immune to the pollen. It would short-circuit their nervous system. The spider herders and the wasps were at a standoff.

When I first stumbled onto the cavern, I got another vision. A group of three spider herders, their veils shifting in the wind of an alien world with a mass of giant spiders behind them; someone with human arms offering a carved wooden box to them; the leading spider herder accepting it; the spiders parting; and a single word spoken: *Bekh-razz*. A gift for safe passage.

I would have to offer a gift to cross.

The spiders couldn't get to the nest, but I could. The ledge I was on curved along the wall all the way to the nest. It was barely seven feet wide near the entrance to the hive. I wouldn't have a lot of room to work with.

I got up and walked along the ledge toward the fissure.

Bear dropped her bone and trotted after me. I halted by the first clump of mauve blossoms and *flexed*.

They glowed with pale lilac. I split the glow into individual layers of light blue and pink. The blue told me they were still mildly toxic to both me and Bear, but nothing our regeneration wouldn't take care of, and the faint pink let me know that if properly processed, the plant could be used as contact analgesic. Made sense. That's why we didn't notice the effect the pollen had on us until it was too late.

The wasps displayed hive behavior. I didn't need a vision to clear that up for me. It was obvious from their patterns. That meant that the moment I attacked the nest, every wasp would fight to the death to kill me. I had no idea how large that nest was. Or how many giant wasps waited inside. I had to be very sure, because once I started, there was no stopping. Earth wasps were vindictive, and it was safer to assume these would be, too. Even if I ran away, they would chase me through the caves and there was no passage narrow enough to lose them anywhere around this cave.

The nest rumbled.

I dropped to the ground. "Down."

Bear hugged the ledge with me.

"Good girl," I whispered.

A large wasp squeezed through the gap and took off, vanishing around the bend.

I wonder how they know when the eggs are harvested? Do the eggs emit a pulse or something...

A hoarse shriek echoed through the cavern. That was new.

The wasp zipped back toward the nest, carrying another silk-wrapped spider egg in its claws. The egg glowed with coral pink. I *flexed*, focusing on it, but the wasp was too fast. Half a blink, and it squeezed into the nest.

I'd seen them steal three eggs besides this one, and nobody screamed the first three times. Also, the rest of the eggs glowed with cream, not pink. There was something special about this egg.

This was my best chance. I had to act now or find a different way.

I flicked my wrist, elongating the cuff into a sharp, two-foot blade shaped like a machete. Bear let out a soft, excited whine.

"Shhh."

I padded through the flowers, my dog trailing me.

This was a foolish plan.

Ten yards to the nest.

Five.

Three.

Something rumbled within the fissure.

I cleared the distance between me and the gap in a single jump.

A wasp thrust out of the gap. I swung the blade and lopped its head off. The blue and yellow body crashed down, and I grabbed it with my left hand, yanked it out of the fissure, and sent it flying to the ground far below.

Bear broke into barks. *There goes our element of surprise.*

The entire nest buzzed like a tornado spinning into life. Another wasp shot through the fissure, and I cleaved it in half, my sword cutting through the segmented thorax like it was butter.

"Sir?"

Elias' eyes snapped open. Leo hovered in his view. Elias sat up.

"We found Jackson," the XO said.

Two wasps tried to squeeze through the gap at the same time and got stuck one on top of the other. I twisted the sword into a spike, skewered the top one, because it was closer and let its dead weight push the second wasp down. It struggled, pinned to the ground, and I hacked at it.

The buzzing was deafening now. The walls of the fissure vibrated as the enraged hive mobilized for an all-out assault. Next to me Bear barked her head off, flinging spit into the air. She wasn't just a dog, she was a guild K9, trained to alert when the breach monsters came near. The monsters were here, and she was alerting everyone.

I grabbed the body of the top wasp, pulled it out of the fissure, and hurled it over the edge.

"He's been detained by the authorities in Japan."

It took Elias a moment to process that tidbit. "On what pretext?"

"They claim he entered a luxury restaurant, ordered a high-quality cut of Wagyu beef, washed it down with Yamazaki Single Malt 55-Year-Old Whisky, which retails for four hundred thousand dollars a bottle, and walked out without paying."

"They're saying he dined and dashed?"

Leo smiled. Technically, it was a smile, but it looked more like a predator baring his teeth.

BODIES CLOGGED THE FISSURE, DRENCHED IN HEMOLYMPH. I stabbed and hacked into the pileup, yanking chunks of the insects out.

Seven wasps.

Eight.

Twelve.

"JACKSON? THE VEGETARIAN WHO DRINKS ONE BEER A YEAR AND only under duress?"

"Yes, sir. Our Jackson."

Elias hid a growl. It was a retaliation for Yosuke.

Two years ago, a star void ronin, a top-tier Talent, had a falling out with the largest guild in Japan and quit. They blacklisted him. No other guild in the country would hire him. The idea was that the pressure of unemployment would force him to crawl back home. Yosuke called their bluff. Cold Chaos welcomed him into the fold eighteen months ago. He was enroute to Elmwood now from another gate and was due to arrive tomorrow.

Publicly, Hikari no Ryu said nothing. Privately, the guild wielded a lot of power in Japan, and they were pissed. Elias thought that they reached an understanding regarding this issue. Apparently, he was mistaken. It didn't matter. Elias had never regretted the decision, and he wasn't about to start now.

"Have they made any demands?" he asked.

"No. Most likely they will hold him and wait for us to come to them."

Guild politics were convoluted and cutthroat. It didn't matter which continent. Elias had dealt with worse nonsense stateside plenty of times. But there was an unspoken rule all guilds followed – healers were exempt from all of the political bullshit. They were off limits. You didn't poach them, you didn't threaten them, and you didn't retaliate against them. They chose who they worked for, and if you got a good one, you did everything you could to keep them.

Someone in Japan had just crossed a very dangerous line.

"How would you like to proceed?" Leo asked.

"I'll make some calls."

THE NEST LAY SILENT.

Bear was still barking.

"Quiet."

The shepherd clamped her mouth shut. I listened for the buzzing.

Nothing.

"Stay, Bear. Stay. Stay!"

Bear sat down.

"Good. Wait right here. Don't follow me. Wait."

I'd killed twelve smaller wasps, probably workers, and five larger wasps, probably guards. Back home wasp colonies had a queen. She was usually larger than the workers and the guards, and if that held true here, she was trapped within the nest. I had no idea what this fight would look like or how much room we would have to maneuver. And, if she looked like her workers and guards, her legs would be almost pure chitin, rock hard and rigid. Bear's jaws wouldn't do much damage, and the last thing I wanted was her rushing in there and getting herself killed.

I slipped into the fissure, moving slowly and quietly. It was about ten feet deep. Beyond that, the passage widened into another cave chamber steeped in gloom and dappled with pools of pale light coming from above. I *flexed*. One hundred and twelve yards to the other wall. A lot of open space, and the floor was unnaturally clear. The wasps must've removed all of the debris that originally littered the chamber. Once I exited the fissure, I would be exposed.

A step.

Another.

A whisper of something large shifting its weight on the right, just outside the passageway. I had expected the wasp to strike from above, but it sounded like it was on the ground instead.

I stopped, poised on my toes. My fingers trembled. Fear filled me. I was overflowing with it.

Another faint whisper. The wasp was waiting just feet away, ready to ambush me the moment I entered. I had to rely on speed.

I darted into the nest, angling to the left. A shadow fell over me and I dove forward, rolled, and came back to my feet.

A massive wasp bore down on me. It was as big as the lake dragon, riding on six huge, segmented legs, each armed with two chitin claws the size of sickles.

Crap.

The wasp charged me. It wasn't flying. It ran across the floor, straight at me, swiping at me with its terrible claws. I darted back and forth like a terrified rabbit.

Right, left, left, too many fucking legs, right...

The wasp swiped at me like a hockey player armed with deadly scythes. It was trying to skewer me and drag me to its terrible mouth where two sets of sharp mandibles would shred the flesh off my bones and rip me apart.

The world shrank to the stone floor of the cavern, the pools of light, and the horrible creature behind me. All my instincts screamed in panic. I had to run away. I had to run from this

145

thing back through the fissure, but I couldn't find it. The walls were a dizzying whirlwind.

I was out of breath. I was disoriented. I couldn't even think long enough to come up with a plan. All I could do was run for my life. Running wouldn't work for too much longer. I would die here, in this nest.

Something dark and shaggy shot out of the wall. Before my brain processed what it was, Bear charged at the wasp.

"No! Bear, no!"

The German Shepherd clamped her jaws on one of the wasp's middle legs. The insect shook it and flung Bear off.

"No!"

One of the wasp's legs sliced like a scythe. I saw it coming. I had stopped running because of Bear and now it was too late. I jerked back, but not fast enough. The blow swept me off my feet. I rolled across the floor, pain smashing into my side. The wasp reared above me. Its front leg came down like a hammer. One of the two claws pierced my right thigh, scraping the bone.

Bear leaped out from the side and bit the leg impaling me. The wasp queen didn't even notice. The other claw clamped on my other leg. The ragged chitin sank into my flesh. I felt myself being lifted, up to where the horrible mandibles clicked.

No.

I sliced at the wasp leg pinning me. My sword cut through chitin like it was a twig. The wasp recoiled. I yanked the severed stump out of my thigh and rolled to my feet.

Fuck this shit. Why the hell was I running?

Bear snarled next to me.

The wasp swiped at me with its uninjured front leg. It was huge and fast, but I was faster. I leaned out of the way. The leg carved through the spot where I had been. The wasp swiped again, and I stepped back again, just out of reach.

Strike, dodge. Strike, dodge. It couldn't touch me.

I *flexed*, stretching time like a rubber band, forcing my senses into overdrive. The uninjured front leg struck at me, slow like molasses. I cut it, dashed under the wasp, severing the other legs with quick strikes as I sprinted past, and emerged behind the monster insect. A second and it was over. The world restarted, and the queen crashed to the floor, the stumps of her legs jerking in wild spasms.

Bear howled.

I took a running start and jumped. My leap carried me through the air, and I landed on the queen's fat abdomen and dashed toward her head.

The queen's huge wings stirred. It was trying to fly.

I slipped on the narrow waist connecting the abdomen and thorax, caught myself, leaped onto the thorax, and scrambled onto her neck.

The wings hummed and blurred like the blades of a helicopter. A gust of wind buffeted me.

I drove my sword into the queen's neck. It sank through, and I ripped it to the side, carving through the exoskeleton. The queen's head drooped, and I chopped at the thin filament connecting it to the body.

The head crashed down.

The wings kept going. The headless body rose in the air, carrying me with it. I clung to it. The wasp corpse climbed twenty feet up...

The wings slowed.

The body fell slowly, careened, and landed in a heap. I jumped, rolled to break my fall, and came up in a crouch.

The queen was dead.

Elias put away his phone.

"Nice." Leo grinned.

"They wanted a fight. We gave them a fight."

All they had to do now was wait.

[8]

"What the hell was that?"
Bear panted at me.

"I said *stay*. I know you know what stay means. I didn't say run into the fight and bite the giant wasp."

Bear looked completely unrepentant.

"You're a butthole. That's your name from now on. Bear Butthole Moore."

Butthole padded over to me and sat with a big canine grin on her face.

"What are you so happy about? I'm mad at you. At least have the decency to look embarrassed."

Bear twitched her ears. Bear and decency clearly had nothing to do with each other.

I looked up. And forgot to breathe. Above me, the chamber climbed to a height of a hundred and fifty feet, expanding into a wider space. Long spiral ledges of something that looked like paper wrapped around the perimeter of the cavern, and between them huge luminous crystals glowed with pale yellow light. Far above, at the very top, a cluster of paper tubes hung together, some sealed with pale paper caps, others empty, their edges ragged. It was like standing inside a gargantuan conch shell, and it felt otherworldly, like a cathedral.

Regret pinched me. I destroyed this.

Yes, it was beautiful, but the spider herders deserved to harvest their eggs in peace, and I needed to get home. I had to get the coral egg and get out.

"Come on, Butthole. Let's find what we are looking for."

The ledges were paper, but they were the sturdiest paper I had ever seen. It had no problem supporting my weight. First, I walked up the ledges to the top, severed the cluster of pupae and let it fall to the ground. I didn't need any more worker wasps hatching while I rummaged around their house. Then I searched the nest top to bottom.

I found the stolen spider eggs glued to the walls still in their web cocoons. Each egg had a bunch of blue coconut-sized spheres by it - the wasp egg sacs containing larvae. In some places, the sacks had hatched into fat three-foot-long grubs resembling maggots and were feeding on the spider eggs.

The lifecycle was clear. The wasps stole the spider eggs and left them for their young. Once the wasp larvae hatched, they would eat the spider eggs and grow until they formed a pupa and finally matured into adults. The spiders weren't the nest's only prey. I found three stalker corpses and the bodies of four goat-like animals the size of a small deer, all glued with that same rough paper near the egg sacs.

Most of the spider eggs were empty or dark. I destroyed any wasp sacks or larvae I came across.

The coral egg had been hidden away near the top of the nest, in a curve of the chamber, with a single egg sack attached to the wall next to it. Perhaps food for the new queen. I killed the wasp egg and gently removed the spider egg from the wall. It was smaller than the others, more like a soccer ball than a beach ball, and it felt warm and surprisingly light. I focused on it, activating my talent. A tiny life slept within, safe in a shell of nurturing liquid.

Oh.

The cream eggs came from the spiders. This one didn't. This was one of *them*, a baby spider herder. A creature of an alien civilization, not just a sentient or a sapient. The official term was sophont, a being not born on Earth with intelligence comparable or greater than human and a capacity for creating a civilization.

I sat down and looked at it. A child separated from its parents, stolen to become wasp food and to be devoured by grubs before its first moment of awareness.

It was so much.

For millennia, humans were terrified of being eaten. It was the most primal of our fears. It drove our progress and our relentless pursuit of technology. We conquered the planet to keep our children safe from the predators that roamed in the night. We thought we put this anachronistic horror behind us. And then the gates appeared, and the ancient fear came roaring back. Once again, we were scared that monsters would attack and devour our children, and all our weapons and our progress would do nothing to stop it.

I hugged the egg gently and stayed like that until the inner storm passed inside me. I would get back to my children. And I would return this child back to its family.

In total I found five spider eggs that were still glowing, including the coral one. Now, I had to get them out and get down to the bottom of the cavern without getting killed. I needed a rope.

Well, there was a lot of spider silk around.

I cut a tendril of the spider thread from one of the hollowed-out cocoons on the wall and pulled on it. It came loose, dragging chunks of wasp paper with it. It was about the width of a thick thread and feather-light.

I *flexed*. One point eight millimeters in diameter, slightly thinner than cooking twine. Wow. The tensile strength was off the charts.

I weighed one hundred and fifty-seven pounds before the breach. I checked my weight regularly. The DDC gym had an abundance of scales. The DDC monitored all government-employed gate divers for any unusual changes. They checked weight and height every three months, bloodwork every six.

I focused on myself. One hundred and fifty-one pounds. A six-pound weight loss. As I suspected, all that healing and fighting came with a price. This tiny strand of spider silk would hold ten times my weight. The eggs weren't heavy, only large. That just left Bear.

I glanced at the dog and froze.

Ninety-four pounds.

That couldn't possibly be right. I had checked her before and she was at seventy-six pounds. She had gained eighteen pounds. It wasn't possible. Even if my sense of time was completely off and we'd been in the breach for a week, a dog couldn't just gain eighteen pounds in seven days.

"Bear, come here, girl."

The shepherd trotted over. I ran my hand over her body, feeling her flanks and back under the fur. There wasn't much fat there, quite the opposite. She was on the leaner side. Judging by feel alone, she could use a few more meals.

I tried to recall her general dimensions, and they popped into my head from memory.

Bear was three inches taller and four inches longer.

I struggled to process it. She was taller and longer, which meant her bones elongated. Growing that fast should have put a huge strain on her body.

It had to be stalker regeneration. She'd been eating every chance she got, and her new accelerated healing must've been putting these calories into her growth.

I *flexed* again, focusing in on her, looking for any abnormalities. Perfectly healthy. Nothing strange. Just a very large dog. Also, her harness was on way too tight. I had noticed that before and loosened it, but she must've grown since then.

I would need the harness to get her down to the floor of the cavern, but once we cleared that hurdle – assuming we survived – I would have to take it off. It was as big as it could be and already pinching her body. If she got any bigger, it would hurt her.

There was nothing I could do about Bear's explosive growth. It was what it was. One thing was for certain, I needed to feed her better. If she was growing, she would need more calories. The next time we downed a stalker or maybe one of those goat things, I would let her eat all she wanted.

For now, I had to concentrate on making a rope. The twine-sized spider silk would hold my weight, but it would also cut my hands. I had to make it thicker and figure out some way to shield my fingers.

I pulled on the silk, and it came loose. If my luck held, it would be one long rope, and I had a lot of cocoons to work with.

THE ROPE TOOK A LOT LONGER THAN EXPECTED. I MUST'VE BEEN at it for about three hours, but in the end, I didn't just have a rope. I had two, braided together from several lengths of the spider twine. I also made a net sack into which I loaded the spider eggs, all but the coral one. That one would come down with me. I pried a paper cap off the cluster of tubes I had dropped to the ground. It was thick like canvas, but flexible, and I managed to work it into a crude sack. I put the coral egg into it and secured it with Bear's leash.

Bear trotted out of the cave and came back in. She started doing it a few minutes after I began working on the rope. I read somewhere that German Shepherds liked to patrol. Nothing could get onto the ledge from below and if something came in from the tunnel, we could hold it off here in the nest, so if patrolling made her feel better, there was no reason to keep her from it.

I coiled my ropes and walked onto the ledge. Below us, about one hundred yards away, the spider herders blocked the floor of the cavern. There were seven of them and behind them massive white spiders splattered with black loomed, each at least twenty feet tall.

Okay then. This altered things.

Bear stared at the spider army and let out a quiet woof.

"Yes. I see."

I went back inside the cave, grabbed the queen's head, and dragged it toward the gap. It barely fit, but finally I managed to push it through. I grabbed it and strained. The head was surprisingly light. I jerked it up above my head.

Look, I killed your enemy.

The spider herders watched, impassive.

I hurled the queen's head off the cliff. It smashed onto the rocks below.

No reaction. Not exactly promising. I'd hoped for a cheer.

I picked up my ropes and walked along the ledge away from the flowers. Bear trotted after me.

We cleared the blossoms. I picked a large boulder, tied one rope around it, secured the other rope around a different chunk of stone and went back to the wasp nest to get the eggs. When I came back, the spider herders had moved directly below my ropes, arranged in a perfect crescent, with the monstrous spiders behind them.

I *flexed*. Some pollen had gotten on the eggs in the net sack. I waved my hands over it, trying to clean them. The pollen was featherlight, and after a couple of minutes most of it was off. I tied the rope to the net sack containing the four regular eggs, tied the other end of it around a rock, and held the sack above the drop.

Still no reaction.

I gently lowered the sack down. The rope was long enough. The trick was to keep from bumping the eggs against the cliff wall.

Nice and slow.

A spider herder stepped forward. I lowered the sack into their arms. The herder sliced at the rope with their hand, cutting the net sack free. There was no tug, no pull. One moment the weight of the eggs was on the rope and the next it vanished. The spider herder moved to the back with their prize, and I pulled the rope back up.

I still had the coral egg, Bear, and myself.

Bear would have to be next. I looped the rope around the rock three more times, then wrapped it around her, threading it through her harness.

"You will be okay, girl. I'll be right down."

I took a deep breath and gently lowered Bear off the cliff, supporting her weight with my arms. When she was about three feet down, I backed up, strung the rope over my shoulders, and began to let it out, little by little, foot by foot, going as slowly as

I could. There was no way the old me could have done this. She would've been too heavy.

I ran out of rope and looked down. I'd calculated correctly. Bear was hanging about six feet off the ground. Letting her down all the way would've been a dangerous gamble. Bear was smart but she was a dog. There was no telling what she would do when facing giant spiders and weird looking beings. She could wait for me like a good girl, or she could decide it was biting time and get herself killed. Leaving her hanging was the safest choice. The spider herders made no move toward her and if the rope snapped and she fell, she wouldn't get injured.

It was my turn. I hung the sack with the last egg around my neck, threading one arm through so Bear's leash crossed my back. The egg was now against my chest. If I smacked into the cliff face, I could use my arms and legs to cushion the impact and keep it safe. I grabbed the second rope. I had never rappelled off anything in my life. Hell of a way to start learning.

It was easier than I thought. The first time I had pushed off a little too hard, but by the fourth bump I got the hang of it.

Push.

Push.

Push.

My feet met the solid ground. I let go of the rope and turned around. The spider herders stood motionless. They were almost eight feet tall, and they towered over me, menacing and silent, their faces hidden behind veils. Only the eyes were visible, two of them per face, large, narrow, with a strange-looking white iris on a solid black sclera that didn't seem the least bit insectoid.

I lifted my paper sack off my back, pulled the paper open, and held the coral egg out.

"*Bekh-razz.*" My voice sounded ragged.

The spider herder in the center stepped forward. A bubble of light popped inside my head, and I knew that the herder was male and the staff in his hand, with the symbols etched into its shaft, meant he was in charge of this cluster.

The herder's robe stirred softly as he moved and I realized that the humanoid shape was an illusion. The top half of him, the upright half, seemed human. His arms, unnaturally white, were long and thin, and his hands had six segmented fingers, each tipped with a black claw. He seemed to float forward rather than walk, and as he moved, I glimpsed the outline of four segmented legs underneath the pale silk.

A soft voice issued forth from the spider herder. *"Horsun, gehr tirr did sembadzer."*

Something inside me recognized this language. The steady cadence sounded so familiar. I knew the words, but their meaning kept avoiding me, as if I was trying to hold on to slippery, wet mud.

"Dzerhen tam dzal lukr tuhta gef."

I used to speak this. A long time ago. I just forgot how... No, wait, it wasn't me.

"...Dzer lohr dzal, Sadrin."

Me. I was *sadrin*. That was more than a name. It was an occupation... no, a purpose. This was my goal in life. It was why I existed. The core of my... The understanding slipped away from me, and I almost growled out of sheer frustration. So close.

Something tore in my mind like a piece of paper and suddenly some of the clicks and odd syllables made sense.

"... hyrt argadi..."

Daughter. *Argadi* meant daughter. I saved a female child.

"...Argadi dzal to na yen sah-dejjit..."

Sah-dejjit. Friend. They considered me a friend.

"Dzer meq dzal bekh-razz danur. Bekh-razz danir."

Safe passage for now and forever. Oh.

The spider herder pointed at my left arm. I stepped forward and held it out. The light on his staff flared into a needle-thin green beam and hit my arm. Pain lashed me. I gritted my teeth.

The light died. A narrow scar marked my arm, twisting into a flowing symbol. My talent focused on it.

The vision burst in my mind. *Groups of spider herders, one after another, different landscapes, different times, all nodding and parting to let me pass.* I had been given a great, rare honor.

The words formed on my lips on their own.

"*Adaren kullnemeq, Sindra-ron. Sadrin issun tanil danir.*"

Thank you for the priceless gift, children of Sindra. I shall be forever grateful.

The spider herders moved aside, and the sea of spiders behind them parted before me.

THE WEIGHT ROOM AT THE ELMWOOD PARK REC CENTER WAS small, but it did have a bench press. The gym stood empty. The gate was considered high risk now and the residents in the immediate area had been evacuated long ago. Elias loaded four plates on each side of the bar. Four hundred and five pounds. He would need an extra two hundred pounds to really get going, but there were no plates left. *A light workout it is.*

Elias slid onto the bench, took a close grip with his fists nearly touching, lifted the bar off the rungs, and slowly lowered it to about an inch off his chest. He held it there for a few breaths, slowly pushed it up, and brought it back down.

The workout wasn't planned, but sitting on his hands was getting to him. He had to let off some steam or he would explode.

Thirty minutes later, he had finished with the chest press and the leg press machine and was on the dip bars, with four plates chained to him, going into his second set of fifty dips, when Leo walked into the gym carrying his tablet. The XO looked like a cat who'd caught a mouse and was very satisfied with his hunting skills.

Elias nodded to him. "Good news?"

"In a manner of speaking. Malcolm has a brother." Leo held up his tablet. On it a man strikingly similar to Malcolm smiled into the camera, poised against a forest. Same height, same lanky build, same dark hair and brown eyes. If you put him into tactical gear, Elias might have mistaken him for the Elmwood gate assault team leader.

Elias kept moving, lifting his body up and down, the plates a comfortable weight tugging on him. "Are they twins?"

"No, Peter is two years younger."

"Is he a Talent?"

Leo shook his head. "He is a biologist. He spends most of his time in Australia."

"What is he doing there?"

"Trying to contain an outbreak of chlamydia in koalas."

Elias paused midway into the lift and looked at Leo.

"Apparently koalas are highly susceptible to chlamydia," Leo said. "The latest strain is threatening to make them extinct in New South Wales."

Elias shook his head and resumed the dips.

"Interesting fact," Leo continued. "Dr. Peter Nevin can apparently be in two places at once. Here he is speaking at the National Koala Conference in Port Macquarie in New South Wales."

He flicked the tablet and a picture of Peter Nevin at the podium slid onto the screen.

"And here he is in Vegas after losing three hundred thousand dollars at the poker table on the same day." Leo swiped across the tablet, presenting a picture of Malcolm exiting a casino, his face flat.

Elias ran out of dips, jumped to the floor, and began to

unchain the weights. "Malcolm gambled under his brother's name."

"Oh, he didn't just gamble. When someone like Malcolm lands in Vegas, a siren goes off and they roll out the red carpet from the plane all the way to the strip."

"How deep is the hole?"

"Twenty-three million."

Elias took special care to slide the weight plate back onto the rack. Breaking community equipment would not be good. Except that whatever pressure he'd managed to vent now doubled.

Twenty-three million. Over three times Malcolm's annual pay with bonuses.

Malcolm was a gambler. Everything suddenly made sense. If the motherlode of gold wasn't an exaggeration, Malcolm could've walked away with a bonus of several hundred thousand.

The casinos had to know who they were dealing with. Nobody would allow a koala scientist to carry that kind of debt, but a star assault team leader from a large guild was a different story. If they had any decency, they would've cut Malcolm off, but then they weren't in the decency business.

"He is on a payment plan," Leo said.

"Of course he is."

And they would let him dig that hole deeper and deeper. Why not? He'd become a passive income golden goose. And all of this should have been caught during his audits. Those payments had to have come from somewhere, and Malcolm would've been at it for years. Any bookkeeper worth their salt would've noticed a large amount of money going out.

"The auditor..."

"Already got her, sir."

Her? Malcolm's auditor was a man... and he had retired two

years ago. The Guild must've assigned him to someone else. "Is it Susan Calloway?"

"It is."

"Are they having an affair?"

Leo blinked. "They are! How…"

"Three years ago at the Establishment Party. He got two drinks, one for his wife and one for Susan, and when he handed the champagne to her, her face lit up. Then her husband returned to the table, and she stopped smiling."

He had reminded Malcolm and Susan separately after that party that rules applied to them. The guild had a code of conduct, and every prospective guild member signed a document stating they read it and agreed to abide by it during the contract stage. Cold Chaos didn't tolerate affairs. If both parties were single, relationships between guild members were fine, but cheating on your spouse, in or outside of the guild, would result in severe sanctions.

Adultery undermined trust, destroyed morale, and eroded the chain of command. That was the official position of the US Army, and during his tenure as an officer, he had seen that directive ignored time and time again. From the senior NCOs who made bets on who would be the first to get into a freshly-minted attractive lieutenant's pants to officers who led double lives every time they went on a prolonged deployment. It never ended well.

He wanted none of that in the guild. If you didn't have the discipline or moral resilience to remain faithful to the one person who should've mattered most in your life, how could anyone rely on you in the breach, where lives were on the line?

He'd made his position quite clear. Both Malcolm and Susan swore nothing was going on, and Elias hadn't seen any signs of trouble since. Meanwhile Susan quietly became Malcolm's auditor and chose to ignore his gambling.

Elias hid a sigh. Some days he was just done.

"Is Legal aware?" he asked.

"Yes. They do not believe that the casino will attempt to collect against Malcolm's estate. They've gotten enough money from him already, and hounding the widow of a dead Talent is a bad look. Not to mention the fraud involved in all of this."

"Jackson?"

"No news yet."

"It won't be long now," Elias told him.

Elias's phone chimed as if on cue. He glanced at it. An 81 country code.

"Speak of the devil."

He took the call.

Yasuo Morita appeared on the screen, a trim man in his forties, dark hair cropped short, a shadow of a beard darkening his jaw and crow's feet at the corners of his smart eyes.

"Elias. Good to see you," Yasuo said. The Vice-Guildmaster of Hikari no Ryu spoke English with the barest trace of an accent.

"Good to see you as well."

"Your healer is on a plane heading home. My people sent over the flight information."

Out of Yasuo's view Leo waved his tablet and nodded.

"This was not done at our request," Yasuo said. "Someone got overzealous in currying favor. This mistake has been corrected."

"Good to hear."

"You surprised me. Nicely done."

"Glad to know I can still keep you on your toes."

Yasuo smiled. "It won't happen again."

There were a couple dozen high-profile US-born Talents working in Japan. This morning nine of them simultaneously asked for leave and booked tickets home. It was a hell of a statement, and it looked impressive, but it wasn't made for the sake of Cold Chaos.

The guild sandbox was small and great healers were rare. Especially healers like Jackson who went out of his way to step in during an emergency. Elias had called every Talent who knew Jackson or benefited from the healer's involvement. Some knew Jackson personally, others through family members, but all agreed that interference with healers had to be off limits.

Explaining all of this to Yasuo was unnecessary. They were much better off letting him think that Cold Chaos had extensive reach.

"How is my brother?" Yasuo asked.

"Yosuke is well. He's been promoted to the lead damage dealer of the Assault Team 2."

"As he should be. When you see him next, I hope you will do me the favor of reminding him that our father hasn't seen him in two years."

"I'll mention it."

"Good-bye and good luck."

"You as well."

Elias ended the call. "When does he land?"

"Not for a while." Leo grimaced. "There is a typhoon heading for Japan. They are rerouting everything. The plane just boarded, and he's on a flight out of Narita with an overnight layover in Hong Kong. I will start the prep."

Even if Jackson was delayed by a day, things were moving. They would finally crack this damn breach. Elias squared his shoulders.

Everything would fall into place once they entered the gate.

[9]

I raised my head from the body of a lake dragon and listened. Next to me, Bear stopped chewing. Her ears twitched.

Something was stalking us through the tunnels.

We left the spider herders behind three sleeps ago. Without a watch, I had no idea how much time had passed, and my circadian rhythms were completely off. There was no sunrise or sunset. There were only the caves. We walked and fought until we got tired, then we ate and rested. It felt like I slept in short bursts, a few hours at a time rather than the full seven or eight.

The last time we bedded down, Bear started barking halfway through. She'd bark, I'd wake up, we'd both peer into the darkness, and then she would settle down and we would go back to sleep. I thought it was some monster making circles around us, but it didn't feel like that anymore. It felt like something was deliberately hunting us, something smart and patient. Our hunter stayed just out of range. Sometimes I would feel a flicker of a presence, and then it would be gone.

I pushed hard after resting, going through the tunnels and caverns at top speed. I thought we'd lost them. Apparently not.

Bear went back to munching on lake dragon steak. The wasp queen was a watershed moment for me. Until that point, I viewed myself as prey. I tried to avoid fights, and I assumed that everything we met was stronger than me.

I was still cautious, but reality had finally set in. I was faster and stronger than a lot of things in this breach, and my injuries healed within hours. I no longer went around. I cut through. And when something managed to get too close, my monster dog tore it to pieces. Bear grew another two inches and reached ninety-nine pounds. The scaredy-cat shepherd who hid behind me when we started was long gone. Now when Bear sighted an enemy, she held herself like an apex predator. When she sensed a fight coming, her tail wagged and her bright eyes seemed to say, "Oh boy, I wonder if this one is yummy."

Perhaps sensing a change, the stalkers gave us a wide berth. We killed an oversized serpent the size of a power pole, a handful of the silverfish bugs, some tentacled thing which I couldn't identify, and now a lake dragon who tried to ambush us on the shore of a deep pond. This one was smaller than the first, but it still made us work for the win. We paused to rest, heal, and eat, and now our unseen tracker caught up.

I shifted the bag on my back. The spider herders didn't just let me pass. Their leader and two of his guard spiders walked us about half a mile through the tunnels. We didn't speak, but he treated me with deference. At the end, one of the other herders caught up with us and brought me a backpack made of spider silk with a length of one of my ropes inside it.

The backpack was weightless and damn near indestructible. Right now, it contained that rope, my helmet and Bear's leash and harness. I had no idea why I kept that stuff around. The rope could prove useful, but the harness didn't fit Bear anymore and the helmet mostly got in the way now. I saw better without its light. My eyes had completely adjusted to the darkness. I was pretty sure I'd passed the human threshold of night vision days ago.

I cut a paper-thin slice from the lake dragon's flank and chewed it.

"Bear, either this dragon tastes like chicken or I'm losing my mind."

Bear ripped into her slab of meat.

"Compared to the stalkers, it's downright delicious."

The more casually we acted, the closer the hunter would get. I took another bite. Come on over, it's just me and my puppy having a picnic. Join us, won't you? We are harmless, I swear.

I chewed and waited.

Nothing.

Hard to look harmless when you are snacking on a monster the size of a moving truck and leaving a trail of bodies in your wake.

I leaned back against the rock. "I'm happy, Bear. My stomach is full, I drank some water, I rested, and neither one of us is hurt."

The shepherd glanced at me.

"When you are young, you think that happiness is made of big triumphant moments. Getting your driver's license. Graduating. Getting accepted into a college of your choice. Your wedding day – that's a big one. But when you get older, you realize that those are the moments you remember, but they are so rare. If you want to be happy, you look for joy in small things. A cup of your favorite coffee. A good book. Vegging out on the couch after a long, hard day at work. Some people might say those are moments when you are content, not happy. But I will take what I can get, and right now this is a moment."

Bear grinned at me.

"When we get out and I get back to my kids, now that will be a huge moment. You will like them, Bear. They will like you, too, because you are the best girl ever."

I would walk out of this gate no matter what it cost me. Even if I was no longer the same Ada who had entered. And when we did exit, Bear would be coming home with me. I would pry her away from the guild no matter what it took. After all, I was *sadrin* now. I would think of something.

Sadrin. The word turned over in my mind. One of my coworkers back at the agency had a crystal cube on her desk with dichroic film paper inside of it. When she turned it, the colors on the inside would change. The same section of the cube could look blue or red or yellow depending on the position and the light. *Sadrin* was like that.

I was sadrin. I am sadrin.

There was a world of meaning in that word, but I couldn't decode it. It felt at once weighty and ephemeral, something I should know, something I already knew, something I had to discover... It was breaking my brain in the same way the lectures on quantum physics I attended as part of the DDC training did. The electron was both a particle and wave, light was a quantum field, and I was *sadrin*.

It was the same strange feeling when I spoke to the spider herders. I knew what I said, and I was understood, and yet, I didn't speak their language. It was more like I formed an intent to communicate gratitude and something in my mind put it into the appropriate sounds.

Technically, that was how speech worked in general. We formed intent to speak, and our body produced the sound, but when I spoke English, that process was instant. With the spider herders, I felt that neural connection happen in slow motion. It was disconcerting.

What did that woman put into my head?

Bear trotted to the pond, drank, and ran over to me. It was time to go.

We trekked across the cavern to another tunnel. I closed my eyes for a moment, checking the position of the anchor. Yep, still straight ahead. It was very close now and it had gotten more distracting. I'd compared it to a psychic splinter before; that splinter had become infected. It wedged itself in my consciousness and throbbed.

The anchor was usually well protected. I had leveled up, figuratively speaking, but I wasn't sure I could take whatever guarded it. A part of me wanted to try. Wanted something to be there, something I could slice to pieces. I wasn't sure if I wanted to punish whoever created the breach in the first place by killing their prized bioweapon or if I wanted to prove something to myself because deep down, I was still scared. Dwelling on it wouldn't do me any good. The anchor was our destination. We would get to it.

Maybe I would get some answers there.

The tunnel ended and Bear and I walked onto another stone bridge. An oval cavern stretched out on both sides of us, not very large but deep, about one hundred yards across and twice that down. The narrow stone bridge spanned it just off center. On the other side, another tunnel waited.

We kept walking, sticking to the center of the path. We were about halfway across when I caught a glint of something below.

"Rest."

Bear lay down. We were working on new commands. Cold Chaos likely taught most of them already, but I didn't know the German words for them, so we had to improvise. So far, she got *rest, up, drop it,* and *back.* That last one was especially useful in a fight. Our battle strategies generally went one of two ways. If the opponent was smaller or roughly the same size as Bear, she rammed them and went for their throat. If the enemy was larger, she usually targeted a limb, clamped on, and used her weight to slow them while I cut them down. Calling her back behind me was crucial, because some creatures, like the lake dragon, were strong enough to fling her away. Although lately when Bear bit something, she stayed on. Her cuspids were now three point two inches long and the rest of her teeth had gotten larger as well.

She also seemed to understand *not food*, but we had mixed success with that.

I had no idea how hard it was to train a dog, but cute puppy videos on Instagram taught me that it required repetition. Command, compliance, reward, rinse and repeat. It took Bear only five repetitions to learn a command, and once she learned it, it stuck. I was sure it wasn't normal, but nothing had been since I walked into this breach. Normal had packed its bags and left the building.

I knelt and carefully leaned over the edge to look down.

Bodies sprawled below. Human bodies in the familiar indigo of Cold Chaos.

I went cold.

They lay strewn around the bottom of the cave like Noah's action figures thrown onto the bed. Some were missing limbs, some had been cut in half. It looked familiar. I had seen this at the mining site. This controlled carnage. One slice. One death.

I forced myself to focus on the corpses. They were too far to fully analyze, but I noticed that when I measured distances with my Talent, it gave me a moment of enhanced distance vision. The body directly under me was lying on its back. I *flexed*, and for a split second my talent grasped its face.

Malcolm. This was the original assault team.

Something flashed by Malcolm's body. I concentrated on it. The cheesecake stone.

My heart hammered in my chest. As soon as London made it out, the gate coordinator would have gone into the breach and activated the cheesecake, the signal stone, twin to the one that was now blinking below me. The moment the cheesecake started flashing, the assault team would've turned around and marched back to the gate. They never made it, which meant they were either already dead by the time the cheesecake started flashing, or they were en route back to the gate when they died.

The assault team went into the gate an hour before the mining team. The mining team died about thirty minutes after entering.

The gate was less than two hours away. Had to be.

If I could get down there, I could walk out of the breach in two hours. Bear and I would be out of this nightmare. We could go home.

I scrambled from the edge and sat, trying to get a grip. I had to calm down.

Could we get down there? Was it physically possible?

I crawled back to the edge and looked down again, measuring the distance with my talent for the second time. Two hundred and eleven feet. The rope in my backpack was only fifty feet long, whatever the spider herders helped me cut from the length I used to rappel down the cliff.

Nowhere near long enough.

I could jump pretty far now, and a drop of thirty feet wasn't out of the question. But that and my rope still only gave me eighty. I would need one hundred and thirty-one feet. At least.

I surveyed the walls. Sheer. No way to climb down. Even if I somehow strapped Bear to myself, we wouldn't make it.

I felt like screaming. We were so close. Damn it.

So fucking close.

I looked below again, surveying the bodies, the floor, the walls...

I had to let it go. There was no way down. We couldn't afford to sit here wasting time and energy obsessing over it.

I felt the weight of someone's stare. The tiny hairs on the back of my neck rose.

I concentrated. The hidden watcher was across the cavern, perpendicular to the bridge.

Slowly I reached into my backpack, pulled out my hard hat, slid the selector on the light to maximum beam, and jerked the helmet up.

Across from us a face with two shining eyes peered at me through the gap in the far wall. My talent grasped an outline of a long humanoid head. A blink and it jerked out of sight, behind the stone.

The light on the helmet sputtered and died.

"And now we know we haven't lost it, Bear."

Something *was* following us. Not just something. Someone. And they glowed bright red.

Red meant value. Our hunter offered something useful, something that, judging by the intensity of the color, we desperately needed.

I got up and stuffed the helmet back into my sack. It was useless as a light source, but it still worked as Bear's water bowl. The anchor was still pulsing on the edge of my awareness.

"If we find the anchor, maybe we can find a way down."

Bear wagged her tail.

"Come on, Bearkins."

I started forward and Bear chased after me.

BEAR AND I TRUDGED ACROSS ANOTHER STONE BRIDGE, A VAST drop below us. This part of the breach seemed to consist of massive caverns and deep shafts connected by short tunnels. Natural stone bridges crisscrossed the sheer drops. Water was scarce. I'd filled our canteens when we killed the latest lake dragon, and half of our water supply was gone. It made me nervous. I kept hoping for streams and not finding any.

We could probably get some moisture from the blood of the monsters we killed, but they had grown scarce too. Nobody barred our path. Maybe the inhabitants of the breach simultaneously decided that we were too much of a threat, but I doubted it. A few times I glimpsed creature corpses below, broken as if they had fallen from a great height. The fall wasn't the only thing that killed them. The bodies were torn, shredded by something with terrible claws. And worse, nothing had touched them since their death. This place was full of scavengers, yet all of that meat was going to waste. There was only one answer: whatever slaughtered the creatures was so frightening, that nothing else dared to touch their kill.

The anchor was ahead and slightly to the right. We had been drawing closer, but our route didn't run in a straight line. We were making circles around it, getting nearer in a spiral that became tighter and tighter.

Behind me, Bear halted. I turned. She was looking to our right, across the cavern. That side of the chamber lay shrouded in gloom.

Bear let out a quiet, deliberate woof.

Something was definitely there, in the darkness.

I *flexed*. My talent rolled outward, trying to measure the distance to the gloom, and falling short.

Woof.

Another stone bridge ran below us, leading to the right. It was a twenty-foot drop. If we got down there, I could use my rope to climb back up.

Woof.

"Okay. We'll go check it out. Up!"

Bear leaped into my arms. I held her the same way I carried Mellow, my cream cat, and jumped down. We landed on the lower stone bridge. The impact punched through the soles of my feet into my legs. I stuck the landing like an Olympic gymnast. Maybe once I got out of here, I would go for a career change. Not many forty-year-old acrobats debuting out there. I'd be a sensation.

I let Bear down, and we headed toward the shadows.

What the hell would I do once I got out? First, I'd need to make sure Cold Chaos didn't have a chance to unalive me, as Tia would put it. I was living proof of their fuckup. A huge liability. A week ago, or however long it had been since we entered, I would have said that a major guild, especially Cold Chaos, wouldn't stoop that low. The risks were too great. But now I didn't just expect the worst, I counted on it.

Assuming that we made it out alive and jumped the Cold Chaos hurdle, the DDC would want the full account of what happened. I had two choices. First, I could demonstrate my newfound powers and come clean. Second, I could hide.

The first option meant ... the end of my life as I knew it. Possibly in more ways than one. I had encountered sentient, sapient lifeforms. I communicated with them, I traded with them, and I witnessed irrefutable evidence of other civilizations. Not just one vague amorphous enemy, but an entire constellation of different sophont species. Not beasts, not monsters. Thinking, feeling beings.

And some of them, like the spider herders, were not overtly hostile. They would defend themselves if we gave them no choice, but that brief flash of knowledge from my gem assured me that they just wanted to be left alone.

The spider herders didn't seem surprised to see me. Looking back at their calm reactions, they had to have seen humans before, and they instantly knew I was *sadrin*. I didn't understand what *sadrin* was, but they did, and they treated me with respect.

The breaches had been active for nearly a decade. Thousands of gates, maybe a hundred thousand gate divers worldwide. Someone had to have seen what I'd seen, and yet there was no mention of non-hostile sophonts anywhere in the DDC archives.

Which meant that somewhere, very high up, a decision was made to keep their existence suppressed.

It made sense. When I was in college, I read a science fiction novel about space marines fighting against insectoid aliens. Bugs. Big horrific bugs. The space marines slaughtered them by thousands and never felt bad about it, because in real life we designated bugs as something that could be killed without guilt. We had exterminators and pesticides, and we never questioned the ethics of it.

Reducing your enemy to the level of a bug or a mindless monster eliminated the guilt of taking their life. When faced with war, humans always dehumanized their opponents. You only had to look at the WWII era cartoons to see it.

Right now, the breaches were filled with monsters. The gate divers fought them, and the rest of us supported them and thanked them for their service. We unified to repel the invasion, and we did not question the morality of that fight. It was okay to hate the enemy, because it was a mindless horde of bioweapons who sought to wipe us from existence.

If I came out and told everyone that I encountered sapient beings, had a chat with some of them, and met a human who spoke to me and put something into my head that was actively changing who I was, I would explode that social construct.

The united front would fracture. Some people would immediately argue for scouring the breach in an effort to bargain and communicate; some people would panic; others would attempt to defect. The major religions would have to undergo yet another series of contortions to try to explain away the multitude of civilizations just like they had to twist themselves into a pretzel a decade ago to explain the gates to their worshippers. Humanity would stew in its own instability and navel gazing, and we couldn't afford to do that. We had to continue to destroy the anchors, or we would be overrun.

If I opened that door, the government, my employers, would disappear me before I was able to make a difference. They probably wouldn't kill me right away. First, they would confine me. I would be interrogated, studied, and analyzed, and either quietly disposed of or made into a weapon. I was ridiculously easy to control. As long as the DDC held Tia and Noah hostage, I would do whatever they wanted. The lives of my children would be hanging in the balance.

No, hiding was my only option. I wasn't ready to become a martyr.

When we walked out of that gate, I had to convince everyone that I was still Adaline Moore, an assessor and non-combatant, who wandered out of the breach by pure luck. Except that I probably looked different, I carried a magic sword, my dog was twenty-five percent larger than when we went in, and I would've survived in the breach for at least a week with no supplies, weapons, or combat Talents to protect me. Now that was truly unheard of.

Piece of cake. Right.

I had no idea how to pull that off. And worrying about it was premature. I had plenty of time to think of some kind of plan.

After five minutes of walking, we stopped before a hole in the wall. It was about ten feet across and roughly semicircular, as if cut in the rock. It reminded me of the small cave where Bear and I took shelter to fight off the mauve flowers. The hole looked empty and dark, except for one thing. A complex dial the size of a dessert plate hung in mid-air in the exact center of the opening.

I *flexed*. The entire entrance fluoresced with bright electric yellow. No touching. A barrier, invisible to my normal vision. Only the dial was free of the glow. It had to be the source of the barrier.

I stared at the dial. Five concentric circles carved out of bone and inlaid with a metal the color of rose gold. Each of the circles was marked with eight smaller round indentations, spaced at even intervals. The top indentation was dark, the second going clockwise was mostly dark with a pale rose gold crescent on the right side, the third was half gold, half dark... Phases of the moon.

Five circles, five moons, eight phases each.

Thousands of combinations.

Something stirred in my mind. A vision flooded me. I saw a hand with slender fingers and brindled skin reach for an identical dial and manipulate the circles with its red claws, selecting the phases. A panorama of a night sky unfolded above me with five moons of different colors in different phases. A holy cosmic combination, part of a twisted faith and a lynchpin of a sacred ritual known only to the initiated.

The vision faded. I had the key now, but not the explanation. Who left the dial barrier here, what was behind it, and most importantly, should I open it?

Was there something dangerous locked in that hole? It could contain treasure, valuable knowledge, or some kind of eldritch horror that would disintegrate us.

I could just keep walking.

I searched my mind for anything else, any other knowledge relating to the barrier or its originator. I found nothing.

This was so frustrating. I knew there was more there, hidden in that glowing gem that somehow lived inside of me, but I just couldn't access it. It showed me glimpses and only when it wanted to.

I stared at the dial. I had to know. If I walked away now, the barrier would eat at me until I doubled back and opened it. It would be a waste of time and effort. And if I walked away, there was no telling if I would ever get the chance to return.

I reached for the dial and turned the top circle. The first moon in waxing gibbous, the second in waning crescent, the third full, the fourth in its third quarter, and the last a dark new moon. The five moon irregular pentagon.

The circles of the dial slid, spinning on their own. The

opening flashed with green, and the dial clattered to the ground. The way was open.

THE AIR WAS STALE AND STANK OF OLD URINE MIXED WITH A harsh odor that reminded me of burned plastic.

I walked into the cave side by side with Bear. She sniffed the air currents and bared the edge of her teeth. Yeah. Right there with you.

The cave was empty. I'd hidden the dial in my backpack. I was pretty sure I could reset it, and a portable impenetrable barrier might come in handy.

We reached the far wall. A dead end on the right, a dark passage leading off to the left. We turned left, then right, through a short hallway, and walked into a small room. A light source glowed on the wall, an apple-sized crystal shining with weak yellow light and wavering almost like a torch. It was on its last legs.

Below the light, a creature lay tied to the wall by some sort of metal cord attached to a collar around its neck. It was probably around three and a half to four feet long and sheathed in thick grey fur. A fluffy tail the color of smoke curled around it, hiding most of the animal from view. All I could see were large triangular ears, tipped by tufts of bright red fur like those of a lynx.

A low snarl rumbled in Bear's mouth.

"Shh," I told her.

Was this a pet? A guard dog equivalent? If so, what was it guarding? There was nothing in the room.

The creature's ears had ragged edges as if something was violently torn out of them. Dried blood caked on the rims. Whatever it was, it hadn't been treated well.

I *flexed*. The beast was alive and breathing, but my talent didn't tell me anything more and the gem stayed silent, too.

I took a careful step forward. Another.

The animal lay still. That wasn't normal. It had to have heard me. Those ears weren't just for show. It was deliberately choosing to ignore my approach.

Another step.

One more.

The fox-thing lunged at me. It was lightning fast, but I expected it and shied away. Dark claws raked the air an inch in front of me, so close they fanned my face. The collar jerked the fox back.

Bear shot forward.

"Stop!"

Bear halted.

"Back!"

Bear snarled, clicking her teeth, but didn't move forward.

The fox bared sharp fangs, the chain on its collar taut.

"Back, Bear."

The shepherd backpedaled until she was one step behind me.

"Good girl. Sit."

Bear sat, but she really didn't want to.

The fox creature retreated to the wall and crouched. It walked on two feet and when it lowered itself, it didn't sit on its haunches. It crouched like a person, like someone used to bipedal locomotion.

A caravan of raccoon-foxes, donkeys, some alien being wrapped in rags, bemoaning its fate... I'd seen its kind before in a vision. Their fur was of a different color, and they wore clothes, but the resemblance was unmistakable. Same species. The leave-you-in-financial-ruin guys.

The fox-thing watched me with big golden eyes. It would be adorably cute, if it wasn't in such a terrible state. Blood had dried into crust on its chest. Long scars covered its arms. Some-thing or more likely someone had either beaten or tortured it.

The room was empty except for the dying light and the pris-oner. No water. No food. No containers indicating that any of that was ever delivered. The fox was chained here and left to die.

And it could see the way out. The light illuminated the passageway behind me. There was no door on the cell. It looked like the exit out was right there, just a few yards away. The fox would watch the light on the wall as it wavered and grew dimmer and dimmer and realize it was a metaphor for its life. Soon the light would die, leaving the cell in the dark, and the fox would die with it, fading from hunger and thirst.

If the fox-creature did somehow break the cord and rush out, thinking it was free, it would run straight into a barrier which would leave it in agony. Once the pain subsided, it would realize that an invisible wall blocked its escape, a wall that could only be opened from the outside. It would see the dial, but it could never touch it.

This was a human level of cruelty. Killing it would have been more humane.

"Can you understand me?"

The fox stared at me, its eyes hot with menace.

For all I knew, it was some kind of criminal sentenced to die in this cell for a horrific killing spree.

I *flexed*. The fox didn't glow. It wasn't toxic, it wasn't an immediate source of pain or danger the way the barrier was. It didn't glow red like the hunter I had glimpsed. It simply was.

I took an empty canteen from my waist, pulled the full one off as well, and poured about a third of our total water supply into the first canteen. The fox watched me with an almost feverish focus. I screwed the lids back on, reattached the fuller bottle to my belt, and held the other one in front of me.

"Water."

179

I tossed the canteen to the fox. It snatched it out of the air. Its long fingers twisted the lid with practiced dexterity, and the fox drank in long greedy gulps. It emptied the canteen and stared at me.

Whatever it had done, I couldn't leave it here to die.

I pointed at the metal cord and shaped my sword into a short thick cleaver.

The fox bared its sharp fangs again.

I waited.

Two burning eyes glaring at me with fierce intensity.

"I don't want to kill you."

I pointed at the cord again, made a chopping motion with my cleaver, and took a step back with my hands up.

The fox rose and padded to the opposite wall, stretching the metal cord as far as it would go. Okay. The ball was in my court.

I walked to the bracket securing the cord to the wall. It didn't seem particularly sturdy, as if whoever put it in place wanted the prisoner to break free. Otherwise, why even bother with the barrier? The cord itself seemed light and felt like a meld of plastic and metal.

Here goes nothing. I swung the cleaver and brought it down onto the cord. The blade cut through the five-millimeter thickness, severing the metal in a single clean strike. The cord fell to the ground.

The fox dashed past Bear into the passage and vanished from sight, dragging the metal cord with it.

Bear tilted her head and let out a puzzled noise.

"I know, right? Not even a thank you."

I looked around. Nothing left here.

"We've done our good deed for the day. Let's see if it goes unpunished. Come on, girl."

We were halfway across the stone bridge when I saw a clump of dark fur up ahead. The fox had made it about a hundred yards before the exhaustion and starvation brought it down. It fell and dropped my canteen on the stone bridge.

I crouched by it. It was still breathing. Bear sniffed it and looked at me.

"No, not food."

I stood over it for a moment. I could just leave it. But it was hurt and alone, trapped in the breach. Just like me and Bear.

I sighed, made my sword into a knife, and sliced through the collar on the fox's neck. The strange half-plastic, half-metal band fell apart. I retrieved my canteen, picked the fox up, and headed forward, back to our original route.

[10]

"I know you're awake."

The fox kept its eyes closed.

"I heard the change in your breathing."

No reaction.

"Suit yourself."

We sat in a shallow depression in the rock, not that different from the little cave that had been the fox's prison. After picking the fox up, I'd carried it to the stone bridge crossing. Getting him and Bear back onto the top bridge with only one rope took some maneuvering, but in the end we made it, and I picked the fox back up. We walked for a few hours - I wasn't sure how long - until eventually Bear and I had gotten hungry. It took us another hour or so to find prey and water, and then we'd bedded down in this hiding spot.

Past the cave opening a large cavern stretched into the distance. Far below a narrow stream ran through a chain of shallow ponds ringed in mauve flowers. A young lake dragon lived in the central pond. It was submerged now but we watched it nab one of the goat-like herbivores earlier, when a small herd wandered out of a side passage to the water to take a drink.

A narrow ledge led to the right, hugging the wall, before diving down and connecting to another tunnel leading into the rock, the only way to access this cave. I had blocked the tunnel with the dial barrier. The irregular shape of the opening didn't matter. The force barrier conveniently expanded until it met solid rock. I'd tested it in different tunnels. As long as the opening was less than twenty-six feet wide, the barrier asserted itself. For the moment we were safe from everything that didn't have wings or couldn't climb sheer walls. If the DDC ever got their hands on this tech, the scientists would faint.

I sliced a sliver from a stalker ham and held it out to our guest on the tip of my sword. "Hungry?"

The fox opened one eye to a narrow slit, looked at the meat, then at me. Its hand shot out, and then my sword was empty. The creature held the meat up, sniffed it, and put it on a rock next to it. Bear stopped eating and watched it.

The fox rolled onto all fours. Its back arched. It strained and hacked. Its body shuddered, gripped by spasms. It hacked again, louder. A small metal object fell from its mouth.

"Lovely." I took a bite from my own stalker tartare.

The fox tipped an imaginary cup to its lips and held its paw out to me. I passed one of the canteens to it. The creature gently unscrewed the lid and poured a little bit of water onto the thing it had regurgitated. It rubbed the object on its fur, inspected it, nodded, sipped from the canteen, and offered it back to me.

"Oh no, that's yours now." I shook my head.

The creature drank from the canteen, hugged it to itself, and put the metal object by its feet. It looked like a large marble with bumps on its surface. The fox must have swallowed it to keep it from being taken.

The former prisoner snatched the meat from the rock and stuffed it into its mouth.

"More?"

The fox nodded. It was so amazingly human-like. I cut another slice from the ham.

About a pound of meat later, the little beast sat back and rubbed its belly.

"Better?"

The fox eyed me, then looked at Bear gnawing on her bone.

"She won't hurt you unless you try to hurt us first. She's my dog and she's a good girl."

The fox's eyes narrowed to slits. It leaned back and giggled. The sound was startling.

It *laughed* at me. The little asshole understood me.

"Which part of that was funny?"

The creature reached for the marble and squeezed it. A beam of light protruded from the sphere, expanding into an image. A fluffy Pomeranian, followed by a Golden Retriever, and then an English Bulldog.

How the hell did it have these recordings?

"Yes, all of those are dogs. Dogs like Bear."

The fox pointed at the device and let out a tiny woof. Then it pointed at Bear and shook its head. Its paws came up, claws out, and he let out a quiet, menacing *rawr*.

Bear was not a dog. Bear was something scary.

"Don't listen to it, Bear. You are the best dog ever."

The fox laughed, then leaned forward. It put one paw on its chest. A quiet voice came from its mouth. If it were human, I would have said it was male and a tenor.

"Kiar Jovo."

That had to be a name. I put my hand on my chest. "Ada Moore."

Kiar Jovo squeezed the marble again. An image of a man and a woman appeared. The man blurred and turned into Kiar Jovo. Male. He was male.

I nodded.

The marble flashed again. An old fox couple, their fur grey, stood side by side, wearing jeweled sashes over one shoulder. Golden hoop earrings flashed in their ears. Behind them a multitude of fox creatures appeared, similarly dressed, most grey or black, their fur like dense smoke.

Kiar Jovo waved his arm over the image. "Kiar." He touched his chest again. "Jovo."

Kiar was the family or tribe. He was Jovo of the Kiar.

I touched my hand to my chest. "Ada."

I didn't have a marble. I looked around, grabbed a rock, and scratched a stick figure drawing into the floor: Me, Tia, Noah, Bear, and our cat. I circled the drawing with a rock. "Moore."

Jovo nodded.

There were so many questions I wanted to ask. How did he know about us, where did he come from, how did he end up in this breach, who made the breaches and why? But right now, I had to stick to the most important one.

I pointed at his ears and the wound on his chest. "Who?"

Jovo bared his teeth in an ugly snarl. The marble flashed, and a familiar figure appeared, wrapped in a grey tattered robe with four arms, each holding a blade. A second figure stood next to it, much smaller, slimmer, its face hidden by a veil of chains. If Jovo put them in the same order as the human pair, the larger creature was male and the smaller was female. That would mean there were only male attackers at the mining site. The head and shoulders of the male matched the outline of the creature that stalked us. Our hunter was one of these. Made sense.

Jovo's voice was a ragged snarl. "Kael'gress."

"I know those. I have seen them." I pointed at myself. "Moore." I pointed at Jovo. "Kiar." I pointed at the four-armed assassin.

Jovo shook his head. He put his hand on his chest again. "Lees." He pointed at me. "Hoo-man." He pointed at the image of the creature. "Gress." He raised his hand as if stabbing and pierced the air with an imaginary knife, mincing an invisible enemy with a flurry of stabs. "Kael."

Gress was the species name. Kael'gress was a gress who killed. Killer gress.

Jovo raked his claws across the image, his fangs bared. He tried to rip the projection, pulling it apart, and looked at me.

"You want to kill this Kael'gress?"

I drew my finger across Kael'gress's throat.

Jovo nodded several times, his eyes bright.

The four-armed fighters were incredibly dangerous. A memory of them spinning through the cavern flashed before me. I still remembered how one of those grey shrouds stretched, trying to kill me after its owner was dead.

"Dangerous," I said.

Jovo frowned at me. Must not have been a word he was familiar with.

I raised my hands, fingers apart, imitating him when he talked about Bear, and made a snarly noise.

Jovo nodded, then raked the image again. Right, we were still stuck on the killing.

"He almost killed you. You were chained." I pointed to Jovo's neck and trailed my finger indicating an imaginary cord. I pointed at the gress and drew a line across Jovo's neck and then mine. He would kill us both.

Jovo put his hands together and bowed to me.

I shook my head. No.

Jovo bowed again, then again.

I shook my head. "No. Dangerous."

Despair shone in Jovo's eyes. He took a deep breath and offered the metal marble to me.

I shook my head. "No."

Jovo shrank from me, clutching his marble with both hands. The marble was his most prized possession, his only possession. He offered me everything he had, and I said no. If he was human, I would have guessed he was close to tears. This seemed more important than just revenge.

I pointed at the gress. "Why?"

Jovo pointed at the gress and made a grabbing motion, snatching something forcefully from the air.

"He took something from you?"

Jovo squeezed his marble. A night sky flared above us, strange constellations glowing. One of the stars shone brighter. Jovo reached for it, his face full of longing.

"Home?" I guessed.

He looked at me. I pointed at my stick drawing. "Home?"

"Home," Jovo said.

He pointed to the gress and crossed his hands forming an X.

Whatever the gress took from him, Jovo needed it to get back home. He was stuck here, alone.

I too wanted to go home, more than anything in the world.

Jovo sagged on the floor, dejected.

"Where is the gress? Where can we find him?" I made a show of looking around.

Jovo raised his hand and pointed over my shoulder. I didn't even need to look. I knew exactly in which direction he was aiming.

Jovo was pointing at the anchor.

Everything we both wanted was at the anchor.

The gress was stalking me. I was sure of it. Four of its kind chased the woman in blue, trying to murder her. Either they wanted to kill her or to take something from her. Before she died, she passed something precious to her onto me, which made me their new target. That wasn't a logical leap. It wasn't even a hop.

This gress would hunt me down. He had followed me but hadn't closed the distance so far. Perhaps he knew that my predecessor killed four of his kind. Perhaps he didn't want to strike until he was sure that I had no escape route. If I lost him in this warren of passageways and caverns, tracking me down would be difficult.

He must've realized by now I was going to the anchor. He would ambush me there. Bear and I could face him alone or with Jovo.

And there was another part to it. I wanted Jovo to go home. I knew exactly how he felt, and I wanted him to get back to his clan.

"Okay." I spread my arms in a gesture of resignation and surrender.

Jovo perked up, his eyes shining.

"We'll try," I told him.

The lees jumped forward, clearing the distance between us in a single leap, raised his hands and hugged me. For a second, I didn't know what to do and then I carefully hugged him back.

ELIAS SAT ALONE IN HIS MAKESHIFT OFFICE INSIDE ELMWOOD Library. Outside the windows, the street was pitch black except for the floodlights bathing the area around the gate in bright electric lights. His phone told him it was just past ten. He hadn't slept well last night, woke up at five, and then spent the entire day catching up on all the admin crap that had piled up in the past two weeks. There was a chance that the Elmwood gate would be his last. Some people would've shied away from that thought. He was a realist who liked to be prepared. If he didn't come out of the breach, the Guild would pass to Stephanie Nguyen. As Chief Operations Manager, she was third in line after him and Leo. The transition would be as smooth as he could humanly make it.

He was tired. He should've gone to bed as soon as he finished, but he couldn't sleep.

Jackson was due to land after two am, if everything went

well. It would take him awhile to clear customs and get his baggage, so he would be on site by four. Leo hadn't come to bother him with any updates. It probably meant that things were going as expected. Elias thought of finding him to check in but decided against it. The kid was running himself ragged as it was. If another calamity fell on their head, Leo would appear and report to him about it.

Elias sipped the last of his cold coffee. The picture on the tablet in front of him was twenty years old. It was taken at the Chicago Botanical Garden on Thanksgiving holiday. Brenda wore her favorite blue coat. She crouched on the stone steps, a wall of picturesque pines behind her, her arms wrapped around six-year-old Ryan. Ryan's face was scrunched up like he'd bitten a lemon. His son had waged a private war against having his picture taken since birth, and the kid had won most of his battles. Brenda was smiling, her soft brown hair spilling from under her white hat.

He didn't know why he fixated on this particular photo. There were other pictures, some at the beach, some during other holidays, a few pictures from the army balls, he and Brenda dressed up and posing. But he always defaulted to this one.

Back then he had just come back to the States, with his second deployment under his belt, and he was done with the Middle East for a while. He'd also made captain on his first try, and a company command assignment had been in the works. He had no idea where exactly it would be, but he knew it would be stateside. They would ship him off again eventually – he had no doubt of it – but for now he'd earned a couple of years of being home in the evenings, if not every night, then most nights. It was that feeling of knowing that wherever they sent him, Brenda and the boy would be there too. That they'd be a family again.

Brenda had finished her Ph.D. in Pharmaceutical Sciences.

She'd postponed the job search until they knew where they were going, but her degree was in demand, and she hadn't anticipated a problem. She'd stayed in Chicago, close to her parents, through his deployments. They wanted time with Ryan, and she needed support while working on her degree. He thought she would be reluctant to leave Chicago, but when he brought it up, she hugged him with that glowing smile and told him she couldn't wait to escape. He could still recall the relief he felt.

That picture was a moment in time when they had everything in front of them. Years of hard work and sacrifice were starting to pay off. The future looked bright.

Happier times. If he could go back to any point in his life, this would be the one.

Ten years later she was dying. The cancer was aggressive and resisted treatment. They thought they had decades left. They had months.

He took emergency leave and when that ran out, he asked to extend it. It was denied. The command wanted to move him up from XO to his own battalion. He was in line for promotion to lieutenant colonel. His CO called him in and told him that he had to think about the future. As tragic as things were, in six months he would be a widower, but he would still have a son and the rest of his life. He had a solid track record. He could go very far if he made the right choices. *Once the funeral is over and your kid graduates and goes to college, what will you do with yourself? Make a smart decision.*

Elias had resigned his commission the next day.

Two months later, he was in the hospital room, exhausted and bleary-eyed, watching Brenda breathe. They'd cut her open again, trying to remove the tumors. He remembered sixteen-year-old Ryan resting his hand on his shoulder. *"Dad, go home. Take a shower, sleep, maybe eat food. You stink, and you look like crap. I'll stay with mom. I'll call you if anything happens."*

He went home and crashed. When he woke up the next afternoon, the gates had burst, monsters overran the city, and the two people he loved most in the world were dead. Before the gates, he was a husband and a father. He had a wife. He had a son. Ten days later, all that was left were two urns of ash. He had awakened as a Talent the morning after the funeral.

It hurt still. Time didn't make it better. Killing shit didn't make it better. He had only two options: to think about it and hurt or to not think about it and carry on.

And here was Malcolm, who had everything he'd lost. A wife, two children, family…

And a mistress.

And a huge gambling addiction.

And a debt he could never repay.

It made Elias irrationally angry.

He was pissed off at Malcolm for not valuing everything he had, while Elias was sitting here wishing he could rewind time. He was pissed off at himself for missing Malcolm's addiction, for giving London a second shot, and for putting both of them in charge of a team and getting everyone killed. He was pissed off at whoever made the breaches. He was just fucking pissed off.

He saw Leo manifest in the doorway. If he didn't know better, he'd swear that his XO could teleport.

"About that typhoon…" Leo started.

Elias' fist landed on the desk. It cracked and shattered into a thousand pieces. His tablet and phone clattered to the floor.

Jackson stuck his head out, leaning from behind the doorway with a small smile. "I heard you're getting the old band back together. Is this a bad time? I can come back."

Elias swore.

"He put me up to it," Leo said.

"I did." Jackson nodded.

Elias just stared at them.

Jackson raised two mugs in his hands. "I brought you some of that swill you call coffee around here. Why don't you come out of this tiny room and have a drink with me?"

"I'll get the desk replaced," Leo said.

Elias sighed and fished his phone and tablet from the wreckage.

They moved into the lounge outside of the office on the second floor, overlooking the library floor below.

Elias gulped his coffee. It did taste like swill, but at least it wasn't cold. "How did you get here so fast?"

"Called in a favor," Jackson said. "I didn't have a choice about the departing flight. They escorted me all the way to my seat. Got off the plane in Hong Kong, got onto another plane instead of cooling my heels, flew around the storm, and here I am."

Elias quietly exhaled.

The healer sipped his coffee and grimaced. "Foul."

"It's hot."

"Well, there is that," Jackson agreed.

He was a lean man, not just thin, but slight, short, and pale, with thoughtful eyes and light brown hair cropped close to his head. Easy to overlook. Easy to dismiss.

"A fine mess we landed in," Jackson said.

"Yes."

"Leo tells me that the DDC will be releasing the update tomorrow."

"That's right," Elias said.

They were out of time. The DDC could only sit on the fatal event for so long, and Leo's contact warned him that things had changed, and she couldn't keep it quiet any longer. A press release would be coming tomorrow. As soon as it hit, Cold Chaos would become the focal point of the country.

It looked bad. An assault team and a mining crew were dead, a week had passed since they were killed, and both the DDC and Cold Chaos had done nothing about it. The media would be all over it. The politicians would hijack it for their own purposes. The rival guilds would accuse Cold Chaos of cowardice and dereliction of duty. Public pressure would be immense.

The law gave the DDC authority to reassign the ownership of the breach if the original guild was unable to close a gate. Tomorrow the country would demand accountability. The DDC would reassign the gate to get the focus off themselves.

The guilds existed in cutthroat competition with each other. It didn't matter how good your track record was; it only mattered how well you closed the latest breach. Cold Chaos couldn't afford to give up Elmwood. If they let another guild recover the bodies because Cold Chaos was too weak to handle it, the DDC would divert the higher difficulty gates to someone else. It would take them years to regain their standing.

Even if that route were possible, Elias didn't want to take it. They lost people inside that damn breach. This was their mess, their responsibility. They owed it to the families.

"We can't lose the gate," Elias said.

"No, we can't," Jackson agreed.

"Our people died in there."

"And we need to bring them home," the healer finished.

"I've got two kids sitting in our HQ. They still think their mother is alive. We must give people answers."

"What do you want to do?"

"The DDC press conferences are always scheduled for ten am," Elias said. "We go in at first light. They can't reassign the breach if we are in it."

Jackson laughed softly.

They would rest tonight. Tomorrow, they would take the breach.

"Do you think you could've cured Brenda if she hadn't died?" Elias asked.

"You asked me that nine years ago, remember?"

He remembered. It was on the day they met. There were eight of them in that original group: Elias, Jackson, Stephanie, Leo, Graham, Simone, Nolan, and Miles. It was the first gate dive for most of them. Leo was barely twenty-two back then, a kid. Stephanie no longer entered the gates; Miles was dead; Nolan took the civil service route and climbed up the ranks in the DDC; Simone became the COO of the Telluric Vanguard; and Graham ran the Guardians. A lot happened in a decade.

Jackson's eyes were kind and mournful. "I'm going to tell you the same thing I told you back then. The past has happened. It cannot be changed. Don't do this to yourself."

Elias drank his coffee. Jackson was watching him with a particular focus.

"Don't do it," Elias warned him.

"Do what?"

"Put me into restorative sleep."

"You look like you need it," Jackson said.

"What I need is to enter that damn breach. I've been sitting on my hands for five days now. What the hell possessed you to go to Japan anyway?"

Jackson smiled. "The trees, Elias. They are good for your soul. Now tell me more about this cave."

THE THREE OF US, JOVO, BEAR, AND I, CROUCHED ON THE LEDGE. Below us the remains of the assault team sprawled on the rocks. We had doubled back to the kill site.

The corpses were still there, untouched. I pointed at the bodies, looked at Jovo, and made a cutting motion. "Knife."

The lees pondered the bodies below.

The first thing Jovo did after we rested was to scale the sheer side of a cliff to a higher ledge to get a better view of the cavern. He'd scrambled a forty-foot wall like it was nothing, which gave me an idea. Jovo needed a weapon, and the only unclaimed weapons in the breach lay there below us. They were out of my reach but maybe not out of his.

The fox took a deep breath, put his marble into his mouth, and leaped off the stone bridge. He bounced off the rock, weightless, bounced again, zigzagging down the wall like a superhero squirrel, and then landed among the bodies.

Wow.

Jovo gagged, coughed, waved his hand in front of his nose, and began rummaging through the corpses. I sat on the stone bridge and watched. Once he armed himself, we would head to the anchor.

Jovo pulled a tactical belt with five pouches on it from a corpse, and wrapped it around himself, over one shoulder, bandolier style.

I could smell the bodies now. The sickening, cloying stench reached all the way up to the bridge.

Jovo picked up a machete, swung it a couple of times, and tossed it over his shoulder. A big ugly knife was next. He waved it around, and over the shoulder it went. It would be almost comically cute if it weren't for the rotting corpses.

Bear stared up ahead, at the darkness beyond.

"What is it?" I whispered.

The shepherd went still, focused on something in the gloom. She didn't woof though.

At the bottom, Jovo raised two small, curved blades. They had six-inch blades shaped like claws and rings in their handles. There was a specific name for that kind of knife… care… kura… karambit. That was it. The style of the knife originated in Southeast Asia.

Those were Ximena's backup blades. She was a pulse carver, a burst damage dealer with enhanced speed who slashed at her opponents. She was like a whirlwind on the battlefield, and now she was dead, decomposing below.

Did we actually have a chance to win a fight with the gress? Or was I deluding myself?

Jovo slid his fingers through the rings in the handle, holding the blades out, and sliced the air in two vicious, lightning-fast strikes.

Okay.

Jovo spun on one foot, danced across the rocky ground, cutting and carving, and leapt into the air spinning like a windmill. The twin blades flashed as he sliced his imaginary opponents in twin X slashes and landed in a crouch.

Holy shit. How the hell had the gress even caught him?

Jovo straightened, looked at the knives, let out a giggle, and bounced from paw to paw, doing a little happy dance.

Bear's black lips trembled. She let out a low, grumbling growl.

"Jovo!"

The lees was still bouncing and waving his knives around.

The darkness at the edge of the chamber shifted.

Bear snarled.

"Jovo!" I waved at him frantically. "Up! Up!"

Jovo glanced at me.

"Dangerous! *Up!*"

Bear broke into barks, snarling.

The shape within the darkness lunged forward.

Jovo leaped at the wall and scrambled up as if he had a ladder. A blink and he was thirty feet up, then fifty.

A creature stalked into the open, its lunge aborted at the last moment. It was definitely feline, but as big as an SUV, with the broad build of a jaguar. Its stocky frame rippled with muscle that shifted and bulged as it walked. Its dense fur was like nothing I had ever seen. Each hair started with a deep ruby, then darkened toward the end into tar black. Like a smoke-colored cat, except that smoke cats of our world went white to black and their coloring was solid, while this creature's pelt shifted as it walked, the multicolored fur forming rosettes and stripes that vanished with the next step. Its paws were enormous, as big as my head, and they had too many toes.

Jovo shot up the wall, conquered the last dozen feet, and landed on the bridge next to me.

The beast below tilted its huge head and stared at us, its eyes a malevolent, terrible green.

I put my hand on Bear's back. The shepherd clicked her mouth closed and glared at the monster.

This thing did not belong in the breach. Every animal that was a native part of this ecosystem – the stalkers, the goats, the bugs - was grey, blue, or purple with fluorescence or a flash of contrasting color here and there. The only exception was the red Grasping Hand, but that was a stationary invertebrate. It didn't hunt or roam.

This cat didn't fit the color scheme and that fur said it was a forest predator. It was as alien to the caves as Jovo and I.

There was a frightening intelligence in those eyes. It reminded me of Bear, the new upgraded version. When I looked into my dog's eyes, something more than a typical canine intelligence looked back. This creature was like that: smart and cunning.

The giant cat took a step back, turned soundlessly, and vanished back into the gloom.

Now I knew why the corpses hadn't been eaten.

"Skelzhar," Jovo hissed.

I pointed at him. "Jovo…"

The fox shook his head and touched his chest. "Lees." He pointed at the beast. "Skelzhar."

Species name.

He pulled his marble out and squeezed it. Five gress walking out of the darkness, two skelzhars flanking them like hounds. When I compared it to Bear, I had no idea how right I was.

"Dan-je-rous," Jovo said carefully.

The gress by itself was bad enough. This took it to another level.

I stood up. "Let's get moving."

[11]

The stench of decomposition started as a faint whiff of cloying odor. It drifted from the warren of passages and tunnels. The farther we walked, the stronger it became.

Jovo waved his hand in front of his nose.

I nodded. It stank.

We kept moving. This part of the breach resembled the inside of a sponge: short roundish chambers connected by a myriad of shorter tunnels, endlessly intersecting. My senses told me we were getting closer and closer to the anchor. It had to be less than a mile away.

This area should have been filled with monsters. The closer to the anchor, the higher the density of creatures. That was a hard and fast rule that had been proven over and over again in the last ten years. This distribution was exactly why the miners stuck to the sites in close proximity to the gates.

The Sponge was deserted. And the stench kept getting thicker.

Nothing in this breach went the way it was supposed to. I wanted answers.

Another hundred yards.

The odor was almost unbearable now.

Our tunnel turned and opened. An enormous cavern unrolled in front of us, its ceiling three hundred feet high and studded with glowing crystals. A narrow river wound its way through the cavern's floor.

Monster corpses littered the ground.

Huge, spiked, armored, grotesque, they sprawled along the banks. There had to be hundreds of them. The scale of the slaughter was horrifying. My mind refused to accept it.

This was too much for any being to kill alone. Had a bomb gone off here? But nothing except the monsters was damaged. The walls weren't scorched, there was no crater, and flowers still bloomed along the banks.

Jovo clamped his hand over his nose and pulled on my sleeve. I glanced down at him. He pointed into the cavern.

I looked in the direction he indicated and *flexed*. A complex metal device sat in the center of the cavern, opened almost like a flower with concentric ridges forming petals.

Jovo let go of his nose and opened the fingers of both hands raising his arms. "Boom!"

Someone had deployed a literal weapon of mass destruction, but instead of destruction, it was just death. Mass death on an unprecedented scale.

I concentrated on the bodies. They didn't look native to the breach. Too large, too many of them, and all clearly nasty in a fight. The mechanism of the breaches was becoming a little clearer. Whoever built them took a section of an actual ecosystem, wedged it between our worlds, and then dumped a large number of predators into it. I had no idea how they transported them in or kept them from immediately killing each other, but it was clear that the monsters were plonked here and then expected to spread through the caves. There was probably enough wildlife for them to survive for the next couple of weeks, but by the time the gate burst, they would be ravenous.

It made no sense for whoever built the breach to stuff it with monsters and then nuke them. This felt like the work of a third party. There were the creators of the breach, us, and then there was the alien woman and the gress.

"Gress?" I asked Jovo.

He shrugged. He didn't know.

It had to be the gress. If the alien woman entered the breach and the gress were pursuing her for some reason, clearing the monsters would make that pursuit much easier. The gress must've killed them shortly after the breach was created, if not right away, because the creatures didn't even have a chance to spread.

But why did the woman enter? Was she escaping? Was she supposed to do something here?

I pointed at the cavern and made a walking motion with my fingers. "Dangerous?"

Jovo took an exaggerated sniff and shook his head.

The anchor lay on the other side of the cavern, through one of the passages puncturing the opposite wall. I took a breath, gagged, and started forward.

JOVO SQUEEZED HIS MARBLE. A GATHERING OF LEES APPEARED, most of them white furred and green eyed. "Sai. Phff!"

He had started this halfway into the monster slaughter, probably out of sheer self-preservation against the horror and the stench. Apparently, the lees existed in large family groups, and there were a lot of them. They greatly varied in fur color, markings, and eye color. A lot of the clans must have been wealthy, because the lees wore jewelry and elaborately decorated sashes, aprons, and kilts. There had to be some meaning to the clothes, but I couldn't decipher it. Perhaps it was regional.

The one thing Jovo made absolutely clear was that Clan Kiar

was far superior to all others. We'd left the monster mass grave-yard behind ten minutes ago, and he was still going.

I was still struggling with the odor. It seemed to stick to us, coating our clothes, skin, and hair. I should've gotten used to it by now, but it still bothered me. My hearing and eyesight had gotten better. My olfactory sense probably got an upgrade as well, and right now it felt like a mixed blessing.

Bear sneezed next to me. She hadn't even tried to investigate the bodies. All of that stench must have been hell on her sensitive nose.

Another squeeze of the marble. A new clan, this one with white, grey, and blue fur colors and turquoise and gold eyes.

"Nuan. Blah."

"Blah?"

Jovo squeezed the marble, projecting an image of a plump pillow and made a squishing motion. "Nuan. Phah!"

Clearly, Clan Nuan was soft like a cushion.

I humored him. "Kiar not phah?"

Jovo pulled his knives out and spun through the tunnel in front of us, slashing left and right. "Kiar!"

Bear barked.

"He is exciting, isn't he?"

Bear was the smartest girl ever, because any other dog would've chased him by now.

Jovo paused, posing on one foot.

I nodded solemnly, acknowledging the warrior badassery of Clan Kiar.

Jovo flipped backwards, slicing with his weapons, pirou-etted to the end of the tunnel, and stopped, dropping into a crouch.

Uh oh.

Bear and I closed in. The tunnel opened into a large space, about a hundred and fifty feet wide and seventy-five feet deep. Multiple openings gaped on the sides, probably leading back to the Sponge. Straight ahead a thick wall rose, with a rectangular doorway dead center.

Jovo hissed.

I *flexed* on the doorway. Beyond it lay a large room. I glimpsed an identical doorway at the other end. Between them a short pillar rose from the floor. It was rectangular and cut from a single block of black stone that seemed to swallow the light around it. White glyphs shone on its sides, carved into the cosmic blackness, and then painted over with an even glow. My eyes told me that the pillar was only three and a half feet tall, but in my mind it loomed, an enormous obelisk, a towering monolith brimming with malevolent power.

We had found the anchor.

The vision of the giant anchor filled my brain. The urge to dash across the open space and into that room gripped me. The anchor was an abomination. I had to crush it.

The pillar throbbed, sending pulses of concentrated power through me. I gritted my teeth.

Get out of my head.

Bear licked my hand.

The connection broke. I reeled, suddenly free. That destructive urge hadn't come from the gem. No, that was something born of my humanity.

I petted Bear's head and forced myself to focus. Something hung above the anchor. Something foreign that didn't belong in that room.

I risked another flex and scanned the object. A knapsack, suspended by a familiar metal-plastic cord. I glanced at Jovo. He was laser-locked on it, his body rigid, compressed like a tightly coiled spring.

This was a trap. The Sponge was a labyrinth. Our hunter didn't want to chase us through it. He wanted us in that room. That was where the last fight would be.

There might have been a way to go around the anchor

chamber, but it would take a long time to find it and I didn't want to look for it. I wanted answers. And I wanted this to be over. Every instinct I had assured me that the way to the gate lay through that room.

A faint whisper of a movement made me spin. A dark form appeared behind us, at the entrance of the tunnel. Darkness pulsed and the form fluttered away like a piece of fabric jerked out of sight, leaving a bone barrier dial hanging in its place. The gress had blocked our escape. It was trying to trap us in the tunnel.

I dashed forward, to the opening that led to the anchor room, pulling my stolen dial out of the pack. Jovo tried to rush past me, and I shoved him back, thrust the dial where the passageway met the wider chamber, and activated it. My barrier pulsed with darkness and settled at the mouth of the tunnel, blocking the exit to the anchor room.

Even if the gress showed up now, he wouldn't be able to place another barrier on top of this one. The forcefield had a twenty-six-foot limit, and it had to reach something solid to activate. Since I blocked the tunnel, the gress' only option would be to set his barrier in the outer chamber, but that space was too wide.

Either the gress wanted to trap us in this small tunnel so he could wait until we ran out of water or food and died, or he wanted to panic us and force us to the anchor. Impulsively charging into the anchor chamber, with Jovo keyed up so high he was practically bouncing off the walls, would be suicide. We needed to be calm and calculating if we had any chance of winning. My barrier bought us temporary safety and time.

Jovo thrust himself in front of me, his face furious, and stabbed his finger at the anchor.

"I know," I told him. "We will go."

He pointed at the anchor again. I pointed at him and waved

my arms frantically, then moved my hands down slowly, spreading them. "Calm down."

Jovo trembled.

"It's a trap." I clamped my hands together, imitating a bear trap closing.

Jovo bounced up and down, slashing with his knives.

"Kiar Jovo!" I went straight to mom voice. "Calm down."

He blinked, stunned for a second, spun around, and started pacing from one side of the tunnel to the other. Score one for the universal parent voice.

I sat down on the stone floor. The anchor chamber was right in front of me with the dial hanging there in the empty air like some bone spider. The gress was nowhere to be seen. He was biding his time. Sooner or later, we would have to leave the tunnel.

If I ever hoped to see my children again, I had to be smart. I had to find out as much about the gress as I could.

"Jovo."

The lees turned to me, his eyes hot.

"Gress." I imitated him squeezing the marble.

Jovo pulled the marble out, put it in front of me, and squeezed it. The image of the gress pair spilled out. I focused on it and tried to relax.

I was never successful with meditation. As soon as I closed my eyes and let my mind off its leash, my thoughts ran in all directions, floating from one topic to another. I would start with something mundane like Noah needing a new pair of glasses, and move on to the car needing gas, then the oil change, then the calendar, then the upcoming meetings, and so it usually devolved into a mess that left me more stressed than when I started it.

This time had to be different. I sensed the power hidden deep inside me. So far it showed me flashes of visions, little fragments, and hints, but it contained so much more. I hadn't even scratched the surface. It knew about the gress. I felt it when it showed me how to open the dial. I had to convince it to let me in. There had to be something there, some information about their weakness. Something that we could use.

Jovo lowered himself onto the floor to the left of me. He leaned forward and placed his hands in front of him, like a cat sitting. The lees took a deep breath and closed his eyes.

Bear padded over and lowered herself, curling around me, her big body bracing mine.

I closed my eyes and *flexed*. This time I wasn't focused on anything. I wasn't measuring distance or trying to determine the properties of an object. I simply entered the state of flexing. My talent splayed out of me like the flames of a bonfire. I let it flail.

My time was almost never my own. I loved my children with all my heart, but they made constant demands on me. They required attention, especially when they wanted to be ignored. Work generated cycles of mind-numbing reports, physical fitness tests, and short, intense bursts of pressure when entering the breaches. The carousel of household bills went round and round, from the expected utilities to the inconvenient emergencies of broken appliances and annual repairs. Everything had to be done. Everything had to be taken care of. My life was so busy, at times it felt like I dissolved into it. I was getting older and older, time was flying by, and I was powerless to stop it. Millions of moments and all of them taken.

But now my life was empty. There were no children in this breach, no tasks, no bills. There were no stalkers, dragons, or gress in this tunnel. There was only my dog, the alien creature I rescued, and me. My body. My senses. My thoughts. This moment was mine. I owned it.

Slowly, carefully, the invisible glow of my talent subsided, until it radiated from within me like soft heat from a low fire. My power stabilized and I let myself sink into it.

THE AIR WAS HOT AND SMELLED OF SOOT.

I stood on an alien planet. Above me a blue sky stretched, but unlike Earth's crystalline blue, this color was a moody, subdued shade, hazy, almost smoky. The sky in perpetual twilight.

The ground was dark stone, triangular hills rising up, ridged with spires of jagged rock. Between the hills, lava flowed in dense currents, a river of it, miles wide, its surface cooled to a grey and purple crust. Here and there, the currents collided, and brilliant red shone in the cracks.

Farther off, at the foot of a hill on the left, where the ground came in contact with the superheated flow, flames rose in a curtain, licking at the hill that had become an island. The fire burned, reflecting in the long stratus clouds and turning them orange and red. Two massive moons hung above it all, translucent grey ghosts sprinkled with glitter.

I'd travelled to someone else's reality. I was still me. When I looked at myself, I saw my hands and my coveralls. But these were not my memories. Fear squirmed down my back. What if I were trapped here?

A faint presence slipped across my consciousness. It touched me and I recognized it. The alien woman who called me her daughter. The ghost of her memories enveloped me, welcoming and warm, the way my biological mother never was. My breach mother embraced me.

It would be alright. I was safe. This world of living memory wouldn't hurt me, because I wasn't an intruder. I belonged. I had a right to be here. This was a legacy gifted to me by my mother, and her mother before her, on and on, stretching into the distant past. It felt at once strange and yet fitting, as if I was a lake at the end of a long river. I was *sadrin*.

The ghost of my new mother whispered something soothing

and reassuring. Strange energy pulsed from her, suffusing me. For a moment the world went white, and then my vision returned, and she was gone.

The transfer was complete. The gem, and everything within it, was now truly mine. I took a deep breath. She had been so kind, my new mother. If only we'd had more time.

I started walking. One step, two... Too slow. I moved the world, spinning it toward me, covering dozens of feet with a single step, then hundreds. I walked and walked, tireless, over the ridges of rock and soil that smelled of tar until I climbed the hill in front of me.

A taller hill waited behind the first. A cluster of six dark towers thrust out of its apex. They were glossy and black, like crystal points of obsidian that had grown ninety feet tall. Time and the elements had eroded their surface, leaving it pock-marked where age gnawed on the stone. No windows inter-rupted the solid walls.

I walked to the tallest tower. Rock flowed like water, allowing me to pass, and I entered. The inside of the tower lay hollow. I was on the bottom floor, on a narrow ledge guarded by a stone rail. The black walls, solid from the outside, turned nearly transparent from within, tinting the sky and the burning flow of lava but not obscuring them. Above me, stone balconies ringed the perimeter, six levels. The bottom three were filled with male gress in dark robes; the top three held female gress with veils of chainmail, clothed in garments made from many layers of diaphanous black cloth.

Below my ledge, lava boiled in a round pit. A narrow stone path protruded above it to a round platform fifteen feet wide carved from a glossy black crystal. It looked like volcanic glass, and yet it wasn't, because lava would have melted it into noth-ing. In the center of a platform, a rectangular table stood.

The body of a female gress lay on the table. She wore the same garments as the watchers on the upper levels, and a chainmail veil hid the lower half of her face. I moved along the ledge to take a closer look. The skin around her closed eyes was lined and wrinkled like old leather. The life within her barely shivered. She was taking her final breaths.

A tall male gress strode to the dais, walking above the churning lava. A priest of his people. He reached the body and thrust his four arms up, metal bracelets sliding down his narrow limbs with a gentle chime. A long wail erupted from him, solemn like a hymn. He reached down and sliced across the garments, exposing her torso. A metal amulet lay on her chest, a dark ring with five moons etched on it.

The female gress exhaled, and the last of her life rejoined the cosmos.

The priest reached for her amulet, touched it, and uttered a sibilant word. The amulet turned red, then yellow. The body of the gress began to disintegrate around it, her skin turning black.

The temple was completely silent. The mourners stood still.

The amulet blazed with white. The clothes of the deceased caught fire. For a breath she shone like she was woven from living flame and then the fire went out, leaving behind a corpse of ash. The priest touched it, and the incinerated body fell apart, raining down into the lava.

Another priest approached, carrying a naked gress baby. The child mewed like a kitten, waving its six limbs. The priests placed it on the table and raised their arms. A spark burst above them and coalesced into an amulet on a thin chain. The first priest reached for it and gently placed it around the baby's neck.

A commotion broke out behind me. A male gress entered the tower. The two priests hissed in unison and three male gress responded, barring the intruder's path. The newcomer shoved at them, trying to force his way in. One of the defending gress slashed at the invader. The dark garment of the intruder fell open, revealing his bare chest with no amulet.

The entire gathering hissed. The sound was so loud, it drowned everything.

The lead priest waved his arm, and everyone fell silent. The priest opened his mouth, showing jagged teeth. Alien sounds flowed and turned into words.

"There is no place for you here, soulless."

The invader dashed out of the tower.

This knowledge was important, but it wasn't enough. It related to the gress as a whole, but my opponent was a Kael. I needed more.

I moved my hand, bending the vision to my will. The temple vanished. I scrolled through the world, looking for the right combination of data. Mountains and valleys rolled around me, the sky darker, then lighter, the moons rising and falling…

There it was. I stopped the memory carousel. A fortress rose in front of me, carved from a mountain side. I took a step forward, conquering miles in a single movement, and landed on its wall.

I watched the gress train within the fort. I walked between them. I listened to them talk. I saw them spar, then learn to kill. I was there when they passed their trials and became Kael. I witnessed them don the devourer shrouds that took root within their bodies. I saw them suffer and inflict that suffering tenfold on others as efficiency mutated into cruelty.

I watched them take their first contracts and step into the cosmos.

I watched them hunt down their prey.

I watched them kill my mother.

[12]

I opened my eyes. Nothing had changed in the tunnel. Bear still napped curled up around me. Jovo's eyes were closed. I didn't know how much time had passed, but I wasn't overly thirsty, so it couldn't have been more than a couple of hours.

I spent years in the gress world. I watched a generation of their young train, grow, achieve their rank, and be unleashed. I knew how they fought. I knew how they thought. I had accessed a layered memory, not just the recollection of a single being, but a collected amalgam of experiences, so complex that they blended into a simulation created in my mind.

I had accepted my inheritance. It didn't sit quite right. And I instinctually knew why: walking through the memories of others was a skill, and I was less than a novice. If it wasn't for the overwhelming need to get back home, I could've gotten lost in the gress' world. The desperation had anchored me. Next time I would have to be much more careful.

And there would be a next time, just not any time soon. The gem had gone dormant. I'd drained whatever psychic battery powered it to nothing. The knowledge wasn't gone. It was still there, deep within me, beginning to rebuild its reserves. The gem required time to recharge – I had no idea how much – and until it replenished itself, I was on my own, without visions and without helpful hints. That was fine. I found what I was looking for.

The Kael'gress were assassins, killers for hire, who spilled into the galaxy by the tens of thousands, taking contracts from the highest bidder. To their planet, they were a lifeline that assured supplies and survival. To everyone else, they were a blight, motivated by greed and reveling in sadistic cruelty. They weren't born cruel. They were conditioned into it, and what happened to Jovo told me that the gress waiting for us to enter the anchor room was no exception.

That desire to inflict suffering was a weakness, and I would use it. I needed answers. If I succeeded, I would get them today. If I failed, I would never leave this breach.

Everything I went through until now was training. This would be the real test. Only one question remained: could I hold out long enough?

I rolled to my feet and stretched, working out the stiffness in my legs and back. Jovo uncoiled and bounced to his feet. His eyes were calm and cold.

I pulled out the spider rope, folded it in half, and twisted the middle into a slip knot. I tested the loop on my arm. When I tugged on the rope, my makeshift lasso tightened around my wrist. I loosened the loop again and wrapped the rope around my left arm, holding the end in my hand.

"Ready?"

He nodded.

I reached for the dial and deactivated it. The barrier vanished. I waited for a moment. The gress could ambush us now, but he would not. The tunnel was narrow, and their bodies were fragile. He would wait until we entered the anchor chamber, where he would have plenty of room to maneuver. Attack and avoid, bleed the opponent and bide your time, wear them down and then strike the final blow, that was the Kael way.

The space beyond the tunnel lay empty. The way to the chamber was open.

I dropped the dial into my backpack, and we started forward.

The gress was watching us. I felt his gaze latch onto me. He was out there somewhere.

We passed through the massive stone doorway. Bright lights came on, flooding the big room in harsh artificial sunshine. The anchor chamber was a perfect square, sixty-eight yards across. The floor, the walls, and the ceiling were identical, built with huge slabs of yellow stone, weathered and rough. Large clusters of pale crystals shone between the ceiling tiles, leaving no shadows in which to hide. The floor was bare, except for the dark pillar of the anchor jutting from the center of the room.

Jovo ran ahead, unhurried, his movements loose and free of tension. He leaped into the air and sliced the knapsack free of the cord securing it to the ceiling. The lees pulled the bundle apart. Things tumbled out, coins, hooped earrings, a sash… He sneered and tossed it all aside. Whatever he needed to get home wasn't there.

The sound of stone sliding made me turn. The gress entered

through the same doorway we'd used, all but gliding across the stone floor. At the other side of the room, the skelzhar padded in through the other doorway, huge and menacing. Behind them, stone slabs descended, blocking the exits.

The trap was sprung. And it was a good one.

The gress studied me. He was seven feet tall and clad in the devourer shroud, a grey, seemingly tattered garment that shifted and moved around him. Neither plant nor animal, it fed on the fluids of his body. In return, it stung anything it touched, applying a powerful paralytic agent and then sucking its prey dry.

The gress were a lean species with six limbs: two that served as legs, and four that were its arms, each pair with its own set of shoulders situated one under the other. They had evolved to climb their rocky world, and their distant relatives still scurried through the stone burrows on all six legs. The gress were terrible at stabbing but amazing at slicing, and the four blades held in the assassin's hands reflected that. Narrow and curved, they were sickles rather than swords.

The gress stared at me, his eyes perfectly round, with huge dark pupils ringed with narrow purple irises. The shroud left a narrow strip of his flesh bare around the eyes and the lizard-like nose. Skin the color of mustard mixed with a pearlescent powder sagged off his cheek bones, the shroud having leeched all spare fat from his body. He was a skeletal killing machine, a lethal whirlwind of striking blades, and he was about to show me how fast he could cut.

Jovo let out a short, sharp yelp saturated with fury and outrage. His fur stood on end, and for a moment, he'd puffed up to nearly twice his size. I glanced to my right. He was looking at the skelzhar. A strange metal bracelet dangled from the beast's collar.

The gress had used Jovo's treasure to decorate his pet. The insult.

The big cat opened its mouth and coughed. It was almost a chuckle.

Beside me, Bear growled. It didn't sound like any growl an Earth dog should have made.

I slipped my backpack off my shoulder. I'd taught Bear four commands, but Cold Chaos taught her others. It was time to put that training to use.

I pointed at the cat. "Fass!"

Bear exploded into a charge as if shot from a cannon. I spun away, shaping my sword into a long narrow blade, a double-edged katana that could thrust or slice. And then the gress was on me.

I *flexed*, stretching time. It bought me a split second, just long enough to recognize the pattern of his attack. I dashed away, running backward, my sword in front of me. The sickles carved at me, and I batted them aside, blocking just enough to keep them off me. The metal rang as his blades struck my sword.

He was fast, so maddeningly fast. If one slice of those sickles landed, it would carve through my arm all the way to the bone.

Strike-strike-strike.

I stabbed through a narrow opening between his slashes. The gress withdrew as if pulled back by a rope, widening the gap between us to twenty-five feet, and charged in again.

Strike-strike-strike.

My arm ached from the impacts. A blade slid too close, almost shaving the skin off my forearm. I leaped back, putting all of my new strength into the jump. I cleared twenty feet. It bought me a second, and I ran backward, right past the skelzhar. I glimpsed Bear and Jovo lunging at the huge cat. Jovo leaped in the air, his blades slicing. The skelzhar snapped at him, its conical fangs like the teeth of a bear trap. Somehow it missed, and Bear darted in and locked her jaws on the cat's hind leg.

The gress was on me again, his sickles flashing. I kept running back, around the chamber, blocking as I moved. It was taking all of my speed to keep up. He was relentless. Unstoppable, untiring. He could do this all day.

I could feel myself slowing down. He was a trained killer who spent years honing his skills, and a week ago I had to ask Google how to best debone a chicken.

The gress knew it. His strikes gained a vicious rhythm. He slowed, then sped up, toying with me, making openings that were traps. Sweat drenched my face. Kael'gress were a cruel breed, conditioned to humiliate their opponents. Their lives were devoid of joy, so they became sadistic, getting off on inflicting pain. And I was such a tempting torture target. I escaped the original fight. I led him on a chase through the tunnels. I released Jovo. And now I was proving difficult to kill.

He couldn't wait to slice me to pieces. He would revel in every moment of my agony.

I stumbled. A curved blade caught the edge of my clothes, its tip drawing a scalding line across my ribs. I shied away, running. Heat wet my skin under my coveralls. The wound was shallow, but it bled as if I was cut with a razor.

Across the room, the skelzhar pinned Jovo down with a huge paw. Bear leaped up and bit into the cat's ear. The skelzhar howled and shook itself, trying to fling her away, but she hung on like a pit bull.

I kept running, veering left and right. The gress drew even with me. There were ten feet between us, and he was looking right at me, his purple eyes filled with glee.

I stumbled again and stopped to catch myself.

The gress loomed in front of me, so fast his movement was a blur. He leaped, spinning, his four arms rotating like the blades of a fan.

I *flexed* and saw him fly toward me in slow motion. He had decided I was done. This was the Kael finishing move, brutal and impossible to counter. He knew he would hit me, and his sickles would carve me apart.

Finally.

I shied to the right, putting all of the reserves I was saving into my speed. He hurtled past me and in the instant his feet touched the ground, his back was to me.

I sliced, shaving a wide section of the shroud off his back. It fell to the ground, a writhing, grey mat. The gress' exposed back gaped in front of me.

The devourer shroud wasn't a garment; it was a symbiotic second skin, bound to the gress by a myriad of nerves. If I had stabbed through it, it would barely react, but I didn't pierce it. I cut it off. The moment my blade peeled a chunk of it off of him, every neuron of the shroud screamed in agony, dumping all of that pain into its host.

The gress shrieked as the excruciating pain twisted his limbs and dropped him to his knees.

I yanked the spider lasso off my arm and looped it around his neck.

He lunged away from me. The gress were fast. They were not strong. The spider rope snapped taut, and I jerked him back and onto my blade. My sword carved through his innards.

The gress tore himself off my blade, the ragged edges of the shroud reaching for me and falling short. He tried to spin around, his sickles lashing out, but I pulled him back, stabbing into his exposed flesh again and again and again.

The gress convulsed. I sliced the top right forearm off his body. Then the top left. The other two arms followed. I jerked him off his feet and dragged him across the floor to the pillar. It took me two seconds to tie him to the anchor.

I straightened. In the corner the skelzhar was snarling, bleeding from a dozen wounds, trying to stay upright on three legs. Its right hind paw hung useless. Its left eye was gone.

Huge angry gashes marked Bear's back. She didn't seem to mind, chewing on the other hind leg, while Jovo clung to the skelzhar's back, sinking his knives into the fur.

I dropped by the gress, sliced the shroud on his chest, and ripped the metal amulet free. He wailed, his voice weak and fading. He thought I held his soul in my hand.

"I'll be right back," I told him in his language. "Don't go anywhere."

IT TOOK LESS THAN A MINUTE FOR THE SKELZHAR TO DIE. I disengaged once the cat collapsed, but Jovo was still stabbing it, drenched in blood and lost to a frenzy.

I made my way back to the gress and crouched by him, holding the amulet by the chain. The small metal disk rotated, suspended from my fingers. The gress' eyes locked on it. His breathing was labored. The stumps of his arms weren't bleeding. The shroud was devouring him from within, trying to repair itself, and it was draining his blood.

The Kael Order believed that during the final rite of their training their god sent a holy demon warrior to inhabit their bodies. The demon raged, and the best way to honor and satisfy it was to deliver pain and suffering. It was a very convenient construct that absolved the Kael'gress of all moral responsibility for their actions.

The ruling elite had to maintain control, and that's where the amulets came in. According to their doctrine, the little metal circles literally contained their souls, safeguarding them from harm, and in case of the Kael, the holy fire of the demon warrior's aura. A gress who lost the amulet was but "a bag of meat," and their soul would never be reborn, remaining bound to the amulet for eternity.

I let the amulet dangle.

"Where is your witness?"

He didn't answer. He was still focused on the amulet.

"Bring your witness to me or die soulless."

His gaze shifted to my face. He squeezed out a single word.

A small metal sphere descended from the ceiling and hung in front of me. I sliced through it with my blade. It fell apart, spilling its electronic guts onto the stone floor. The gress recorded their kills, both to prove they completed their contracts and to boast.

I looked back at the gress. "Who hired you?"

He took a deep breath. "Rakalan."

No reaction from the power within me. The gem was still dormant. "Did the Rakalan make this breach?"

"Rakalan do not invade. They are the invaded."

"Who does the invading?"

"Tsuun."

"How many worlds did the Tsuun invade?"

"More than six of greater of six."

Greater of six in their counting system was six squared, so thirty-six. Six of thirty-six was two hundred and sixteen. So many...

"Why do the Tsuun invade? What do they want?"

He blinked slowly. "Power. Resources. Territory."

He was fading fast. I had to get to the important questions.

"What were the terms of your contract?"

"Find *sadrin*. Bring her back. Kill her if you fail."

"Is that why you hunt me?"

"Yes." His voice was a soft sibilant whisper. "You are *sadrin*. I must take you back."

"How do you know I am *sadrin*?"

His breath was a soft rasp. "I feel it..."

That wasn't good. If he felt it, did that mean anybody could feel it?

"Was the previous *sadrin* a Tsuun?"

"She was Rakalan."

"Her own people hired you to kill her?"

"Yes."

"Why?"

"Rakalan submitted. She did not. Rakalan resisted for greater of greater six of their rotations. Their *sadrin* held much knowledge. She was of value to Tsuun. Rakalan failed to deliver her. They feared destruction."

The Tsuun had invaded the Rakalan world, and the Rakalans fought them off for one thousand two hundred and ninety-six years. In the end, the Tsuun won the interdimensional war, and the Rakalan surrendered. Turning over their *sadrin* must've been a condition of that surrender.

A death rattle clamped the gress. He reached for the amulet with a handless arm.

"How did you come to be here?"

"*Sadrin* fled. We pursued."

"What makes *sadrin* valuable?"

"Knowledge. Knowledge accumulated, knowledge passed from parent to chosen offspring, again and again."

"Why didn't the Rakalan order you to bring the knowledge back?" They could've just carved that stone out of my mother's head.

"Cannot be taken. Only gifted. If not gifted, knowledge dies with *sadrin*."

I always wondered why the last Kael'gress had switched targets back in the cave. He was fighting my *sadrin* mother, and then he abruptly tried to kill me. It was because he knew he would lose the fight, and I was the only other creature in the cave capable of becoming a sadrin. Bear wasn't sapient enough.

The gress trembled.

"What does it mean to be sadrin?" I asked.

His voice was barely audible. His eyes were desperate. "Everything."

I placed the amulet on his chest.

"You can let go now. I will make sure the shroud of the holy power cleanses your passing."

Relief shone in his eyes. He took one last shuddering breath and went still.

I *flexed*. The gress no longer glowed red. In the moment I had scanned him on that stone bridge, I wanted to go home, and I wanted answers. My talent tagged him as key to either one or possibly both. Now the way home was clear. I had my answers, too, but they just led to more questions.

Somewhere out there a civilization named Tsuun waged interdimensional war. They invaded world after world. They probably had it down to routine now. Earth was just the latest of their targets. Some worlds must've been conquered immediately. Others, like the Rakalan, fought back for centuries.

When I sank into the gem, looking for the information on the gress, moving through their world didn't feel like accessing a specific memory of a single being. It felt like a compilation of memories from different individuals, woven into a semi-cohesive whole. Like an encyclopedia article come to life, a summary of collected information from many sources presented in a concise format.

The assassin said that the Rakalan resisted for almost thirteen hundred years, which was why my mother was "of value." This and the memories in the gem suggested that my mother wasn't the original *sadrin*. She inherited her knowledge just like I inherited mine. If my guess was right, each *sadrin* added to the gem and passed that gift to the next, on and on, through generations. The longer their world resisted, the more knowledge the gem accumulated, and the more value it had.

When the Rakalan surrendered, my mother must've fled into a Tsuun breach linked to Earth. I had no idea how she ended up here, but she did, and the gress chased her into it. It had to be more than just an attempt to escape. What I saw of the gress was just a tiny sample of the information hidden in the gem. My mother had access to so much, she could've gone anywhere, and yet she decided to enter this breach. She didn't just choose me, she chose humanity. My mother picked Earth and gave us this priceless gift. Her world's war against the invaders was done, but ours was just beginning.

She let herself die. Had she kept the gem, she would've survived, I was sure of it. She didn't want to continue. The invasion of the Rakalan began with a breach, and my mother had chosen to die in one, closing the whole tragic saga full circle. She passed, betrayed by her people and never knowing if I and the knowledge she gifted me would survive.

I felt strangely hollow.

The gress didn't say *"sadrin."* He said *"their sadrin."* That meant other worlds had them as well. Was that something that occurred naturally or just in response to the invasion? Whatever the answer was, the Tsuun wanted *sadrins.* Perhaps they had a way to harvest our knowledge.

The Rakalan resisted for almost thirteen centuries. Thirteen hundred years of war. The enormity of it slammed into me. I sat down on the ground by the gress's body. My legs refused to hold my weight.

How many gates was that? How many deaths? Generations and generations, born with the war already burning and dying while it still raged. Thirteen *hundred* years. We've been fighting for only ten, and it already completely changed our lives. Over a thousand years of this?

And in the end, the Rakalan still lost and gave up their *sadrin.* If the Tsuun found out I existed and carried all of that generational knowledge in my head, they could pressure the Earth to turn me over.

Would my planet give me up? Was there even a point to going on?

Something nudged me. Bear brought me a bloody feline

222

femur with shreds of flesh on it. The claw marks on her back weren't bleeding anymore.

I *flexed* on autopilot. Well, the meat wasn't poisonous, and she had already eaten some of it, so it was probably too late to make a fuss about it.

Bear nudged me again.

"Hey, Bear."

She dropped the femur at my feet. I crouched. I'd read somewhere that dogs didn't like being hugged. I had hugged her before because I was too far gone, but I was calm now, so I leaned against her, stroking her side. She leaned back against me and licked my cheek.

The flat, empty feeling inside me faded.

I felt more like myself.

There were so many fucking questions I didn't have the answers to. What happened to the worlds after the Tsuun won? They could be destroyed, occupied, vassalized... Did anyone ever win against the Tsuun?

The answers to all those questions were likely in my head and out of reach for now. The most pressing question was, what do I do now? How do I fix this mess?

Staggering out of the gate and announcing to the world that I was *sadrin* was out of the question. I had no intention of becoming a bargaining chip. Nor would I let the government collect me like a weird specimen or turn me into a weapon by keeping my kids hostage. If they understood what I was, I would face the choice of being eliminated, confined, or controlled for the rest of my life. Not going to happen.

My priorities were the same: get out of the breach alive and return to my children. But now there was one final part to that awesome plan. Once I managed to escape, I would end this invasion.

There would be no thirteen centuries of conflict. My children deserved a safe future. I deserved it.

The Tsuun wanted my mother because she was a threat. I would use her legacy. I had to get out and study the gem. I needed to learn what it contained, how to access it quickly, and where to find the information I required. I needed to know what we faced. I needed to learn the limits of my new body. All of this meant I would need to hide until I accomplished that.

Bear and I had been stuck in this breach for at least a week. Whoever had the rights to this breach – whether it was still Cold Chaos or some other guild – would be sending a new team in. For all I knew, they were already inside. That team would attempt to blast through the passageway London collapsed, because they would want to recover the corpses and the incredibly valuable adamantite.

London's face flashed before me. Soon. We would meet very soon.

When the second assault team entered that cave, they would find the corpses of four alien humanoids and my mother. I couldn't let that happen. I had to avoid anything that drew attention to the existence of *sadrin*.

If our government already knew about the Tsuun and other sophonts on the other side of the breach and were actively hiding it, they could disappear the entire assault team for just discovering the bodies. Not to mention that the devourer shroud required living hosts. By now it would have fallen into a semi-dormant state from starvation but the moment a human approached one of the gress corpses, the shroud would strike. People would die.

London was pond scum, Melissa was a selfish coward, but the rest of the Cold Chaos members didn't deserve to die or disappear if I could prevent it.

I looked at the anchor. It still loomed large in my mind's vision, an ominous evil thing that had to be destroyed.

I focused. Still solid black, impenetrable to my talent. I didn't know what it was made of or how it came to be, but I understood what it did far better now. It was a pushpin. The breach was a notecard. Someone picked it up from its place on a desk and used a pushpin to stick it to a corkboard. Once the pushpin disappeared, the note card would fall back to its place on the desk. The caves, the spider herders, the lake dragons, they probably wouldn't even notice the shift as their little slice of biosphere returned to its rightful spot in the world that had spawned it.

If I shattered the anchor, the gate would collapse in three days, as the breach ran out of energy to stay wedged between dimensions. But it wouldn't solve the problem of the bodies, because it left enough time to search the mining site. The corpses would still be found.

Besides, everyone would know that I had destroyed the anchor. The anchors didn't just spontaneously collapse on their own. I couldn't stagger out of the breach and have it collapse behind me. My life would be over.

The compulsion burned in me. I had to destroy it.

No. I was my own person. I had other things to do. I had to clean this up. The sooner the better.

I turned to the body of the gress, squeezed the amulet until it clicked, and spoke a single word in an alien language. *"Irhkzurr."*

The amulet on the gress' exposed chest turned red, then orange. The assassin's flesh sizzled. The devourer shroud hissed, trying to crawl away from the heat and failing, trapped by its roots with the alien body.

The amulet grew yellow, then finally a blinding white, and the corpse turned to ash, the grey shroud writhing as it too was incinerated. A moment and the pile of ash collapsed onto the floor.

Jovo stood up on the dead skelzhar's head, his bracelet clutched in his hand. He was splattered with blood and his eyes looked a little wild.

I gave him a little wave.

The lees hopped off the corpse of his enemy, shook himself, flinging blood everywhere, ran over to me, and showed me the bracelet. It was a metal band about two inches wide, that looked to be made of copper. Thin red lines crossed it, carving it into smaller sections.

He grinned at me.

"Home," I said.

"Home!"

He jumped from foot to foot, spinning in place, then turned around, and hugged me. "Ada."

"Jovo."

He took my hand, squeezed it to his chest, and pointed to the exit, toward the gate. "Home."

I nodded. "My home."

Jovo put his paw on his chest and said, pronouncing the words very carefully. "Help." He pointed at me. "Ada. Dan-ge-rous. Help."

He waved his knives around and struck a dramatic pose.

It took me a minute. My nice new friend from a different world, who helped me kill an assassin from an alien planet, was determined to walk me home. Because it wasn't safe. Gentleman Jovo.

I sat on the floor and laughed.

THE TREK FROM THE ANCHOR CHAMBER TO THE GATE WAS SHORT. So short, I nearly cried. Only a few dozen yards on the other side of the anchor chamber the ground sloped downhill into a wide tunnel that led pretty much straight to the gate. I had wandered through the tunnels for days. I must've crossed above this tunnel several times, never finding access to it.

After the first few minutes I started running. Jovo kept up with me and we bounded through the passage, with Bear in the lead. The way was clear. All the monsters were either dead or too scared to get in our way.

We'd crossed the killing site of Malcolm's team. I stopped long enough to pick up some aetherium charges. I didn't look at the bodies.

The assault team had marked their path with white arrows painted on the walls. Following their route was easy.

We'd been running for what felt like an hour, when I saw an orange arrow on the wall. I remembered when Hotchkins drew it. We had reached the turn off to the mining site.

Finding London's cave-in took no time at all. Two aetherium detonations later, we blasted a hole through the rubble. With my new strength, I could've dug through it, but I was in a hurry, and when I *flexed*, my talent conveniently marked the best place for an explosion.

We made it into the mining site. The bodies lay where they fell. Nothing fed on them, nothing touched them. They had been decomposing for a week and some were beginning to bloat. The four gress, however, had shrunk as the shrouds drained the last of their body fluids. I set off the remaining amulets one by one, until the dead gress became ash.

My mother was decomposing too, although much slower than the humans around her. I wrapped her in her robe, carried her into a side tunnel, to one of the dead ends, and placed her on the bottom of a shallow pool while Jovo stood guard. I used the last aetherium charge to collapse the passageway. Cold Chaos had no reason to go this way and with luck, her body would remain undiscovered.

I stood there by her tomb in silence for a long moment.

Thank you for your gift. I promise I won't squander it.

The secret of the breach was hidden. It was time to go home.

Elias turned away from the table filled with his gear. Something was going on outside. He headed to the library's entrance. Outside the window, the sunrise barely began, the street and the gate awash in the early dawn light.

Elias stopped by the tinted window. The gate was on his left. In front of it, Leo stood with his arms crossed. Kovalenko was on Leo's right, lean, dark-haired, holding his bow. The cryo ranger was poised on his toes, the bow casually hanging in his hand. Kovalenko summoned energy projectiles, which his mind shaped into arrows. Contrary to the misleading name of his talent, they didn't encase things in ice. When one of Kovalenko's arrows struck, his target seized up, frozen in their tracks for a couple of moments, as if tased. The bow wasn't strictly necessary, but it helped him aim.

To the right, at the mouth of the street, ten people had disembarked from a personnel carrier, grouping themselves around their leader. Tall and broad-shouldered, he towered over his team, and his bulky tactical armor, reinforced with adamant, only made him look larger. Anton Sokolov, a bastion Talent, a good solid tank with just the right amount of aggression. The woman next to him was older and willowy, her dark blond hair pulled back into a French braid. JoAnne Kersey, otherwise known as the Bloodmist. For some reason, a lot of women awakened as pulse carvers, high-burst damage dealers who used bladed weapons and diced their opponents into pieces in a controlled frenzy. JoAnne was one of the best.

Elias recognized a few other faces. All ten had the same charcoal and white patch on their gear: a dark square showing a shield with two stylized wings spreading from its sides. A faceless human bust rose out of the shield with a sharp corona of triangular rays stabbing outward from its head. It was meant to evoke guardian angels and general badassery, but to him it looked like some winged crash dummy thrust its head through the shield and was now stuck wearing it like a yoke.

The ten people on the street wore it proudly. The Guardian Guild had sent their A team to claim the Elmwood gate.

He didn't hold it against Graham. It wasn't personal. Graham was like a shark: always hungry and looking for something to sink his teeth into.

Krista walked out of the library's depths and stopped next to Elias. A faint red glow traced her long dark fingers, a precursor to an inferno.

"Look at them all dressed up. Bless their hearts."

"Are we ready?" Elias asked.

"We're good."

"London?"

"Geared and armed. If he isn't happy about it, he's keeping it to himself."

"I'll need you to watch him in the breach."

She smiled. "No worries. If he sneezes the wrong way, I'll be on him like a hawk."

On the street Anton shrugged his massive shoulders. "You're standing between me and my gate, Leonard."

"Funny, I thought I was standing between you and our gate."

Anton sighed. "Don't be fucking difficult. We both know the DDC is going to announce the gate change."

"If they reassign it and if the Guardians get that assignment, we'll revisit the issue." Leo's voice was cold and light. "Until then, you are trespassing. This is your only warning: turn around, sashay back to your soccer dad minivan, and get the fuck out of here."

"Your healer is stuck in Hong Kong," Anton boomed. "And the old man isn't here to pull your ass out of the fire."

The old man, huh?

"We know he left for HQ last night."

Elias's eyebrows crept up. Last night he and Leo returned to

HQ. It was late but he wanted to speak to Ada's children one more time before the news broke. Leo came with him for that conversation and then went back to the site in the Cold Chaos vehicle. Elias stayed for another hour, finishing up some last-minute things. He'd taken a ride-share back, had it drop him off several streets away, then ran the last couple of miles to clear his head. It worked – he'd slept well for the first time in a week.

Someone from the Guardians must've been watching the site and noted Leo coming back without him.

"We all know you can't go in," Anton continued. "There are ten of us here and we're ready to enter. Why don't you step aside and let us fix your mess?"

"He did just say that there were ten of them?" Leo asked.

"Yes," Kovalenko confirmed. "He learned to count."

"Did that sound like a threat to you?" Leo wondered.

"It did."

Leo's eyes blazed with white. Two huge dark wings thrust from his back, ethereal as if woven from a thunderstorm. Lightning crackled and danced across the phantom contour feathers.

A pulse of deep green shot from Anton and contracted back into an aura that sheathed the big man like second armor.

"Persistent," Krista said. "What do they know that I don't?"

"There is a big adamantite vein in that breach," Elias said.

"Someone has been talking."

"Mhm."

And he had a very good idea who. The pool of suspects was limited to four. Wagner was too pessimistic, Drishya was too young and inexperienced, and Melissa thought the guild completely had her back, thanks to Leo's gentle style of interrogating. Only one person's future was in doubt. London had taken an opportunity to open another door for himself.

"They aren't normally that aggressive." Krista frowned.

"This is being recorded," Elias said. "They are hoping to provoke us and then splatter it all over the media."

"You are in violation of Article 3 of the Gate Regulation Act." Leo's voice was an eerie, unnaturally loud whisper underscored by the roar of a distant storm. "Retreat or we will be forced to remove you for your safety."

Anton took a step forward. The team behind him fanned out into a battle formation. Anton took another step. A third.

"That's my cue." Elias picked up his coffee mug and stepped out the door.

JoAnne was the first to see him. She put her hand on Anton's arm and when he didn't react, she said something under her breath. Anton stopped walking.

For a moment nobody moved.

Elias sipped his coffee and started forward. Behind him, Jackson came out of the library and leaned on the wall.

Elias reached the middle of the street, took a deeper breath, and let go. Power roared out of him, snapping into an invisible half-sphere. Twenty yards ahead of him a mining cart slid out of the way.

Anton glanced at the cart and back at Elias.

Elias kept walking. His forcefield moved with him. The two heavy trailers just ahead of the Guardian group slid to the sides, gouging the pavement, pushed out of Elias's path.

The rival guild group backed away. Anton remained and pulled a sword off his back. The seventy-five-inch-long blade was solid black. Pure adamant. Nice.

The forward edge of Elias' shield touched the rival tank.

Anton gripped his sword, and the oversized blade burst into purple glow. The big man swung. The sword smashed into the forcefield and bounced off.

Elias kept walking.

Anton took a step back and slashed again. The sword rebounded.

Anton slid backward. Two feet. Three. Four. The tank

reversed his sword and raised it above the pavement, about to stab it into the ground to anchor himself.

"It will break," Leo called out.

"I'd listen to him." Elias said, pausing. "It's a good sword."

Anton stared at them for a long second.

Elias drank his coffee.

The Guardian tank sheathed his sword. Elias dropped the shield. Another moment and it would be tapped out anyway.

The Guardians eyed him, wary.

Elias took the final swallow of his coffee. "Tell Graham that if he feels some way about this, he's welcome to give me a call after I'm done with this gate."

Anton turned his back to him and went back to the van. His team followed.

Elias watched them go, then turned around. "Alright people, I want us in that breach in ten minutes!"

THE GATE LOOMED BEFORE ME, HUGE AND DARK. I TURNED TO Jovo and pointed at it.

"Home."

He grinned.

I opened my arms and hugged him.

He hugged me back and said something in his language. If my gem was awake, I might have understood it, but it was still dormant.

Jovo tinkered with his bracelet. A pale hole formed in the middle of the tunnel, with a fiery rim that spun like a pinwheel, throwing long trails of sparks. I glimpsed a strange city of sand-colored stone poised against a purple sky with a huge, shattered planet hanging above it.

Jovo pointed at the portal. "Baha-char. Kiar sae Baha-char."

I had no idea what a baha-char was.

He grabbed my hands, looking into my eyes, and pronounced the words slowly.

"Baha-char, Ada. Kiar sae Baha-char."

This seemed vitally important. "Kiar sae Baha-char."

He nodded.

"I'll remember," I promised.

Jovo grinned, let go of my hands, bowed to me, and dove into the portal. It snapped closed behind him, vanishing into thin air.

The tunnel lay dark and silent.

I took a deep breath and pulled my phone out of the pocket of my coveralls. I had carried it with me all this time, in a military grade shatterproof and water-tight case. I had turned it off when I entered the breach and hadn't fired it back up even once. Even when turned off, phones still lost charge, and I needed it to power on now. My life literally depended on it.

I pushed the power button.

ELIAS SURVEYED THE NINE-MEMBER ASSAULT TEAM IN FULL BATTLE gear. The best Cold Chaos had to offer. They looked ready. Everyone was rested. The sun was up. It was time.

He turned back to the black hole of the gate. "Alright. Let's do this."

THE ELECTRIC GLOW OF THE PHONE SCREEN LIT UP THE TUNNEL. Only two percent of the charge left, but it was enough. Just enough.

The camera wouldn't work and I couldn't waste any charge on it. I couldn't see myself. I didn't know what I looked like now or if I had enough humanity left in me to exit. My hands shook from the pressure.

I scrolled through my contacts, found the right name, and tugged the sleeve of my coveralls over my sword bracelet. Here is hoping I won't need it.

I was still me. I was Ada Moore. It had to let me out.

There was only one way to find out.

"Come, Bear."

My dog wagged her tail, and we strode into the gate.

I half-expected an impenetrable barrier to stop me, or a flash of pain, but there was none. I sank into the gate, pushing my way through the invisible Jello. The familiar pressure squeezed me. I pushed through it.

The heaviness vanished.

I smelled Earth's air.

The sky spread before me, gorgeous and blue, backlit with the first rays of sunrise, and I had never seen anything more beautiful.

We were out. We were home. I'd been trapped in the damn breach for so long, this didn't feel real. It felt like a wishful dream.

Now I had to stay alive.

In front of me, an assault team was walking to the gate, their gear dyed in Cold Chaos indigo. They saw me and froze, their faces shocked. A large man in the front, enormous in his adamant armor, stared at me as if he'd seen a ghost.

I pushed the contact on my phone and put the call on speaker.

"You have reached the Chicago DDC office," a female voice said into the phone.

"Assessor Adaline Moore," I spoke into the phone. "Personal code 3725. I'm out of the Elmwood gate. I'm alive and uninjured."

The voice on the other end vibrated with urgency. "Do you require immediate assistance?"

"Not at this time."

I hung up. My phone died.

It was done. I had reported in. Cold Chaos couldn't disappear me now.

To the left, behind the large man, a familiar face swung into view, bleached white. London.

I moved forward before I realized I had done it.

He just stood there.

I cleared the distance between us in a single breath. My hand drew back almost on its own.

Control your strength, control your strength, control your strength...

Panic burst in London's eyes. His talent shot out of him, trying to shield him from me, but I was already swinging, and my fist tore right through his blade warden force field like it was a soap bubble.

I hammered a punch to London's jaw.

The blow took him off his feet. He flew backward and landed on his back.

Yes! That felt amazing. I wished I could rewind time so I could punch him again. If only I had that power, I would just sit here and do this all day.

London tried to rise. Bear lunged forward like a bullet and pinned him to the ground. Her fur stood on end. Her mouth gaped, big teeth bare and wet with drool. She snarled like a monster from hell and clamped onto London's right shoulder.

Well, at least it wasn't his neck. That would've been too fast and easy.

London cried out.

"Drop him."

Bear growled, her mouth full of London's arm.

"Not food," I told her. "Just human garbage. Back."

Bear let go, snarled at London in case he didn't get the point, and ran back to me, tail wagging.

London collapsed back onto the pavement. A man dashed to his side, knelt by him, and put his hand on the blade warden's chest. A faint golden glow bathed London.

The big man in armor looked at the healer. The smaller man nodded. I finally recognized the two of them. The one kneeling by London was Merrick Jackson, Cold Chaos' miracle healer. The man in armor who looked like he popped out of some medieval knight film was Elias McFeron. The Guildmaster of Cold Chaos.

Behind London, someone made a strangled noise. I looked up. Melissa was standing by one of the trailers next to a man in mining coveralls. Our gazes met. Fear slapped her face. She shoved the man out of the way, pushing him between us, and took off running.

The site was silent like a tomb. Nobody moved.

Melissa kept running down the street, to the intersection. She turned right and ran out of view.

"Leo," Elias said in a deep voice. "Please inform HQ that Melissa Hollister has turned in her resignation, effective immediately. And call Haze."

"Yes, sir."

The man who answered was in his thirties, handsome, athletic, and his eyes were pure white. The light tactical armor fit him like a glove. I knew him, too. Leonard Martinez, Vice-Guildmaster of Cold Chaos. Cold Chaos had brought their best guns to take on the gate.

Elias McFeron turned to me. He was in his late forties, with short blond hair that was going grey. His face was harsh, with a square jaw and broad angles. He might have been handsome if he'd led a different life, but the breaches must've purged all softness from his soul and his face. Only hard resolve remained. His light blue eyes evaluated me with methodical precision. He saw my face, my expression, my coveralls, Bear at my feet. He missed nothing. Elias McFeron was very dangerous, and he'd decided I was a threat.

I didn't want to kill anyone. I just wanted to go home, but if I had to cut my way through Cold Chaos to get back to my children, I would do it.

He opened his mouth.

I braced myself.

"Assessor Moore, welcome home. Perhaps we could have a word?"

[13]

L eo held the library door open. "Please."

Adaline Moore walked into the library side by side with the dog. If that creature could be called a dog. She strode in and sat in the nearest chair.

Leo followed her.

Jackson approached, his eyes wary.

"London?" Elias asked under his breath.

"Shattered jaw, cracked teeth, torn brachial artery. I put him back together. Krista is watching him. If it wasn't for the shield, he would be dead."

Adaline Moore, a consummate noncombatant, punched through a warden forcefield and hit London so hard, he flew twelve feet. And she had held back. He saw her slow the punch halfway through. Had she hit him with everything she had, London would have stopped being a problem. Permanently.

And if Elias was honest with himself, he wouldn't be shedding any tears over it.

"Did you get a chance to scan her?" Elias asked.

Jackson nodded. "Kid gloves, Elias. Treat her like a nuclear warhead. You want me in for this meeting."

238

"Is she human?"

"She *seems* to be."

Elias held the door open for Jackson and walked in. He was too large for a chair in his gear, so he just leaned against the nearest desk. Leo took up a similar position to his left and Jackson stood to his right. They had formed a U with Adaline in the center. The significance of being flanked wasn't lost on her. She noted it but didn't seem bothered.

Adaline leaned back in the chair. A harsh, familiar stench emanated from her. He'd smelled it on himself hundreds of times – the odor of alien blood and ichor, acrid and tinged with decomp. Layers of brown stains marked her coveralls. Dried blood caked on her scalp. She looked like someone in an assault team's vanguard after a week of hard fighting in the breach.

The dog at her feet was supposed to be a guild K9, a two-year old German Shepherd, according to the files. He'd seen a picture of her, a typical guild GS with big eyes and a happy dog smile, panting. The picture did not match reality.

For one, Bear was too damn large. She had to be over a hundred pounds, and those teeth were longer than any dog's cuspids he had seen. More importantly, she watched him with something other than canine intelligence. He knew their German Shepherds, the guild took them on every gate dive, and he'd interacted with them and gave them treats. This creature was something else.

There was an eerie similarity in the way the woman and the dog were looking at him. He had a feeling that if he said the wrong word or moved the wrong way, both would go for his throat.

Kid gloves. Right.

"Do you require medical assistance?" he asked, keeping his tone casual. "Jackson is our best healer, and he will be happy to assist."

"No."

No emotion, nothing in the eyes. Unreadable and cold.

"Your children are safe and on their way here," Elias said.

She focused on him, and it was like having a blade to his throat, pressing against his carotid. "Why do you have my children?"

The challenge in her eyes was so sharp, he had to force himself to speak instead of simply staring. On his left, Leo tensed. A faint gold shimmer rolled over Jackson's hands.

"You spent a week in the breach. Since you were presumed dead, we brought them to Cold Chaos HQ. They are under the care of Felicia Terrell. She doesn't work for Cold Chaos. She is representing them directly. The DDC doesn't have the best track record when it comes to taking care of survivors, and the political infighting between the guilds is vicious."

"We felt it would be best to shield them from media scrutiny and from being used to influence public sentiment," Leo said.

"We have the cat as well," Elias added. "The children insisted on bringing Mellow with them. Although from my interactions with him, I believe the name to be a misnomer."

The pressure in her eyes eased a little.

"We are not enemies, Ms. Moore," Elias said. "We mean you no harm. We just want to know if London was honest in his report. He stated there were no survivors."

"He lied." Her voice was ice-cold.

"Are there other survivors?" Elias probed.

She shook her head. "Just me and Bear."

The monster dog twitched her ear.

"Could you walk us through what happened?" Elias asked.

She studied him. This woman didn't trust him at all.

"London stated that there were humanoid hostiles. We need specifics and confirmation," Leo said.

She ignored Leo. She was looking straight at Elias instead. Their gazes met.

"Did you know? That he was a coward?"

He could've lied but he didn't want to. "Yes."

"And you put him in charge of the escort anyway."

"The best escort captains are cautious," he said.

"The best escort captains don't look you straight in the eye and throw an aetherium grenade at the people they are supposed to protect."

"Is that what he did?" Elias asked.

"Yes. There were hostiles at the mining site, but we were not their targets. We simply got in their way. Some of us died instantly. The rest of us ran for the exit. He murdered four people with that blast, activated his shield and got the fuck out. When you find the bodies, look at their injuries."

"I will," Jackson said. "I will confirm exactly how they died. My Talent identifies the cause of death. It's never wrong."

She ignored him.

"What about Melissa Hollister?" Leo asked.

"What about her?" Adaline asked.

"What was her role in this?"

"She reacted exactly as you saw. When the slaughter started, she shoved people out of her way and ran for the exit. I believe her last words were, 'Throw it!'"

He almost flinched from the venom in her words. "Thank you."

"For what?"

"For confirming my worst fear and giving me the justification I needed."

"Are you planning to fire him?" She raised her eyebrows.

"For starters."

"You will have to do better than that."

He had this weird feeling that they were the only two people in the room, circling each other, their blades out, looking for an opening.

"How did you survive?" Leo asked.

She didn't answer.

"Where did you get this bag?" Leo asked.

He'd noticed her backpack too. It was made from a fabric he didn't recognize.

"What's in it?" Leo asked.

She finally gave him a flat look. "Don't worry about it."

Leo blinked.

She looked directly at Elias. "Do you keep your promises, McFeron?"

"Yes."

She studied him for a long moment.

"I gave London a second chance," he told her. "The buck stops with me. I made an error in judgement. Two, actually. Everything that happened to you in that breach is the result of my mistakes. I can't bring the dead back to life, but you are not dead. Tell me what I can do for you."

She was still watching him with that disconcerting focus. He finally identified what it reminded him of. He'd met intelligent monsters in the breaches. That was exactly how they looked at him before deciding the best way to strike.

"You could've requested assistance from the DDC," he said. "You didn't. You want something from us."

Adaline tossed one leg over the other. "The DDC knows I'm alive. In about thirty minutes, they will descend on this site to take me into custody under the pretense of medical care. They will expect a full report. This can go one of two ways. I can tell them that Cold Chaos betrayed me, left me to die, and then delayed entering the gate, hoping the creatures of the breach would finish their dirty work. Or I can make you look like heroes, who rescued me against impossible odds."

"What will it cost me?" he asked.

"London must never enter another breach."

"We cannot guarantee that," Leo said.

"What he means is that it's not within our power," Elias explained. "The law shields him from being tried for murder for his conduct within the breach. They leave other punishments to our discretion."

"So what can you do?"

"We can Sontag him," Leo said.

"We can fire him and revoke his combat certification with a Sontag code," Elias explained. "It means that there will be a code by his name in the international Talent database that states that he killed his team members to save himself."

"The code is named after Steven Sontag, the man who murdered his team members and fed their bodies to monsters to buy himself time to escape." Jackson added. "No legitimate guild will hire him after that. Nobody wants to go into the breach with a killer who'll stab you in the back."

"That doesn't mean that he can't get hired by some desperate minor operation," Elias said. "But I can guarantee you that he will never work for any guild above third level."

"And it will follow him to the civilian employment market," Leo said. "Talent standing is factored into the background checks."

Elias could tell she wanted more. He watched her mull it over.

"Good enough," Adaline said.

Practicality won.

"What else?" he asked.

"Bear stays with me."

"No," Leo said.

He knew exactly why Leo wanted the dog. Something happened to Bear in the breach, something that made her what she was now, and his XO was desperate to find out what it was.

Adaline turned toward Leo and stared at him. The dog at her feet rose, looking at Leo as well. It was like they were in sync. She would kill them all to keep this dog. Elias knew it but he wanted to see what she would do.

"That dog is the property of Cold Chaos," Leo said.

Adaline leaned forward. It was a tiny movement.

The fur on Bear's back rose. A terrifying growl rumbled in the shepherd's throat. The dog snarled and erupted into barks, biting the air with huge fangs.

Leo took a step back.

"Back," Adaline said.

The shepherd stopped barking and sat at her feet.

"Does she seem like your dog, Vice-Guildmaster?"

Leo opened his mouth. Elias shook his head.

Adaline turned back to him. "The dog is mine. It's non-negotiable. I cleared the cave-in London caused. The adamantite is marked. The way to the anchor is open, and resistance should be minimal. Give me the dog, and you can be mining all that adamantite in half an hour while I sing your praises to the DDC. Or I will make sure you lose the gate and three days from now you will be testifying before a congressional committee. You might keep the guild, you might not. Your choice."

Elias stared at her. "Are you threatening me?"

"Yes. That's exactly what I'm doing."

"Hmm."

He looked into her eyes and saw steel-hard resolve staring back. She wasn't bluffing. He knew that if he tried to contain her, she and that so-called dog would explode with violence. A part of him wanted to do it just to see how strong she was.

He hadn't felt so alive in years.

"But will Mellow be okay with it?" He couldn't resist baiting her.

"What happens in my family is none of your business, Guildmaster. Do we have a deal?"

"We do," he said. "The guild record will reflect that K9 47 died in the breach with her handler."

Her posture eased slightly.

"We're going to give you everything you want," Elias said.

"As a gesture of goodwill, would you tell us more about what we can expect from this breach?"

"Stay away from the flowers with mauve petals. The pollen goes airborne quickly and will kill you. Stay away from red coral growth. Their thorns secrete poison. It will kill you. Any water source larger than a small pond might have dragons in it. They wait under the surface, ambush you, and will kill you."

What the hell happened to her in that breach?

"Malcolm marked his route in white. Stick to it, don't deviate. You won't encounter resistance."

"Even at the anchor chamber?" he asked. *Did you reach the anchor?*

"Even at the anchor." *Yes I did. Don't worry about it.*

He almost asked her to go back in the breach with him.

"If you see the spider herders, you're going the wrong way. Leave them alone and backtrack…"

What in the world was a spider herder? "Or they will kill us?"

"Not unless you piss them off. They keep to themselves, but I have seen their war spiders, and it will be a hard fight even for you."

The doors of the library opened, and Tia and Noah ran inside.

Adaline spun off her chair, so fast, he barely registered the movement. The hard mask on her face broke. Her eyes shone, and she smiled a beautiful, glowing smile, as she threw her arms around her children.

Twelve hours later

ELIAS STOOD ON A STONE BRIDGE. BELOW HIM THE RECOVERY crew bagged the last of the assault team's bodies and loaded them onto a mining cart.

Adaline's prediction proved correct. Less than an hour after she exited the gate, the DDC arrived and whisked her away. He led the new assault team into the breach five minutes later, right after he'd informed London that he was fired with a Sontag code. Alex Wright didn't even argue. He seemed shellshocked, as if the world had suddenly kicked him in the face.

True to Adaline's word, they encountered no resistance in the breach. The way to the anchor chamber was well marked and deserted. They reached the anchor in three hours.

Considering the chamber's proximity to the gate, he made the decision to shatter the anchor. They had three days before the gate collapsed, more than enough time to remove all of the bodies and mine the rest of the adamantite. The miners were already working, under much heavier guard this time and with all three northern tunnels collapsed to ensure their safety.

While the mining and recovery crew worked, he scoured the area around the anchor. Something had happened to Adaline in this breach, something that turned her from a regular person into a dangerous, calculating... he didn't even know what to call it. Survivor seemed inadequate. Combatant didn't do her justice. He wanted to know what she went through.

They'd found a cavern filled with dead monsters and some sort of weird device. He tried to detach it, and it disintegrated into dust. They found a pile of ash in the anchor chamber and the body of a massive feline-looking monster. He had seen hundreds of creatures in his time in the breaches, but nothing quite like that one. Jackson informed him that it died from being repeatedly stabbed, and that the puncture wounds all over its body came from canine teeth.

He glanced at the darkness at the other end of the bridge. She had come this way. Just her and the dog. Without weapons, without food or water. How did she manage it?

"We found something," Samantha said at his side.

He almost fell off the damn bridge. There were twenty yards between him and the side passage she came from, and he neither heard her nor saw her approach.

The phantom ranger tilted her head to look at his face. "Are you alright?"

"Yes." *Make some damn noise next time.* "What did you find?"

"A doohicky. Leo wants you to see it."

Elias followed her through the tunnels to a narrow side passage. A strange disk hung in the center of it. A dial of some sort made of concentric circles carved from bone or ivory with circles gouged in the rims. Leo stood next to it, pondering the dial.

Elias stopped next to him. "What is this?"

"It's a forcefield," Samantha told him.

Leo raised his hand. A thin tendril of lightning snaked from his fingertips and licked the space around the dial. A wall of light flashed, sealing off the tunnel, and vanished.

"Carver touched it," Leo said. "It zapped him. Stopped his heart."

"Is he okay?" Elias asked.

"He's fine," Leo said. "Jackson was right there, so he brought him back. Carver said it was the worst pain he ever felt. I tried overloading it, but it eats energy like it's nothing."

There were only two reasons to have a forcefield block the tunnel: to keep something from getting out or to keep them from getting in.

Elias pulled his sword off his back. Leo and Samantha backed away.

He concentrated on the blade. A pale red glow slicked the adamant sword, and vanished, sucked into it. The weapon turned translucent. A familiar feedback hummed against his hand, as if he was holding onto the rail of a rope bridge while people marched across it and the impact of their footsteps reverberated into his fingers.

Elias swung. The massive blade sliced through the barrier. The two halves of the dial clattered onto the rock, split in half.

Elias walked into the passageway. It opened into a roughly rectangular cavern about twenty-five yards long and roughly half as wide. Veins of jubar stone crisscrossed the ceiling and the walls, illuminating the rocky walls and floor. At the far wall, a creature sprawled on the ground. It raised its head, and he realized he was looking at a smaller version of the dead cat they found in the anchor chamber.

The feline beast stared at him with big green eyes. It was sturdy, with a broad squarish frame that reminded him of a jaguar or maybe a lynx, except it was the size of a cow. Dense fur sheathed it, rippling with black and red.

The two of them looked at each other from across the chamber.

The imbued energy in his sword would dissipate soon. If he was going to strike, now would be the time.

The cat made a noise. It sounded almost plaintive. It didn't move.

"It's tame," Samantha said by his left ear.

Damn it. "Samantha, stop sneaking up on me."

"The cat is tame."

"What makes you say that?" Leo came up on his right.

"It has a collar."

He saw it now, a metal collar wrapping around the cat's neck. Something hung from it, some kind of metal device. Someone had locked this creature in the chamber. He didn't see any food or water. It was probably thirsty and starving.

Elias sheathed his sword, pulled a canteen off his belt, opened it, and let a little water run out.

The cat rose jerkily, stumbled, and sat, holding its front paw off the ground. A deep cut split the flesh. Something with a very sharp blade had nearly sliced through the limb.

"Awww, it's hurt," Samantha said. "It's very weak, Elias, and very, very thirsty. It's been locked here for a while."

The cat whined softly. It wanted water. Elias could practically feel the desperation rolling from it.

"A tiger's paw swipe is estimated to generate over ten thousand pounds of force," Leo said.

"So?" Samantha asked.

"This thing is three times larger. It's dangerous."

"One of us is a phantom ranger with a feral discernment skill that lets her evaluate breach monsters, and the other one is you. Elias, that cat is at the end of its rope."

Elias crossed the cavern. Both Samantha and Leo followed, keeping a bit of distance. The ranger's tactical crossbow was in her hands and Leo's eyes had gone white.

The cat watched them come, its big green eyes sad.

Elias pulled off his helmet, poured the water into it, and offered it to the cat. The big beast crouched and lapped the water out of the helmet with a wide pink tongue. Its fangs were the size of Elias' fingers.

"What a nice kitty," Samantha said.

"This is a terrible idea," Leo said.

"We should get Jackson to heal it," Samantha said.

"No need," Elias said. "I've been meaning to try this."

He concentrated. A faint golden glow slid from him and clutched the cat's injured limb. The bleeding stopped. The severed muscle began to knit itself closed. It wasn't instant the way Jackson's heals were. It was slow and Elias could feel his reserves draining from the strain of it, but it was healing.

"You can heal?" Leo's jaw hung open. "Since when?"

"Since this morning."

For almost a year now he felt a vague stirring of something, some aspect of his talent that he couldn't quite grasp. It was just like the time he learned to imbue his blade. He'd felt the ability building for months before he finally learned what it was and how to use it. This morning, as he watched Adaline hug her children, it came to him in a flash, like a door suddenly flung open deep inside his soul.

The cat leaned its massive head and butted him in the chest.

"Oh my God, how cute!" Samantha cooed.

Elias reached over and gently scratched the cat's jaw.

"You've lost your minds," Leo announced.

"Can we keep it?" Samantha asked. "Please, please, can we keep it, Elias?"

"We can't take a beast out of a breach." Leo shook his head. "It won't be able to get through the gate."

"It will," Samantha said. "It isn't part of the breach."

"How do you know?"

"It feels different. More like that dog the assessor brought with her than a breach creature."

"That was our dog," Leo said.

Was being the operative term.

The cat stretched a little, trying to get more pets.

"You can't abandon it here," Samantha said. "This cat isn't part of whatever this is. It will die on its own."

"Where would we keep it?" Leo asked.

"In the HQ," Samantha countered. "We have an R&D department. We can claim it's for research."

"No! The DDC would lose its shit."

"The DDC doesn't have to know. We can sneak it out tonight."

"Sam!"

"'You become responsible, forever, for what you have tamed,'" Samantha quoted.

"That's great. When we are hauled before a congressional committee and the guild is in danger of being disbanded, you can tell them we did it because The Little Prince said so."

The cat pressed its head against Elias' arm and made a low rumbling noise.

"It's purring!"

"It's growling!"

"Keep it!"

"Kill it."

The cat looked at him with big green eyes.

"You know, your kind usually doesn't like me," Elias told it.

The beast purred louder.

"Guildmaster?" Sam prompted.

"We're keeping it," Elias said.

"Yessss!" Samantha jumped three feet into the air.

Leo spun away waving his arms. "Why doesn't anyone listen to me?"

"I can't leave it here without food or water," Elias said. "The wound is closed, but it will need time to recover."

"This will end in disaster. Mark my words…"

"Leonard," Elias said.

Leo stopped.

"What I say now stays between the three of us. Adaline mentioned spider herders. I didn't get a chance to find out more, because getting our story straight before the DDC showed up took priority, but I'm certain she encountered sophonts in this breach."

In nine years of gate diving, he'd only seen sophonts twice and even now he wasn't sure exactly what he'd witnessed.

"The DDC actively suppresses any news of sophonts. I don't know why. It may be political. It may be that someone somewhere up the chain of command decided that hiding their existence was in the interests of national security. That means they won't tell us what they know until they absolutely have no choice about it. They are withholding information while we are risking our lives in the breaches."

Leo and Samantha stared at him.

"This cat is evidence of sophont activity. It's a working animal. It was left in this cave guarded by a piece of technology we've never seen before. It has a collar. We cannot rely on the mercy of the DDC to keep us informed. We must obtain our own intel. We're going to gather everything in this chamber, including the cat, and we're going to learn as much as we can from it. And we'll need to figure out what this is."

Elias reached over and picked up the metal device hanging from the cat's collar. It was a sphere about the size of an apple. Something shifted under the pressure of his fingers. He heard a faint click.

A beam of light emanated from the sphere and flared into a massive image on the cavern's closest wall, like a projector streaming a film. An anchor chamber, filmed from above, as if from a drone camera. Adaline Moore dashed across the floor, chased by a four-armed alien wrapped in some sort of garment. There was a sword in her hand.

Adaline stumbled, slowing. The four-armed creature threw itself at her. She dodged in a blur and sliced at his back, cutting through the garment. A chunk of it fell off onto the floor. The creature shrieked and fell to its knees. She yanked a rope off her arm and looped it around its neck. The creature tried to run, but she'd tethered it to herself, and she jerked it back and stabbed it in a controlled, cold frenzy. She severed its arms off one by one, dragged it across the floor to the pillar, and tied it to the anchor. She bent over it, doing something he couldn't see, and then she hissed something in a language he didn't understand and walked away.

The camera panned, following her. At the other end of the chamber, Bear was fighting a massive cat. And there was something else there, something short and furry, and covered in blood. It had two pulse carver knives in its furry hands, and it lashed at the cat, screeching like a pissed off racoon.

Adaline moved in with the grace of a dancer. The cat swiped at her, but she was too fast. He saw her drive her sword into the beast's throat. Blood gushed in a dark torrent. She watched it for a few seconds with a dispassionate look on her face, until it collapsed, then turned and walked back to the four-armed creature. She crouched by it, holding something suspended from her fingers. He heard her voice, cold and sibilant, shaping words that didn't belong to any human language.

The camera streaked to her. He saw her raise her sword. The recording went black and died. The cave fell silent.

"Holy shit," Samantha whispered.

I SAT ON THE BIG COUCH IN OUR LIVING ROOM. NOAH SPRAWLED next to me, asleep. Tia curled up on the other side under a blanket. Mellow sat on my lap, while Bear lay on the rug by my feet. The cat and the dog had sniffed each other once and declared a watchful truce. Mellow truly was a sweet cat, and Bear would never attack something I treasured. I had thawed two pounds of ground beef to feed Bear and shared a small clump of it with

Mellow. I'd been low-key worried that Bear wouldn't be able to eat regular food, but she liked the beef just fine. Tomorrow I would order a big bag of dog kibble.

After the kids arrived and I was finally able to stop hugging them, I spent another half an hour getting the story straight with Cold Chaos. I took the bracer off my wrist, slipped it into my bag, handed it to Tia and told her and Noah to take Bear to our house and wait for me. Elias ordered a guild car to take them home. The way Tia looked at me when she climbed into that SUV, as if she was terrified she would never see me again, made my heart hurt.

The DDC descended onto the site in two black Suburbans. I was whisked away under guard, examined, poked, prodded, my blood and vitals were taken, and then I was allowed to shower, given clean clothes, and brought before three interrogators to be debriefed.

I spent the next four hours singing praises to the heroic conduct of Cold Chaos leadership, who purposefully delayed entering the breach so their scouts could find me and bring me back after an unfortunate monster attack wiped out the mining escort and London bailed on us. I kept that part in.

Finally, I was cleared to go home. My tests had come back one hundred percent human. Once at the house, I finally had a chance to look at myself in the mirror. Someone who didn't pay attention to me probably wouldn't have noticed any changes. But I knew my body. I'd lost weight and gained muscle. It wasn't the attractive muscle resulting from carefully structured workouts, but the kind one got from fighting for their life. It wasn't pretty. I looked half-starved and almost feral. Even my face was sunken in.

I took another shower just because I wanted the comfort of my own bathroom and the familiar scent of my shampoo. Tia ordered pizza. We huddled together on the couch and talked. I told them a little bit about what happened in the breach, but I kept my breach mother and the gem out of it. They told me what happened while I was gone.

Apparently, the Cold Chaos HQ was the stuff of legends and a wondrous place of food brought to their door on demand, video game systems, and indoor pools.

After Cold Chaos brought them to their HQ, they'd called their father.

He didn't take their call.

They left a message explaining that I was dead and they needed him. He never called back. Then Tia found the death folder on my laptop.

Noah had a rough time with it. In his mind, his father hadn't abandoned him. He just left because of some weird misunderstanding and if only they could've sat down and talked, my son was sure that his father would see things his way and come back. This was Roger's last opportunity for fatherhood, and he threw it away. Noah finally understood, and it hurt.

I'd met Felicia Terrell, and she was a cobra in a business suit. They wouldn't let her into my debriefing with the DDC but she waited right outside until I emerged and then ran interference as the media swarmed me. Her services were expensive, but worth every penny.

Elias had taken excellent care of my kids. It was so unexpected.

I pushed away from the couch and carefully got up.

Tia stirred under her blanket. "Mom?"

"Yes, sweetheart?"

"You're not leaving?"

"Of course not. I'm going to take Bear to go potty in the back yard and then go to bed."

"You promise?"

"I promise. Don't worry, kiddo. I'm here to stay. I'm still me."

"I know," she murmured. "I checked."

What did that mean?

"What happens now?" she asked.

"We keep going. The crisis is over. I told the DDC I needed two weeks off to recover. I have a lot of leave saved up. We'll have a little staycation, pick up the pieces, and go on with our lives."

"Will it be okay?" she asked.

"Yes," I told her. "Everything will be okay. I'll make sure of it."

She sighed happily and closed her eyes.

I crossed the house to the back door. Bear followed me like a large silent shadow. I opened the kitchen door, and Bear bounded onto the grass, making a perimeter along the fence of our backyard.

I sat on the porch steps. Above me the night sky stretched, vast and beautiful. I was finally home. The nightmare of the breach was over.

I thought of Elias McFeron. There was a lot of power there, and willingness to use it. I asked him to lie to the DDC, and he didn't even blink. He went along with my plan because he wanted to keep his guild safe. And all of that adamantite would ensure the DDC would abandon any disciplinary action against Cold Chaos. Before they took me away, I heard Elias tell someone that the families of the dead guildmembers would be entitled to their bonus. Money was cold comfort when you lost your husband or your mother. But bills didn't go away because you had a personal tragedy. I knew that better than anyone.

Elias would make a very dangerous opponent. A very capable ally, too, but it was too early for that. I needed to plan long term, and I had to choose who I trusted very carefully.

I looked at the night sky, closed my eyes, and reached deep inside myself, to the soft glow. It was still weak, but it had recovered enough. I tapped it, and it responded, eager to connect.

It was time to keep my promises. I took a deep breath.
Tell me about the Tsuun.

The End

CLASSES AND TALENTS

P eople who acquired extraordinary abilities in the wake of the first gates rupturing are called Talents. Their special new skills are also called talents. Talents are sorted into classes based on the nature of their abilities. The two largest groups are noncombat and combat talents.

Noncombat Classes

Noncombat classes encompass a wide variety of people with unusual skills that have no direct use on the battlefield. Some of the talents are valuable, others less so. Preservists project a personal aura that keeps whatever they are carrying in stasis; foragers harvest valuable plants; artisans work with breach resources to create equipment. Although none of them offer any advantage in combat, without their efforts and the resources they gather, fighting to close the breaches would be a lot harder.

Class Examples

Assessor – the most mysterious of all noncombat classes,

assessors evaluate their environment and gain information about it through means they themselves do not fully understand. They detect valuable ores, medicinal plants, and useful biological resources and identify environmental dangers, such as poisonous gases and liquids. To be an effective assessor means to devote a lot of time familiarizing oneself with minerals, ores, plants, and monster components that are brought out of the breaches. No guild can hire an assessor; in the US, they work exclusively for the government, specifically the Dimensional Defense Command (DDC), where their official designation is Dimensional Breach Assessor, or DeBRA for short. Adaline Moore is an assessor.

Orefinder – orefinders can sense ores even when they are buried under rock. Melissa of Cold Chaos is an orefinder.

Combat Classes

Tanks are well-armored fighters with defensive capabilities, who try to draw the attention of the enemies and keep it focused on themselves. Most tanks deal significant damage but not as fast as the dedicated damage dealers.

Class Examples

Bastion – Bastions project a forcefield over their shield that damages and stuns opponents on contact. Because the shield provides so much protection, they tend to be lighter armored than other tank classes. In battle, they often plant their shield, shock their opponents, and then advance and repeat. They favor spears and lances for their long reach. Bastions are the most defense-oriented of all tank classes and are particularly useful in cave breaches. If you need to block a tunnel, no other tank class is better. Aaron Ford of Cold Chaos Assault Team #3 is a bastion.

Vanguard – heavily armored fighters that fight with large, two-handed weapons. Vanguards possess the stalwart aura talent. When activated, it sheaths them in a protective force-field. Unlike the blade warden shield, which covers an area around the caster, the stalwart aura only affects the vanguards themselves. For as long as it's active, they are very hard to damage. In a fight, vanguards are the tip of the spear. They mow through the enemy line like bulldozers, always pressing their advantage. Anton Sokolov of the Guardian Guild is a vanguard.

Damage Dealers

Damage dealers, as their name suggests, concentrate on dishing out damage, the faster the better. They are the most numerous cross-section of combat gate divers and encompass many varied classes.

Class Examples

Pulse carver – pulse carvers are dual-wield melee fighters who favor short swords or long knives and deliver damage in brief, devastating bursts. When they pulse, activating their special abilities, they become incredibly fast and agile, capable of dizzying speed and bouncing off the walls. On the battlefield, the pulse carver is a whirlwind, slicing their opponents one moment and dancing away the next. For some reason, women manifest this talent more often than men, although male pulse carvers do exist. Ximena of Cold Chaos and JoAnne Kersey of the Guardian Guild are both pulse carvers.

Interceptor – interceptors are fast, maneuverable damage dealers who teleport short distances, summon "plasma" projectiles, and imbue their melee weapons with dangerous energy. In a fight, interceptors move around the battlefield, appearing where they are needed most. One moment they might hurl a plasma javelin over the tank's shoulder, the next they stab an enemy on the other side of the fight with their spear. They usually have heightened situational awareness. Malcolm, the leader of the Cold Chaos Assault Team 4, is an interceptor.

Stormsurge – stormsurgers are a rare but very sought-after class. They appear to command wind and lightning, but scientists have yet to agree on the exact nature of their powers. In battle, a stormsurge rises above the fray on dark incorporeal wings and unleashes a variety of lightning attacks that often kill on contact. Leo Martinez, Vice-Guildmaster of Cold Chaos, is a stormsurge.

Scouts

Scout classes require three things: stealth, speed, and enhanced senses. Scouts move quickly and silently, and they usually don't get lost. Lightly armored, they are snipers and assassins, and if trapped alone in the breach, they are the most likely of all classes to escape unharmed. In the fight, they tend to hang back, often protecting more vulnerable support classes.

Class Examples

Pathfinder – light on their feet, pathfinders have enhanced hearing and an unerring sense of direction. If you walked a pathfinder into a maze, blindfolded them, and spun them around, they would be able to retrace their steps and get out within minutes. Elena of Cold Chaos is a pathfinder.

Phantom Ranger – the stealthiest of all scout classes, phantom rangers can camouflage themselves. They move silently, and when they activate their phase aura, they become virtually undetectable and untraceable by sight, scent, or even body heat. They also possess feral discernment that allows them to evaluate creatures of the breach. How much they can discern is a matter of debate, since phantom rangers don't volunteer information unless absolutely necessary. Samantha of Cold Chaos is a phantom ranger.

Support

Support classes encompass Talents who can aid during combat but do not engage the enemy directly. Healers who treat the wounded, hazardists who lay traps, and catalysts who enhance their allies' abilities all fall into this broad category.

Class Examples

Burst Medic – burst medics are powerful single-target healers. Unlike zone restorers, who slowly heal everyone within their area of effect, burst medics deliver focused surges of healing to one ally at a time with nearly instant results. One-on-one, they are the most powerful of all healing classes, capable of near miracles at top-tier. Jackson of Cold Chaos is a burst medic.

Hybrid

Hybrid classes possess abilities that allow them to play dual roles. Rushblades act both as melee damage dealers and as support by enhancing their teammates' speed. Recon strikers unleash devastating ranged attacks but can double as scouts in a pinch. Hybrid classes are highly prized, because in the breach flexibility is priceless.

Class Examples

Blade Warden – a hybrid class that is both a tank and a damage dealer, blade wardens project a forcefield around themselves that makes them nearly invulnerable for a short time. The warden shield moves with them, which makes them incredibly effective at shielding their allies. They are usually well armored, and while they are not the fastest or most maneuverable fighters, top-tier blade wardens can imbue their weapons, making them capable of cutting through large opponents in a single strike. Elias McFeron is a blade warden.

ALSO BY ILONA ANDREWS

Maggie the Undying

THIS KINGDOM WILL NOT KILL ME

Roman's Chronicles

SANCTUARY

Kate Daniels: Wilmington Years

MAGIC TIDES

MAGIC CLAIMS

Kate Daniels World

BLOOD HEIR

Kate Daniels Series

MAGIC BITES

MAGIC BLEEDS

MAGIC BURNS

MAGIC STRIKES

MAGIC MOURNS

MAGIC BLEEDS

MAGIC DREAMS

MAGIC SLAYS

GUNMETAL MAGIC

MAGIC GIFTS

MAGIC RISES

MAGIC BREAKS

MAGIC STEALS

MAGIC SHIFTS

MAGIC STARS

MAGIC BINDS

MAGIC TRIUMPHS

The Iron Covenant

IRON AND MAGIC

UNTITLED IRON AND MAGIC #2

Hidden Legacy Series

BURN FOR ME

WHITE HOT

WILDFIRE

DIAMOND FIRE

SAPPHIRE FLAMES

EMERALD BLAZE

RUBY FEVER

Innkeeper Chronicles Series

CLEAN SWEEP

SWEEP IN PEACE

ONE FELL SWEEP

SWEEP OF THE BLADE

SWEEP WITH ME

SWEEP OF THE HEART

Kinsmen

SILENT BLADE

SILVER SHARK

THE KINSMEN UNIVERSE (anthology with both SILENT BLADE
and SILVER SHARK)

FATED BLADES

The Edge Series
ON THE EDGE
BAYOU MOON
FATE'S EDGE
STEEL'S EDGE

ABOUT THE AUTHOR

Ilona Andrews is the pseudonym for a husband-and-wife writing team, Gordon and Ilona. They currently reside in Texas with their two children and numerous dogs and cats. The couple are the #1 *New York Times* and *USA Today* bestselling authors of the Kate Daniels and Kate Daniels World novels as well as The Edge and Hidden Legacy series. They also write the Innkeeper Chronicles series, which they post as a free weekly serial.

For a complete list of their books, fun extras, and Innkeeper installments, please visit their website www.ilona-andrews.com.

Made in United States
Cleveland, OH
31 December 2025

30013336R00154